Last Graffiti Beıore Motorway

Shani Solomons

To Maggie,
Do hope you enjoy!
Shani

Also by the same author:

"All Things Bright and Beautiful"

Published by YouWriteOn.com, 2011

Cover Drawing: Stephen Browne

Design and Editing: Naomi Stolow

****

Verity Macklesworth had "delusions of shrinkage". At least a size 22, she had somehow managed to heave her poor tortured body into a size 16. You could almost hear the flesh gasping for breath, as it strained against the fastenings.

Across from Verity sat her P.A, Angela who wished Verity wasn't her boss. Angela could fit at least three times inside Verity's body, and for this alone, Verity felt Angela should be made to suffer severely.

The P.A observed how Verity's brassy blonde hair was scraped back with an Alice band which was something she always did when it was growing too long, but when she had it cut, her bob was very severe with a fringe that emphasised her permanently frowning brows – brows which were much darker than her hair.

Her foundation was also slightly too orange and the eyelashes were always disconcertingly clumped together. It wasn't so much that the eyelashes looked so uncomfortable that bothered Angela – it was the way Verity would sit at her computer clicking her mouse with one hand and tugging at her caked-up eyelids with the other.

But the very worst thing about Verity was the shortness of her skirts, combined with the way she sat like a man. In the winter it wasn't quite as bad, although it would take an extremely frosty day to make Verity don a pair of tights. At least then you were spared the excruciating journey from white, goose-pimpled flesh to the red underwear, leading to a place that few dared to enter.....

As she caught a glimpse of something nylon and frilly in between Verity's legs, Angela was glad that lunch time was a long way off. She pondered on how Verity appeared to eat nothing and yet seemed to remain so large. She could only guess it was a result of the copious amounts of "client entertaining" her boss did and the fact she could drink any man under the table.

For everything Angela disliked about Verity, Verity did seem to bring a huge amount of business to "Mort and Grey" and for that reason had climbed the corporate ladder to her prestigious position.

It was cold outside and freezing in the office, as Verity always liked to have the heating low and watch her skinny colleague shiver; Angela ate lots – even chocolate, and yet never seemed to gain an ounce. Occasionally Verity would make back-handed compliments - she'd mention how lovely a blouse was that Angela was wearing, but then say that you really needed curves and her own voluptuous shape to carry it off.

Somehow, Verity would always labour the point that Angela had virtually no breasts to speak of, whereas she herself was a veritable Marilyn Monroe. In truth, Verity's bosom needed a serious restriction order. Her breasts appeared to be strung up with something so flimsy, it really made no difference whatsoever.

Consequently, whenever Verity stood up, one breast would swing so far out to the left it would almost knock over the table lamp, whilst the other would make a loop, like a well-rehearsed burlesque dancer. Even though Angela didn't really need a bra, she'd buy tiny teenage-size ones in pretty colours – something to make her feel feminine, at least.

Verity bent down and lifted a huge black box file from behind her desk. She smiled a slightly nauseating smile at Angela. Angela tried to smile back. She knew what was coming next.

****

Marisa Brown looked up at the large damp patch on her living room ceiling. The bathroom above her was leaking again and dripping persistent little drops into the bucket she'd placed underneath. She sat at the kitchen table with her head in her hands unable to hold back much longer; eventually her tears started to drip, just like her walls. She didn't think she had the energy to go on – the council had been called so many times and still fixed nothing.

The smell of damp in the tiny flat had now become all pervading, invading her nostrils and overwhelming her. Callum's cough was getting worse as well and she was sure the damp was the cause. She hadn't dared look in his bedroom for a while, but every time she opened the door, a stench of wet and rotting plaster board filled the air. It was getting worse and as if that wasn't bad enough, she really had no idea how she was going to continue paying for his private tuition – something he badly needed in this school year. For now, all Marisa could do was put her head in her hands.

****

Verity leaned across Angela's desk and the right breast performed its burlesque trick. She plonked down the black box file.

"Filing."

If only it were as simple as that. Not that filing wasn't simple, but it was Verity's long and tedious description of the alphabet which seemed to take forever. If she found the tiniest aberration in the "St's" or the "Mc's" or something where a secretary might hesitate, Angela would receive the lecture aimed at a grown up office worker, but delivered as though Verity were speaking to three year old child.

Alas, Verity found a mistake. Angela took a deep breath and tried to think about George Clooney, whilst silently nodding at everything Verity said. Then she sat quietly, pretending to file, whilst sneakily looking at a job advert she'd printed off her computer. It was definitely time to move on, but Angela had no idea where to.

She'd now been at Mort and Grey for two and a half years and liked her job, but detested the omnipresent shadow of Verity Macklesworth. Every time she thought about putting herself back out in the job market, she became gripped by anxieties and excuses. She was thirty-nine and her C.V had so many holes, one of them might turn into a crater. She was fed up with moving around, even though she had never really found something awfully satisfactory. Whenever her self-esteem was low, Verity would always manage to crush it even further.

Verity originally joined Mort and Grey as a temp, but never ceased telling the story of how she had worked her way up from her humble beginnings. Angela thought it far more likely that she had bullied her way up, but every time she heard the tales, Angela nodded and marvelled and gave appreciative gasps of ooohs and aaahs, just like a good P.A should.

****

It was the way she was handed the cup of tea that told private tutor Beverley Ofori she would no longer be required. She knew the score and the little ritual well, by now. First of all she would finish the lesson and then the parent would usher the child into another room, saying they'd like a "bit of a chat". Then, she would always be offered another cup of tea and that would be handed over very slowly and deliberately as though there were a death certificate attached to it.

To be honest, she was surprised that Marisa Brown had managed to keep her son's tuition going for this long. The run-down property had been falling into further and further decline and Beverley was much more concerned for the health of her young student and his struggling single mother than she was for her own salary top-up. She wondered what to say to Marisa.

First of all, she dealt lightly with the fact that the tuition would need to be terminated. She understood it was an expensive option and that she was very pleased with Callum's progress anyway. Then, because it was hard not to notice, she expressed her concern about the smell of the damp and asked if anything was being done. She didn't realize she'd opened a can of worms.

Marisa placed her own mug down and let out a long, deep sigh. Then she coughed and went over to the side cabinet, reaching for a room spray and let a long squirt burst into the room.

"I'm really sorry about that – I hope it hasn't been too awful to work in"

"It's not affecting me" replied Beverley, "But I just hope the council are doing something?"

Marisa shook her head.

"Is there anything I can do? Write a letter maybe? I can say I'm very concerned for Callum's health."

Marisa gulped and Beverley could see she was choking back tears.

"Mrs Brown.....?"

Marisa stuttered, "Perhaps.....yes. Thank you. Maybe a letter would help."

Beverley didn't push it further. She was there to listen, not to probe.

"Really, it's no trouble at all. Just let me know. And please keep in touch."

Marisa nodded, then fished in her handbag for her purse. She looked very embarrassed, realizing there were only a few pound coins in it.

"Oh God, I'm so sorry....forgot to get cash....can I give you a cheque?"

Beverley nodded, knowing full well that the cheque would bounce. It was mid September, a time of year when tutoring work should have been plentiful, but this year much of her work either didn't take off or people just had a few lessons. There had been a mild hint of impending recession in the air, but so far it hadn't really affected her or anyone she knew – besides, she still had her full-time position as a local primary school teacher. Anyway, this was just a blip, wasn't it? It was surely only affecting the city and people who worked in banks.

****

Verity was going out on a date. Angela knew that because the "performing bosom" actually looked quite well contained and Verity had her "pulling shoes" on. Angela didn't want to admit it, but Verity actually looked quite nice. She complimented her.

"I know" said Verity. She wasn't the most modest of women. "Just got the top yesterday – down in the sale to £79. It's pure wool."

This was said with a smug little smile out of the corner of Verity's mouth, indicating that she could afford to spend that sort of money on a cardigan. Angela tried to work out how a "corner of the mouth smugness" could take over an entire face. Verity always managed to make it known how self-important she was and how lowly Angela was, due entirely to their conflicting salaries.

Verity walked back to her desk and crossed her legs, admiring her shiny stilettos like a girl who'd just got into the ballet school of her choice. Angela started to wonder what Verity's date looked like, and to this end started playing with Photoshop. She morphed a hybrid creation of John Prescott and Anne Widdecombe and then when she was satisfied with her creation, emailed the picture to her friend.

It was almost four o'clock and she knew her friend would probably be as bored as her and frantically checking her inbox for amusing attachments. A few minutes later, a reply came back with the subject line "Tasty!" The reply also questioned how the "P.M.T. Rex" was. God help anyone who tried to have a joke with Verity at her time of month. Unfortunately, Angela had fallen victim to her boss's hormones the previous month, and was caught playing on the internet. She was punished by having to put the entire client account folder in date order, instead of its usual alphabetical order. It took two and a half days. When Angela had finished, Verity decided she'd changed her mind and wanted the files put back in alphabetical order.

Just to make sure Angela was really going to suffer, she asked her for her opinion first. Did Angela think this system would work better left in date order, or would it be easier to locate documents if they were filed alphabetically? Angela knew she was over a barrel. Verity would disagree with her whatever she said and she'd have to re-file. She thought carefully before telling Verity she thought it was half a dozen of one and six of the other.

Verity didn't like that. She placed her hands flat on Angela's desk, so that the scary bosom loomed from above.

"But Angela.....which one do you think is *best?*"

Angela wouldn't be pushed.

"Hmm, well I guess if you're looking for a purchase order then date order is best –"

Verity lifted her hands, supposedly in triumph, but then Angela continued.

"However, if you want a quick reference then it might be best to have them alphabetically."

Angela knew that one moment longer and Verity would kill her, but she took the risk nonetheless. Verity looked to all extents and purposes like she was about to morph into the Incredible Hulk. Only she wasn't green. She was actually going a very bright shade of scarlet – so much so, that Angela was worried.

Verity started coughing and staggered back to her desk.

"Verity – are you ok?"

Angela rushed to get some water and watched as Verity amazingly remained silent for a full ten minutes. She couldn't allow her blood pressure to rise any further. Once she was sure Verity had returned to her normal colour, Angela said nothing, but just carried on with some other work. She couldn't resist throwing in a little pièce de résistance, however.

"Dear me Verity – what happened just then? It's a bit worrying, isn't it? Do you think it might be.........*hormonal......?*"

****

Callum was late for tea. Marisa was more worried about the lack of hot water, as she was desperate for a bath. Her lank locks hung down her bony back and she boiled up the kettle, so that she could at least give her hair a wash. She wondered what was going to go wrong next in the flat, but just as she pondered asking her neighbours if she could use their shower, she heard Callum's key turn in the door.

"Where the hell have you been?"

"S'not your business" replied Callum, treading mud into the threadbare carpet.

"What do you mean it's none of my business? I'm your mother – of course it's my business. Don't you dare talk to me like that!"

Callum didn't reply, continuing in a line towards the kitchen. Marisa ducked in front of him and grabbed the tea utensils off the table.

"I don't think so, young man! Not until you tell me why you're so late!"

She expected her son to argue – he usually did. Instead, he stamped a muddy foot and skulked off to his bedroom. As he did so, Marisa noticed a small cut on the side of his cheek. The hair washing would need to wait.

****

In bounced Brian. Brian was a fairly frequent visitor to Verity and Angela's office and sometimes annoyingly too frequent. He was a tall, bulky man with a mop of black hair and dark bushy beard, somewhat reminiscent of Brian Blessed. Were it not for his voice, one might have thought Brian was a thespian, but when he spoke the sound was high-pitched, nervous and nasal. He also had the most awful giggle known to man and when he and Verity were in unison with their cacophony of chuckles, Angela had to make an excuse to leave the room.

They also flirted in a highly sickening manner, making Brian chuckle even more. He was married, but it never stopped him trying. Both Verity and Angela were single and Brian loved that, feeling it gave him carte blanche to be in there whenever he wanted, foolishly believing both women would be flattered.

Verity always seemed to have some hapless bloke on the go, but there had been a null and void place in Angela's love-life for quite some time. If it were a choice to go home to a packet of Kettle Chips or Brian, then the Kettle Chips would win every time.

The flirting reminded Angela of the last Mort and Grey Christmas office party. That time was almost upon them again. She'd always found Christmas office parties to be quite awful affairs, but Mort and Grey abused the privilege. Angela had come into work last year to discover the extremely sad decorations had already been hung. Across the window sill in their office, Verity had fixed some home-made paper chains which she'd attached with a mixture of Blu Tack and drawing pins.

A sales chart on the wall had a piece of red tinsel pinned around it, so that one end hung a good several inches lower than the other. But the real treat was on the printer desk. A miniature colour-changing plastic Christmas tree with a sort of strobe light flashed annoyingly for a couple of days before its battery finally died.

As it approached death, the tree would "hold" one colour for a while, then flicker madly as though desperately gasping for breath before passing through to the next colour. Eventually, no colours showed other than pale grey plastic spikes, silent in their final expiration and journey to the afterlife....

The main hall where there would be drinks and a D.J fared little better. There was a larger plastic tree in here, but thankfully this one didn't light up. Someone had cut out the face of Mort and Grey's Managing Director from their in-house magazine and stuck it onto a fairy doll, placed rather lopsidedly at the top of the tree. Everyone but Angela seemed to find that absolutely hysterical.

Whilst Angela looked forward to spending Christmas firstly with her mother and then inviting friends over for mince pies and mulled wine, she was cornered by drunk Mort and Grey colleagues in the kitchen, adamant that this was "event of the year". For Mort and Grey, it was.

Angela spent a whole day wondering if she could get out of it this year, but didn't want to lose face with the company bosses – one had to mingle, if one wanted to get on. But there was worse to come. Verity wanted Angela to join her one Saturday morning to shop for outfits for the "event".

****

Marisa tried to figure out the best way to tell Callum that Beverley wasn't coming any more. He really liked her, and was doing well with her. It was also a really important year for his school work. Marisa had agonized over stopping the tuition, but there was food and travel and the rent was about to go up – she was struggling enough without having to worry about finding extra.

Over breakfast, just before school seemed the best time to bring it up. The Wednesday morning she chose to tell him, was different from other mornings. Marisa had noticed her son had become sullen, withdrawn and not like his usual chirpy self. He must have picked up on her anxieties. She decided to go for the gentle approach.

"Cal, sweetheart, finish your toast – I need to speak to you."

Callum already knew by the tone in his mother's voice it wasn't going to be something he wanted to hear. Marisa took a deep a breath.

"I'm afraid there's no easy way to say this, but.....Beverley won't be coming anymore."

She waited for the protest. Callum stared ahead for a moment then buttered another slice of toast.

"Ok", he said, nonchalantly. Marisa was taken aback.

"Ok? You're ok with that? I thought you really liked Beverley."

"Yeah, I do, but s'alright. I've got other stuff to do anyway." Callum got up from the table.

"Wait – sit down. What do you mean "other stuff ?"

"Like.....like lots of homework. What does it matter, anyway? She's not coming back, is she?"

With that, Callum shrugged his satchel over his shoulder and half-stepped into his scruffy trainers, then headed out the door without tying them up. A moment after he left, the postman arrived and Marisa put another pile of bills on the kitchen table before shoving them to one side and then rifling through her handbag for a packet of pills.

****

There was only one thing worse than working with Verity and that was socializing with her. Angela figured she'd get through it – it was only one morning of the year; Verity only needed one outfit. What she wasn't exactly thrilled about was that Verity wanted them to meet at 8.30am at the station, just to "have a cappuccino first".

Getting up at the same time as she would have done for work, purely to be Verity's " image consultant" on a cold, wet Saturday morning, didn't harmonize well with the comfort of Angela's duvet. She cursed her alarm clock and rolled back over. It was only October. Why did Verity need to get party clothes now? She'd supposed she'd already got all her cards and presents. Angela's Christmas shopping usually consisted of last minute dashes to the pound shop – her salary wasn't exactly huge and rent took up most of her income.

The alarm went off again. Angela cursed. She was really going to be late. She pulled open a drawer full of clothes, into which some crumpled jeans were stuffed. So much for a "capsule wardrobe". In a higher up drawer, she pulled out underwear and a t-shirt and then rifled through the rest of her clothes to find a warm enough jumper. It was freezing – way too cold for the time of year.

Alas, Angela's only really decent jumper was in the wash basket, along with her best jeans. She found herself pulling on a pair of cheap supermarket jeans and wearing two thinner jumpers, which together, were too thick under her coat. Dragging a hairbrush very quickly through her unwashed locks and reaching for a scrunchy, Angela fished around for her glasses; no time for make-up. After all, she didn't bother with it for work, so couldn't see how it could matter at the weekend. Especially when Verity saw her with her bare-faced naturalness all the time. How wrong could she be. Verity was fuming.

"Oh my God, Angela – you could at least have made an effort."

"I've made an effort to be here, Verity. I wasn't aware that this was an occasion that called for dressing up."

"Do you have any idea what you look like?"

"Yes. About 5ft 8", size 10, dark hair and glasses."

"You are *not* a size 10."

"Am too."

"Well" huffed Verity grabbing her handbag, "We'll soon find out, won't we?" She tottered over to the coffee bar.

"S'pose you want a *skinny* latte?"

"Oh no, not me", Angela grinned "Full fat version, please. I don't know why it is, but I just never seem to put on weight....."

Verity scowled and plonked her money down. Angela was relieved the day would take place at an indoor shopping centre – it was dreary and drizzly outside and the thought of the weather combined with spending her free time with Verity was not making her weak coffee taste any better.

The drink however, was warming and a few minutes later Angela was almost looking forward to browsing. Verity began in Marks and Spencer's. She picked some dresses off the rails, then took a very small black shirt off another rail, which she threw at Angela.

"Here, try that" Verity sniffed.

"What for?" asked Angela, "I already know what I'm wearing to the party."

"God, how boring. Try it on anyway."

For a moment, Angela actually thought Verity was picking out something she thought might suit her. The truth was, she wanted to see if it fitted. It did.

"Let me look at that label" said Verity angrily.

"It's a 10" said Angela.

Verity tried to heave herself into a skirt smaller than the diameter of her knee.

"Huh", she muttered "M and S make their sizes at least one size smaller than everyone else"

"Shame you'll need two sizes bigger then, Verity...."

Verity had no choice. She had to admit defeat before there were broken zippers and bloodshed. The women boarded an escalator to an outsize shop, where Verity couldn't find Angela anything to try on. After a few minutes, Angela heard muffled little squeals of delight coming from the changing room, as Verity discovered that the clothes not only fitted, but also looked good. She bought them all.

"I thought you were just after a Christmas top?" queried Angela.

"Christmas?" replied Verity "Oh, we haven't even started that...."

Verity smirked and Angela sighed deeply.

At the other end of the mall, Marisa was ferreting through some trainers in the discount store, desperately trying to find something in Callum's size.

"Don't want them" said Callum "They're naff trainers." He stomped over to another aisle.

Marisa was weary now. "Cal – your school shoes are full of holes and the sole is going. You've got to have something on your feet."

"But the other kids will laugh at me if I wear those."

"Laugh? Why should they? They're just plain black trainers – regulation school wear. They're not pink with yellow spots and lime green ribbons, so why should anyone laugh...?"

Marisa knew full well why. Callum wanted a designer name on anything he wore. But he wasn't the only child of a poor, struggling single parent in his class. The betting was lots of kids would have to do with cheaper clothes. Callum looked down at his mother's own scuffed boots.

"Aren't you gonna get new shoes, too Mum?" he asked.

Tears welled up in Marisa's eyes. He might have been a handful lately, but deep down Callum was still her own, sweet son. Still a good heart in there.

"Well, let's just sort you out first, shall we?" Marisa turned to put a pair of trainers back down, so that Callum couldn't see the tear rolling down her cheek.

****

Five hours later and Angela was exhausted and famished.

"Verity – I really have to get back. If you want to go anywhere else, you can manage without me, can't you?"

Verity gave Angela a hard, Paddington-Bear stare.

"I *know* you're not teaching later. It's half term." Verity knew Angela ran Saturday music courses for children – apparently she was a trained pianist, although Verity assumed she couldn't be a very good one as she had ended up in secretarial work. Angela tried to out-stare Verity, but eventually had to concede.

"I may not have my group today, but I do have other things to do" said Angela firmly.

" That may be" replied Verity, "But I think you'll stay and shop with me for as long as I want you to." Verity doubled the intensity of her stare.

"What's that supposed to mean, Verity? Are you..........are you saying you're going to make things difficult for me at work if I don't do as you say? But we're not at the office and that's – blackmail!"

An extremely evil smirk spread across Verity's face, like the kind you see in horror films. It was so scary, that Angela physically recoiled.

"Blackmail, Angela? Oh, that's a bit extreme, isn't it? I think it might be a good idea if you read your job description again. Remember, your role is to 'generally assist' me, which is what you're doing right now. And you do remember that bit about 'occasional need for out of office hours', don't you......?"

****

Callum detoured round the back of the recycling area at the park, where he wasn't allowed to go. Inside the concrete tunnels, someone had sprayed the words "This Way Up", upside down - Callum bent his head into strange positions to try and read it before realising that it was a joke.

The length of the tunnels was sprayed with graffiti and stunk of urine, but they held a dangerous kind of thrill for Callum and besides – Daz and his younger brother Benji might be lurking. Daz was fourteen and fast becoming a manipulative little ring leader. He was a handsome boy with thick afro-style hair, golden skin and a taut, lithe body. He was also well aware of his own charisma.

Daz's real name was Jermaine, but Daz was short for "Dazzle" on account of his sparkling white teeth. Eight year old Benji hung onto his every word. The boys had different fathers so didn't much look like brothers, but Benji absolutely worshipped Daz and personality-wise was fast morphing into him.

Callum was short and skinny, but it wasn't his brawn that Daz wanted him for. Callum was smart and most of all - he was discreet. As he slid down the grass bank and into the tunnel, Callum wasn't disappointed.

"Cal – our main man. Pleasure to see you." Daz stood tall with his hands in his pockets, dazzling his bright smile. Benji tried to copy, but his teeth were nowhere near as straight or white and he just looked funny with his crooked little smile and counterfeit swagger.

Daz continued, "Got some important news for you Cal, so glad you're here." Callum felt the adrenalin surge through his body.

"We've got a few weeks n'that's all."

"Yeah, that's all" repeated Benji.

"It's gonna be a big one Cal – Halloween. You like Trick and Treating, don't ya?"

"Yeah, you betcha!" gushed Callum. His eyes lit up. Something really exciting and special was about to happen and he was going to be part of it.

"Thought as much" said Daz. "I need you on board, Cal. Gotta get you trained up fast." Daz's dark, intense eyes held Callum transfixed for as long as Daz required.

"So.....you know how to behave with your mum when she starts asking lots of questions, don't you?"

"That's easy, yeah" replied Callum, "Sweet as pie."

"Sweet as pie" echoed Benji.

****

Marisa started polishing over the scuffs on her boots with some black polish.

"You shouldn't have to do that, Mum" sighed Callum.

"Well, you know I can't get new ones. Anyway, a few rubs and these will be as good as."

"I mean – let me do it, Mum. I'm good at polishing. You'll hurt your back, all bent over the table like that." Marisa stopped rubbing. In the midst of all the stress and hopelessness and drudgery, one little beacon of light shone through that made it all worthwhile. Her son.

****

Verity wore her new boots to work. Every so often she would spin on her office chair, stretch out her legs and flick her toes up and down, like a podgy, hopeful girl on her first day of the new term. Kevin from Accounts walked in with some papers.

"Nice boots, Verity." He winked. Angela always watched with great amusement the interaction between Verity and Kevin. Kevin was young, single, heterosexual and every inch the flirty, cheeky chap. Technically, Verity should have been flirting back on all four cylinders. But Kevin was also a dwarf.

This always made Verity extremely awkward around him. She wasn't entirely sure how politically correct it was to flirt with a dwarf and sort of kept him at a distance whilst trying to pout at the same time.

"Heard about the City?" said Kevin, plonking his papers down on Verity's desk, "Shocking, all of 'em jobs going, innit?"

Angela had briefly glimpsed the BBC news the previous night and seen footage of people leaving their jobs with nothing but cardboard boxes.

"Mate of mine just got laid off. Just like that" continued Kevin, "Seems it's all happened so quick."

Verity hadn't watched the news, but wanted to join in the conversation. "Oh, yes, yes....I heard", she replied quickly.

"So....." Kevin had his horns out. Angela could always tell when he was about to wind Verity up. She sat back and decided to enjoy the ride. Kevin kicked at a cardboard box under Verity's desk. It was her boot box.

"You sure that's gonna be big enough, Verity?" It became apparent very quickly that Verity had absolutely no idea what Kevin was talking about. Angela tried to stifle a giggle as Kevin continued.

"If I were you, I'd pop up to Waitrose at lunchtime and get a bigger one there, although I'd better warn you – they're going fast." The hapless Verity just nodded and went very red as both Kevin and Angela roared with laughter, but knew the situation wasn't really so funny. No one really thought Mort and Grey would be making any severe staff cuts, but there were rumours that Christmas bonuses wouldn't manifest this year and pay rises would become a thing of the past.

Angela cursed her timing. Just as she was about to broach the subject of a pay rise, something would always happen. This year there were mutterings about a recession, last year her department lost a big contract and in previous years she'd either been temping or laid off before she could claim much in the way of redundancy. She asked Kevin what he knew about the bonuses.

"So – do you think we'll get anything then, Kevin?" Angela had kind of been relying on hers for Christmas presents. "If it came down to it, I'd much rather have my bonus than the office party – look at all the money they're throwing on that."

Verity rose up on her heckles. The office Christmas party was her raison d'être, her time – her entrance in her ball gown.....life would not be worth living without this annual event. Much to her distress, Kevin gave Angela a big wink, before adding that he'd miss snogging her under the mistletoe and they both howled with laughter.

That was too much for Verity. Just who did the dwarf think he was? Fancy flirting with a woman who never wore any make up, not to mention having the audacity to flirt with someone else anyway, when Verity couldn't flirt with him because he was a dwarf....

****

Daz and a large group of other boys including Callum and Benji gathered round the back of the tunnels for their briefing. An older boy of fourteen or fifteen with cropped hair, a broken front tooth and scary eyes addressed his "congregation".

"We've got to remember brothers, we've only got a few weeks. I want you all in on this now. I need you to know how important this is. We can all get what we want if we unite. We know that there are many who are undeserving and we know that we are the deserving ones, aren't we?" At this point, a huge roar of agreement came from the throng. Callum joined in.

"So...." continued their speaker as he unpacked his hold-all. Callum stared as the boy laid out bundles wrapped in black cloth and then carefully unwrapped them to reveal a selection of knives, chisels, hammers and other weaponry. Callum gasped as the metal edges glistened in the moonlight.

"Tonight", grinned the speaker, "We begin.......*training*......."

* * * * * * * * * *

Beverley couldn't stop thinking about Callum. He was academically weak, but incredibly talented in other ways. When his brain struggled with adjectives and adverbs, Beverley would do role-play games and drama with him, helping to ease him back into learning his English grammar. His imagination was particularly fertile when he and Beverley played "Pretend".

It was 4.30pm and after finishing some marking, Beverley was heading home. As it wasn't completely dark yet, she thought she'd cut through "The Tunnels". This wasn't a particularly nice walk, but it saved time, and just after school, there'd be plenty of people around.

Rounding the corner from the main street, Beverley clocked a gang of boys hanging around the entrance. There'd always been groups of teenagers smoking and hanging out in the park, but just recently Beverley had started to feel ill at ease, even though none of them had taken much notice of her.

Occasionally the odd boy from her school would shout out "Hello Miss!" whilst his friends would chuckle and smirk. Beverley would smile and wave hello back and carry on walking. This afternoon seemed much like any other late autumn afternoon, only this time she spotted a face amongst the gang which shocked her. Callum.

Luckily Callum was too absorbed with the other boys to notice Beverley, but after a few yards, she suddenly felt very queasy and overwhelmed with anxiety. She decided to ignore the feeling, putting it down to a dodgy curry, but had she followed her instincts she would have known it was something other than that. It would be what her Grandmother used to call "The Knowing".

****

After her draining shopping expedition, Angela felt the need to treat herself to something nice. She certainly needed some new work clothes and the best place to shop for basics was the main mall, a short bus ride from home. On the bus she debated whether to go for quality or quantity – whatever, it had to be quick – she wasn't really one for clothes shopping and would decide on something instantaneously. Unlike Verity.

Armed with a few bags full of the cheap and cheerful section, Angela was about to catch her bus, when she saw "It". The Dress. The definitive Christmas party dress. It was off-the-shoulder, royal blue and sparkly in a Celine Dion sort of way. Angela gasped and instantly fell in love. She automatically found herself going into the store and staring up at the mannequin.

Just as she was about to summon a shop assistant, Angela stopped herself. What on earth was she thinking? That dress was for Oscar ceremonies, dinner at the Dorchester – a red carpet event. Did she honestly think it was suitable for a Mort and Grey function? Angela felt torn in half. She may not have looked like she cared about her appearance very much, but the little girl in her had always dreamed of having a princess dress.

Beneath the glasses, strands of grey and lack of mascara, lay a veritable siren with twinkly eyes, a wicked sense of humour and a fabulous figure. Angela just knew that deep down inside, she could pull it off. The fantasy jarred greatly with her reality, but maybe, just maybe, she'd have to check the price tag and then that would clinch it.

Angela climbed onto the display stand and reached inside the neckline for a label. Unfortunately, so transfixed was she that she didn't secure her handbag and felt a sharp tugging all too late, realising it was gone. Angela swung round in a panic, only to see a fair-haired young man running down the corridor of the mall with her bag.

"Hey!" Angela tore after him, not slowing down to think of anything else but stopping him. As he darted out of the automatic doors onto the street, Angela had almost caught up and a crowd of shoppers and a security guard followed closely behind. The young man was almost thwarted, sensing he had to navigate the busy main road without being run over. In a split second, he shoved an elderly woman aside, dodging the beeping traffic.

There was a sickening screech of car breaks as the old woman tumbled off the curb. Almost as though it were a slow motion scene unfolding, the woman threw her hands up in the air, crying out in pain as her leg twisted in an impossible shape beneath her body. Then she crumpled into the roadside, her handbag landing on top of her.

The car missed her by inches. Suddenly oblivious to the thief and her bag, Angela shot to the woman's side and watched her gasping – her face contorted in agony. Angela's immediate instinct was to reach for her mobile, before realising it was in her bag. She yelled for someone to call an ambulance, took hold of the woman's hand and gently asked her name.

"M....Maggie. Maggie Buxton" the woman stammered through anguished gasps.

"I'm going to look after you until the ambulance gets here" said Angela reassuringly. Her phone, her purse, her keys – none of that mattered now. All that mattered was this woman.

****

Callum was now a fully-fledged member of "The Tunnel Boys" – an underground schoolboy gang who saw no hope for their future, other than violence. Callum had come a long way since he first heard that gripping speech in the tunnels at dusk and had been sworn in. As he approached the meeting place, Callum spotted fresh graffiti in the tunnels. He wondered if one of the gang was responsible. This time the big black spray painted letters read, "Abandon hope, all ye who leave here". Callum knew something about that quote wasn't quite right, but he couldn't put his finger on it.

The gang members had been practising stabbing oranges with knives; the texture was said to be the closest thing to human flesh, as well as plunging larger weapons into tree stumps and self-made bundles, used as target practice. But for their first operation, knives were only to be used in extreme circumstances and even then only to cause minor flesh wounds.

The boys were gathered that evening to be briefed on "Trick or Cheat", to be carried out on Halloween evening, October 31st. Callum was quick to process the title.

"Trick or Cheat..... doesn't that mean the same thing?"

"Exactly" replied Daz . "No one gets an option. None of us want those pissy little penny sweets that some stupid mothers stock up on, thinking they're being oh so clever."

"Yeah!" began another boy. "No one wants their pathetic demented smiles with their 'Oh boys, you scared me soooo much! An' then they go and tip these horrible sugary things into your bag, thinking that lets them off."

Daz grew more serious.

"This year, we're going for the *big* stuff, so don't anyone think otherwise. I'm talking TV's, DVD's , iphones – whatever you can lay your hands on. We need you to listen up very carefully on our brother's methods here – we've been working very carefully on this for weeks."

Callum's heart pounded and his ears burned, dying to hear what Daz had to say. This was the most exciting thing he'd been involved in, ever. The Tunnel Boys were even going to provide disguises. Traditional Halloween costumes with masks for every boy. A winning formula for looting, if ever there was.

****

Seated at her coffee table with a pile of marking, a mug of tea and her obligatory plate of chocolate digestives, Beverley got a queasy feeling in her stomach again. It wasn't just the sheer volume of the marking she had to do – there was this much every time at this time of year. Besides, chocolate digestives had virtually been invented for the job at hand.

But something was nagging at her – for some reason she just didn't feel safe. She glanced over at the photo of "Grandma", no longer in this world, but omnipresent just by sitting above the fireplace. Beverley wasn't afraid in the flat – anyway, her boyfriend would be home soon and she had more than enough to focus on without worrying about dinner as well.

But just the thought of dinner made her feel nauseous; somewhere, somehow, there was an ominous feeling in the air. Whilst Beverley would not exactly have described herself as psychic, she would certainly have used the word "intuitive" and she would also allow herself to be guided by gut instinct.

Without knowing the direction her fear lay in, she knew something was heading her way. Something she really wanted to avoid at all costs. Gut instinct made her hand hover over the phone, about to dial Marisa Brown's number, but what was she going to say? What evidence did she have? All she'd seen was Callum hanging around the park with a group of older boys. What harm could they possibly have been doing......?

****

Angela insisted on accompanying Maggie Buxton in the ambulance. Not only had she witnessed the whole accident, but she felt awfully guilty for her part in it and the old woman was in so much pain she had started to drift in and out of consciousness. Maggie managed to mutter something about living on the Drayton Estate, but the rest was largely incoherent. Angela held her hand the whole way to Drayton General.

****

Beverley frantically dialled and re-dialled her boyfriend Mark's mobile number. It was late and he wasn't answering. She started pacing the living room trying to tell herself he was just stuck in traffic and couldn't pick up. When he finally did answer, she screamed down the phone with a mix of relief and release of panic.

"Mark! Are you OK?"

"Yes sweetheart – of course I am. But you don't sound like you are. Has something happened? Has there been an accident?"

"No...." Beverley paused. "I just.....I need you to come home now!"

Mark laughed and Beverley felt her stomach turn again.

"Well, I'm not far away. I'm just at the curry house getting something nice for us both. It was meant to be a surprise. Didn't think you'd feel much like cooking, given all the work you have to do tonight."

"Oh...." Beverley's breathing slowed down. "That's really lovely, thanks. Really thoughtful. I'll see you soon."

Mark asked Beverley again if she was OK, but she'd already hung up.

****

Angela would not budge from the hospital waiting room until someone had come to give her some news. Any news. The police had been and gone, taken a statement and handed back her handbag which still had everything completely intact. For some reason, Angela felt she needed to stay close to this woman – find out if she would be alright.

Maggie's agonised face kept flashing in front of her eyes and she couldn't let it go. But it was more than just that. From the moment she took her hand at the roadside, Angela had already made a deep connection with this stranger – something that came from a warm, honest and yet determined place of truth that couldn't be named. Before she did anything else, Angela needed to know that Maggie Buxton had survived her operation.

****

"Stupid bloody bastard!"

The boy with the broken tooth slung his jacket across a log and thumped his backside down on the stump.

"Whassap Spencer?" asked Daz. The stupid bloody bastard was Spencer's older brother.

"He's only gone and got himself arrested, innee?"

"Why? What's he done?"

"Went and snatched some silly cow's handbag. Right in broad daylight. Right in the middle of the shopping centre."

Daz frowned then looked Spencer in the eye very seriously.

"What's got into him? That's not the way we do things."

"I know" spat Spencer, "But Tony's twenty and he ain't one of us, is he? He acts independent, like. Random acts of theft. Just does what the hell he likes."

Daz forgot the age gap between Spencer and his brother. He'd make sure nothing like that ever happened between him and Benji. He'd train him well – make sure he knew the rules and how imperative it was to abide by them - what would happen to him if he didn't.

"Well, nothing we can do" said Daz. "He's not for us to deal with."

"It gets worse" sighed Spencer, "He knocked an old lady in the road n'all. He'll get A.B.H. An' what if she dies? He's in for good, innee?"

Daz went silent and his golden skin paled a shade. "Then listen carefully to me. Your brother doesn't live with you, does he? You don't go near him. You don't talk to him. You're a Tunnel Boy now. It'd be far too dangerous for any of us. You got that?"

Spencer gulped as his shoulders sunk. It was like the graveness of the situation had finally hit him. You couldn't take risks if you were a Tunnel Boy. Even if it meant disowning your own.

****

A nurse came and found Angela and told her to go home. Mrs Buxton was sleeping peacefully now and there was no more anyone could do. The operation was successful in pinning her leg back together, but recovery might take a while due to her age. Now they needed to see if they could track down any relatives.

Angela glided through the automatic doors of A & E, walking along cold, antiseptic corridors that seemed surreal, until she found herself back on the cold pavement and the harsh screeching of some car breaks followed by the burst of an ambulance siren suddenly brought her back to reality and recent events passed.

****

"C'mon Bev, out with it." Mark spooned out some curry and plonked it in front of his girlfriend. "When you won't touch a chicken korma, I know something's badly wrong." Beverley stared at the mountain of food in front of her. Mark tried to coax her.

"Have you been getting grief from the kids? The head? Tell me, sweetheart."

"No, nothing like that. School's fine. It's some other kids that I'm worried about. Some boys hanging around the park."

Mark placed the cutlery down carefully and took Beverley's hands in his.

"Have – have they threatened you, Bev?"

"Good God, no – they just give me the creeps."

"So....so you've seen them getting up to something? Think they've got drugs, or have you just seen them drinking?"

"That's just it" said Beverley quickly releasing Mark's grasp and standing, "I haven't seen them do anything. They just keep gathering – meeting near The Tunnels. A whole gang. I just know there's some evil plot going on." Beverley spoke faster and faster and waved her hands, gesticulating wildly.

"Know?" queried Mark. It wasn't like Beverley to get so worked up. Her breathing became more rapid and she tapped her chest. Mark gently guided her back down to the sofa.

"Hon – I think you've been overdoing it. Take a few days off. That extra paperwork – it's stressing you out. I'll phone Mr Martin, if you like."

But Beverley wasn't placated. She nodded, seemingly in agreement, but stared vacuously into the distance, her face pale. Now it was Mark's turn to get anxious. Just as he was worrying about who else he should call other than Beverley's boss, Mark realized she was staring hard at the picture of Grandma.

****

A woman who looked too young to be Maggie Buxton's daughter and who had a little boy with her, left Maggie's bedside as Angela watched from the safety of her orange, plastic NHS chair. She supposed this woman must be a relative, as she herself had been asked to wait – maybe a niece? Finally, a nurse beckoned her to the ward. Angela walked slowly and with some trepidation, having been warned that the old woman may not recognise her or even want to talk to her.

Angela stood over the bed, still in her coat and scarf in case she needed to make a hasty exit. The full-on hospital heating was turning her cheeks pink. Maggie turned her head.

"H .. hi. I'm Angela. The lady who came with you in the ambulance." Maggie's eyes twinkled with recognition.

"Oh! I'm so glad you've come! With me in the ambulance? My dear – you did so much more than that!"

Angela smiled guiltily. She wasn't sure how much Maggie knew yet about what had happened. Maggie looked frail, but also well rested. Angela couldn't see her leg as it was covered with a blanket, yellow toenails and bruised toes peeping out from under a plaster cast.

"That looks a bit nasty" said Angela, awkwardly.

"Does it?" replied Maggie "I've never broken anything before, so I wouldn't really know. I can't feel much." Then she chuckled, "Hopefully they'll be giving me lots more drugs – I shall enjoy that bit." When she saw Angela looked a bit taken aback, Maggie realized she wasn't used to being around people who didn't understand her black sense of humour.

"Oh, I'm so sorry my dear – did I shock you? Not really the sort of thing you'd expect from an eighty-seven year old, is it?" Maggie realized Angela was laughing. Someone who *did* get her sense of humour.

"On the contrary" said Angela, "It's kind of – refreshing." In that very moment, a little acknowledging glance, a tiny smile, and two strangers formed a strong bond of understanding, showing they knew each other perfectly. No words were needed – just a sort of Knowing.

****

Benji's young heart leapt for joy. Daz was going to make him his assistant. Halloween was almost upon them and Daz had been allocated the task of choosing each boys' costume. Thinking that Benji might find that fun and absorbing, Daz gave him the job of selecting masks. The best way to match costumes was by height and size, but Daz needed to keep back some "special masks" without giving too much away about what these were for. Besides, he hoped to keep Benji sufficiently occupied not to notice that the older boys were doing stuff he couldn't be involved in – things too harsh and sinister for Benji to even be allowed to get a whiff of.

His pulse pumping with enthusiasm, Callum turned up at the shed early. Daz, however didn't greet Callum with his usual dazzling smile. Instead, he frowned and ignored him. Callum's heart sunk – had he done something wrong? Upset Daz somehow? Worst of all, did the Tunnel Boy leaders think that he wasn't somehow up to scratch?

He wanted to say something, but Benji grabbed his hand.

"Yeah, Callum! Come and see what we've got for you!" Benji led him round the back of a rail of cloaks and masks and handed Callum a plastic scythe. "We thought you'd make a really good Death, didn't we Daz?" Callum smiled. He was going to be used after all. What he wasn't aware of was just how he was being groomed.

Callum was small, quiet, discreet and clever. He'd slip in silently, but deliver short, sharp blows swiftly, before creeping away unnoticed. Yes, he would certainly make a very good Death.

****

Verity was most certainly twitching and twitching was not something that Verity did. Snort with contempt, scowl maybe, but definitely not twitch. This unnerved Angela. She crossed the room to lift some papers from Verity's desk and Verity didn't look up. This was even more disturbing, seeing as Verity usually monitored her every move.

Angela waited to be chastised, asked to re-file, generally scolded, but Verity seemed to be fixated on her screen. Angela put the papers in her own in tray.

"Coffee?" Angela was at a loss. Verity didn't answer. She just mumbled and her frown became so pronounced that Angela thought her eyebrows might lose contact with her face. This was really getting quite distressing now. Something had really gotten to Verity big time. Feeling distinctly uneasy with the negative energy, Angela took herself for a breather in the kitchen, whereby she saw Kevin looking solemnly at the ground.

"Oh no – not you too."

"Eh?" Kevin looked up.

"Verity's in a really funny mood. Not being her usual obnoxious self, at all."

"Yeah, well" was all Kevin said in reply.

"Kevin.....what's going on?" Angela needed to know. Kevin peered around the door, checking that no one was in earshot.

"I shouldn't be telling you this, but.....well, we're not doing that well. I got some sales figures in and I had to forward them to Verity. It's not looking good Ang– I'm sorry." Angela took a deep gulp and then trembled slightly as she spoke again.

"So....are you saying ..." Kevin cut her off.

"I'm afraid so. I didn't think it'd affect us, either. Thought it'd just be my City mates, but that's not the case. It's all had a big knock-on effect."

"B .. but people still need paperclips, don't they?" ventured Angela.

"Yeah, but they can get them cheaper if they're imported from India. And right now, everyone needs cheaper." Kevin just about managed one of his cheeky grins, but Angela couldn't bring herself to say any more. Kevin tried to put her at ease.

"Hey, look. I could well be jumping the gun here. It might not be all doom and gloom for Mort and Grey."

Angela resisted the urge to say *how can you expect anything else from a company name like that?* and instead started to register anger and irritation – unusual for her.

"Don't try and play this down, Kevin. You're our accountant. You, out of anyone must know how bad it is."

It was Kevin's turn to look at the floor now, before he looked Angela directly in the eye. He liked her, she was fun and she was honest – something of a rare find in the company nowadays. She deserved to know the truth. Kevin's normal twinkle seemed to have retreated to a safer hiding place. His eyes registered a mix of deep worry and heavy-heartedness. All he would say was, "It's bad."

Angela took her coffee back to her desk, where Verity was still fixated in her catatonic state. Angela said nothing and tried to focus on doing some work. Just as she thought she had found something to divert her mind, the phone rang. Verity finally spoke.

"Is it for me?"

"Yes" replied Angela. She'd taken the call from Head Office.

"Thank you......I um.....Angela, I wonder if you'd mind stepping out the room for a few minutes?"

Angela obeyed. This was something Verity had never asked her to do. As Kevin had just solemnly revealed – it was bad.

****

Beverley told Mark to stop fussing. After spending the weekend being pampered by him, she insisted she was absolutely fine to go back to work. Having had time to relax, she was also sure it had just been the stress of being a school-teacher getting to her; it had been a long time and the bureaucracy of paperwork just seemed to pile up.

Now however, thanks to her lovely boyfriend bringing her breakfast in bed, cups of tea and magazines all weekend, she felt refreshed, on top of it, and ready to face year six. It was a fine day for late October and Beverley decided the Tunnels route would be fine this time of morning.

She wasn't wrong. The winter sunshine brought out the best in people as joggers and dog walkers smiled at her and some young children and mothers from her school waved.

She slung her backpack over one shoulder and reached into a pocket for her diary. Almost Halloween. That was a fun time at school – it gave her opportunity to be endlessly creative as she helped children construct lanterns, masks and paper cobwebs. She wondered if there'd be a good supply of powder paint this year, as she started to formulate some designs in her head.

She watched younger children keen to get to school and tugging at their mothers, whilst the older ones were being tugged by *their* mothers. Beverley smiled at her observation and for that moment at least forgot all about boy gangs. Some amusing graffiti on the outside park toilet wall made her chuckle; someone had painted some grinning pumpkins and scrawled "Buy one, get one free".

****

Angela tried to sit on a chair in the corridor outside her office, but if she crossed her legs one way a muscle would twitch and if she crossed them the other way, her calf would go numb. She found herself anxiously tapping her fingers on her knees and when she could stand it no longer, she got up and paced instead.

Angela also needed to get an irritating tune out of her head that had been playing in a loop. The tune was from the children's television programme "Sesame Street", followed by cheery American accents announcing the letters and numbers of the day. But all she could hear was...

"And today Sesame Street is brought to you by the letter P and the number 45!"

The door to the office swung open. Angela gulped.

"Come in" said Verity, smiling.

So. That was it, then. Verity wouldn't be smiling unless she were about to deliver bad news. Funnily enough, now that she knew what was coming, sitting down and facing Verity, Angela found that her legs were keeping obediently still. She let Verity deliver the full speech about sales dropping, difficult times, not just her being cut back etc, but then Verity surprised Angela.

"So, I'm sorry, but it looks like from mid-November onwards your contract will only be three days a week."

Angela sat up.

"You, you mean I still have a job? A little bit of a job?"

Her relief was visible, which annoyed Verity. Angela shouldn't have been taking it so well.

"Well....yes, you do. You'll still get your full salary for another month." Then, Verity's smile found its way into an evil little curl. "Of course, I do quite understand if you'll need to find something else...."

"Yes. Thank you Verity" was all Angela said before returning to her desk. She didn't want to give Verity the satisfaction of seeing her tearful or shaky or pleading in any way. Angela had far too much dignity for that. Quietly, she appeared to be working diligently, although any thoughts of doing so were very far from her mind.

Verity was uneasy at first, but then certain things started to occur to her and she relaxed more. Perhaps Angela was just putting on a brave face. That was it – it was her reaction to shock. So the next time Angela looked up, Verity gave her a smile that Angela noticed was unusually nervous. It seemed to say, "Thank goodness it wasn't me."

It was nothing like victory on Verity's part and she knew it. She also quietly continued with her own work, but both women kept occasionally glancing at the other, just to gauge reactions. Who would crack first? They knew they weren't really entirely out of the water – not now noises had been made. It was interesting to note both of their reactions to the thin ice they suddenly found themselves skating on.

Verity's initial relief gave way to future anxiety and Angela's nerves pleasantly seemed to be replaced by the thought that maybe this was the light at the end of the tunnel – a way forward, a way to think about and put into action what she really wanted to do and where she wanted to be. For now, she had no idea what this might be, but she had the strange Knowing that something was just about to happen.

* * * * * * * * *

Marisa Brown was in a very bad place. She had been growing increasingly depressed and stared at the pack of white pills in front of her. She'd been steadily losing weight from her already emaciated frame – partly due to anxiety and partly because she couldn't afford enough good, healthy food for herself and a growing boy.

A piece of semi-burnt toast popped up from the toaster and Marisa reached for the butter, but her stomach knotted up. The condition of the flat was getting worse and just to add to the general misery, she was now worried about keeping her job. A cashier at a large local chain store, cutbacks were already filtering down through her colleagues. There was more than enough to worry about without parents' evening looming.

Callum seemed fine – a little more withdrawn than usual perhaps, but he hadn't really been giving her any more cause for concern. In fact, he seemed quite buoyant and focussed, like he'd found a really good new interest. Marisa decided to skip parents' evening - she'd say she was ill. Surely they'd phone her if they found any cause for concern.

She flipped over the shiny silver pill packet and popped one pill out of its bubble. Then she grasped it between her thumb and first finger and held it up to the table lamp so that it resembled a miniature planet. She revolved the little planet until it appeared to glow and the rest of the room, and Earth faded into the background.

If she could just leave this world and go to that planet – a brighter one that shone like that....everything would be ok. She'd be happier. There'd be no damp. She started to pop the other little pills out of their "space bubbles" and tip them into the palm of her hand. Just as she was about to swallow them all down, the door swung open. Callum was home.

Marisa made a tight fist around the pills and slung them into the breadbin. Callum couldn't help but notice the big dark grey circles beneath his mother's eyes, her permanently furrowed brow and most of all, how thin she was getting. He knew she was ill, but please – don't let her get worse now. Not before Halloween. Not before "Trick or Cheat". He did his best to adopt an upbeat attitude.

"Hey, Mum – shall I go and get us some fish n' chips?"

Marisa stared blankly.

"Mum? Mum - you gotta eat *something*." Marisa nodded and Callum jangled lose coins in his pockets as he headed back out the door. Just for this one evening – just let her eat some food – just let her go up to bed and be ok. Just let them get through the next couple of days and then Halloween would be over and everything would get sorted.

****

Beverley noticed that there seemed to be a particularly excited, unusual buzz especially with the older children about Halloween this year. When she'd done a student placement in America, Halloween was a much bigger deal than it was in England. There, almost without exception, every child from a very young age dressed up and went out "Trick or Treating".

Adults also seemed to join in the buzz, not showing the same hostility as people did in the UK. The treats could also be quite elaborate, ranging from small one cent sweets up to little puppets or toys. It was an evening that people looked forward to. Maybe as the world appeared to shrink, this had now filtered through to England, spurred on by tales from relatives or friends in the States. Children in other parts of the world now wanted all the same joy and fun.

Beverley had wondered whether to discuss the pagan ritual of Samhain with her students, but thought she'd get grief from some of the parents, despite the school now having multi-cultural assemblies. She would be accused of indoctrinating the children with "New Age" ways or even enticing to devil worship, or something extraordinary like that. Beverley chuckled to herself, thinking just how ridiculous all the politically correct rules of her school were.

It was 5pm and the Tunnel Boys were gathered in the park for their briefing. They were greeted to a gripping slide show, constructed on the laptop of one of the older boys in a Power Point presentation. The show featured clips from medieval practises, horror movies, devil worship and Trick and Treating around the world.

This was intended to whip the boys into a frenzy, excite them – get them to execute their tasks to perfection. But Callum started to feel nervous. He couldn't put his finger on it and he thought about his mother – he knew she'd not been herself for a while, but he knew that wasn't what was bothering him. The mission ahead was far more vital and the adrenalin surged through his body. Callum gulped hard as a frightening image flashed on the screen.

Half the boys giggled, whilst others screeched and some whispered fearfully. Callum remained silent suddenly taking in the gravity of where he was and what he was about to do. But it was too late now.

****

Angela was also having problems understanding her feelings. She was being forced to take a substantial pay-cut and really should have been feeling anxious and depressed, but as she boarded her bus back home, she felt like an incredible weight had lifted off her slender frame. Apart from the fact that was two days a week less from Verity, she suddenly found thoughts flowing into her head of all the other jobs she could apply for – things she'd actually like to do; things well away from the world of Mort and Grey.

She knew she'd just got sucked into P.A work following on from her original temping and secretarial college because it was safe, and it was just what you did when you were in her class. It was what you were *expected* to do. Her mind whirled into re-wind, rhythmically with the motion of the bus wheels as the bus pulled in and out of lanes, against the flow of rush-hour.

Today, for maybe the first time ever, Angela started to really look at and think about her fellow travellers. She noticed their differing ages, clothes, creeds and colours, but mostly she noticed the sameness; the vacuous stares, a wash of grey, black and brown clothing. No one seemed to really stand out until a schoolboy of about thirteen or fourteen suddenly caught her eye.

The boy was very good looking with clear, almost luminous golden skin and dark afro style hair. He had eyes almost as dark as his hair and a look twice as intense. Angela noticed him rub the mist off the window and move closer to the edge of his seat to peer out. At first he appeared to be looking out for someone – maybe a friend, but then Angela took in his body language.

This was no ordinary schoolboy on his unremarkable way home. The boy's body was tense and his eyes shining. He was incredibly excited about something and seemed to be scanning the world outside as though he were waiting to observe some kind of happening. Angela ingested his energy, and found herself also rubbing a clear space in the window, only she had no idea what she was looking for.

The bus trundled down the local high street, past the familiar shops. Some people that she knew went in and out of shops – nothing unusual seemed to be going on. A woman wearing a leather jacket and sporting sandy-coloured dreadlocks, made a grab for a young boy as he ran along the pavement. She looked very out of place and Angela knew she had seen her somewhere before.

Suddenly recognising the young woman as the same one she had seen leaving Maggie's hospital bed one afternoon, Angela stared to replay images of Maggie and her twisted leg and twisted face – yellow lines and kerbs suddenly flashing before her eyes. She suddenly felt really anxious about the little boy and pressed her nose closer and closer, up against the glass to try and see him.

When both the boy and the woman disappeared from view, Angela felt her heart racing and sweat pouring down her brow. Suddenly she cared about them with an intense urgency and tried to move to the other side of the bus desperately to see if she could see them. At once the piercing eyes of the teenager's met hers. Angela froze as she got caught in the stare of the golden-skinned boy. She felt threatened, but didn't know why. It was as though he was drinking in her very features, making sure he'd remember her. She averted her gaze and Daz stepped off the bus.

Angela felt her stomach churn and a raw nerve deep in her body felt suddenly very exposed. She just had to know what had happened to the woman and the boy. When she looked up again and out the window, Daz was looking up at her again and behind him, the young boy and the woman were holding hands, skipping and laughing down the high road. The boy caught Angela's eye and he smiled up at her. Unlike Daz, his gaze melted her heart. But why had she been so afraid of Daz? He'd just shown her the people she so cared about were ok. She wanted to leap off the bus and hug the boy, but why such a strong feeling for a complete stranger?

What had Daz set fire to inside her that made her want to act from a place of raw emotion, above all else? Angela felt sick. It was like aliens were invading her body. Suddenly, the calm, quiet, rational Angela stayed on the bus whilst a new, impetuous and vital woman jumped off the bus, leaving an empty seat between a frowning OAP and a flustered young mother with her baby. She didn't understand what was happening to her, but she was having a very strong touch of The Knowing.

****

7pm Halloween evening. After months of preparation, blood sweat and tears, careful recruiting and rigid planning had all come down to this night. This was a first – this would mark the Tunnel Boys initiation into the world of fully-fledged gangs. They'd watched what had happened to their older siblings and the kids on their estate and didn't want lives of deprivation and poverty forever.

They'd already been written off at school, no matter how high their real academic ability. Maybe an older brother had already condemned the family name, making any other siblings already labelled as troublemakers before they'd even set foot inside a classroom. Their school experience was that any bad behaviour was automatically blamed on them.

Brought up in a run-down area, attending one of the roughest schools and having role models who felt they had the bleakest of futures anyway, these boys were not inspired to try and improve their lot in any conventional way. They were already labelled guilty without having any opportunity to declare their innocence.

Spencer remembered when his brother Tony was expelled. He himself must have been very young and didn't know much about what was going on, but he heard the rows and the screams and slaps as one parent or the other was always telling Spencer to disappear – go to his room; basically make himself invisible.

Tony would always come into their bedroom with cuts or bruises or rubbing his backside, cursing and then taking it all out on Spencer's pillows. They would burst and then Spencer would be punished – a punishment would always be preceded by him being sent to his room and told to stay there. It felt like the worst command in the world.

Then, one day Tony just disappeared and there were policemen in the kitchen and more swearing and Spencer's mother howling. Then his father disappeared.

When Spencer started big school, the first words from his form teacher on his first day were, "I'm keeping an eye on you." Eight years later he remembered his first day at school very clearly. The crunch of the gravel as reception classes lined up in the playground, seemed to get louder and louder until someone blew a whistle and a hushed silence fell.

Then he remembered the big metal doors with their chipped red paint which seemed enormous, pushing into the building and being led through endless corridors of grey walls littered with art and craft work. One painting caught his eye. It frightened him. It was a Halloween picture made from thick black paint, tissue and sugar paper and egg cartons.

Red egg box demons with even redder eyes seemed to be leaping off the wall whilst a yellow-eyed and brown-toothed witch with a mangy black cat circled the blue and purple swirly sky above them. Spencer "heard" the demons groan and grunt in croaky dry voices – "We've got an eye on you......" Suddenly he cried out loud.

A hand gripped his shoulder hard and he cranked his neck to see a stern older man with a dark moustache.

"I can see why we're going to have to watch *you*" scowled the man as he firmly pushed Spencer back in his class line. But that was just it – didn't this man understand? The demons were already watching him, always had been and had just confirmed that they intended to continue. Always.

****

"I love this one, its great!"

Mark beamed as Beverley produced a selection of child-made masks from her bag.

"Isn't it fab?" Beverley giggled as she tried the mask on, tugging the elastic strip under her chin. The mask was far too small, but she was determined to get it as far down her face as she possibly could. Finally the mask squashed her bottom lip so that it protruded from underneath, making it look more like some kind of tribal African headwear than a Halloween mask.

Beverley did the obligatory dance in front of the sofa whilst Mark cheered and clapped. Then he raised his hands to his face and shouted in mock horror, "Oh no! Puuurleeese Miss Galbraith! Please don't give me any more homework!"

"What?" Beverley frowned and lifted the mask up.

"Seriously, you do" said Mark, "You look like your colleague Tanya Galbraith."

Beverley pulled the mask off and looked directly at it.

"See?" said Mark "The hair is perfect, isn't it? Just need to add some dark roots!"

Beverley fell about laughing. The mask really did bare a resemblance to a deeply disliked form teacher. "Mark" she said, "That's really cruel – to Mary-Anne's mask!"

Mark grabbed one of Beverley's large perfumed candles off their coffee table and reached into the top drawer of a cabinet for some matches. He lit the candle and started chanting, "Back off, evil woman! You voodoo, voodoo!" Beverley didn't like this. It reminded her of something her Grandma used to do and her eyes darted towards Grandma's picture on the mantelpiece.

Suddenly, all the lights went out.

"Mark?" Beverley called out. He didn't answer and the candle flame was out as well, so she couldn't see anything. She felt her heart pumping as she edged forward, trying to grope her way towards him in the darkness. She stopped still and heard only silence. Suddenly Mark screamed "Aaaahhh!" as he grabbed her ankle. Beverley screamed.

Her fear turned to anger as she pulled her leg away.

"Bastard! Fuck you, fuck you!"

Hot tears started to prick the back of Beverley's eyes as she crawled around on the living room floor, trying to feel for a candle to light. Mark was shocked at her reaction.

"Hon – it was just a joke....I didn't mean to scare you....hon.....where are you?"

Mark tried to feel around for his partner when he felt a sharp blow under his chin as Beverley kicked him hard.

"Oww! That's me you're kicking!"

Rubbing his chin and looking up, Mark realized Beverley was well aware she was kicking him as she held a lit candle above his head.

"Jesus, Beverley – what the hell are you doing? It's just a power cut!"

"How could you, Mark?" Angry tears started streaming down Beverley's cheeks.

"You know – you know what my Grandma meant to me. She said the spirits....." Her voice trailed off and she started sobbing. Mark felt a helpless mix of bemusement, anger and concern. He rubbed his chin and reached out for Beverley's hand to guide her to the sofa and sit with her and put his arm around her and reassure her like he would if she were ever troubled about anything. But she wouldn't take his hand.

****

A sea of black and white and grey and red covered the grass peak at the entrance to The Tunnels. There stood a resplendent army of Halloween masks and costumes, varying heights of the boys wearing them from the very youngest to the ring leaders. The broomstick was raised and hence the signal was given.

The boys split into their separate groups and marched down the banks onto the suburban streets. They'd all been extremely well drilled and had been waiting for this moment so long they could hardly contain the adrenalin any longer.

Warned against running or making too much noise, they marched obediently onwards towards the local houses, until they realized there was no street lighting. Some of the boys half ran onto the street not sure what to do next, others held back and froze, looking towards Daz, Spencer or one of the older leaders.

"Shit!" muttered Daz under his breath, "Looks like there's been a power cut or somethin'!"

"What are we going to do?" panted Spencer, "We can't call it off – not now, not after all our work!"

Daz found his brain cells going into overdrive, then he went onto methodical mode;

"We go back to base and we wait."

"Wait? What for?" yelled Spencer. "Look at them! Our boys want to do this *now!*"

"Well they *can't*" dictated Daz firmly. "They – *we* need to exercise some control."

Daz was the master of that. When the going got tough, Daz was the coolest cookie around. He had the sort of mind that made meticulous plans and could re-organise his calculations if nothing went accordingly. You could almost see the grey matter ticking as he worked out what to do next.

"Get everyone back" he ordered. "The lights might come back on later."

"But..."

"We don't have a choice Spence! We've gotta wait. We've all waited this long haven't we? Well, we can wait a few hours longer."

Spencer's shoulders slunk down as he realized there was really nothing else they could do. He rounded up all the boys and got the message spread to all those who had run on ahead. But he was also open to other options – maybe, just maybe there was something else that could be done – some great idea someone could come up with. He couldn't conceive that mission "Trick or Cheat" would be over before it had begun.

Maybe Daz was right – maybe the lights would come back on. After all, if there was still lighting in the park, then the power cut was only affecting a very small area. Unfortunately, that was also part of the area they'd targeted to carry out their scheme. Perhaps they could re-group; send some boys down to see if other streets not so far away were also affected. It would hold everything up, but at least they could still go ahead.

Back at base, the mood had changed considerably. Starting out that night on top of the hill, looking down upon the concrete tunnels, there had been a sense of euphoria. There was a feeling that something quite magnificent, magical and even historic might be about to happen, even if there was also a strong smell of danger in the air.

It felt like a battalion of troops, psyched up to fight to the death and yet also believing they themselves were impenetrable, immortal, protected. They would win something great. That's what it had felt like. Now, thwarted by something as pathetic as the modern day invention of electricity, the atmosphere was one of deflation and defeat.

Some of the boys had flung their masks off and were crouched with their heads in their hands, staring stony faced at the creepy mask-faces.

"Brothers!" Daz's voice roused everyone to attention. "This is a setback – not the end. It's just a delay. We know we've got lights up here, so the chances of everything coming back on soon are high. If we can't get down into the places we've mapped up, we're gonna get you to look at another area and set to there, instead. You can't hang your heads and give up, just 'cos things aren't how you expected – who'd ever have gotten anywhere with that attitude?

If your plans don't work out, do you just pack in all your dreams then and there? No – you dream up other plans. You try again. You go out there, and you keep on going. You keep going til' you make it all happen. We're gonna make it happen, brothers – we're *still* gonna make it happen."

Daz practically got a standing ovation. He was a great orator, worthy maybe of looking towards doing a Politics degree in later life and becoming an M.P. Maybe even Prime Minister. But because of his "labelling" and up-bringing and circumstances, for now at least, he was becoming a gang leader. An enticer – a charismatic and powerful little icon, representing every boy who had ever had it tough, just couldn't make it through school and who thought the only way ahead was via pillaging and violence.

****

Verity had the corner table at the "Dog and Bucket", whilst Kevin was perched with his friends at the bar. The bar stool was big in comparison to Kevin, but he was used to scrambling up on one – usually his friends liked to lean on the bar and chat to the staff rather than sit at what they called the "girly" table.

The conversations between the sexes at either end of the pub were different as well. The men were quite subdued, whilst the women were chatting and animated.

"Gosh, that's lovely Verity!" gasped her friend, as Verity pulled a sequinned red vest top out of her work bag.

"Oh – it's just a little something," she gushed, "Thought with a black skirt – Christmas do's?"

"Absolutely perfect!" said another friend.

"It's designer, but it was reduced" said Verity, "I got it for £52.99 – it was originally reduced to £55, but I argued a few of the sequins were coming lose, and so the sales girl reduced it even further." Several girls in the group looked at Verity with envy, whilst others chuckled and said things like, "Well done! What a bargain!", but none of the women would admit to being "financially terrified" given the undercurrent in the economy or confess to not being able to keep up with office fashion.

Not that Verity dressed in a way that was exactly what you'd call "high fashion", much as she saw herself that way. Her clothes were expensive, but hardly stylish, giving her the look of a very desperate prostitute when she wore too much make-up and high heels. Verity liked to think of herself as a bit of trend setter.

She had become peculiarly middle-aged before her time, wearing what she thought was expensive enough and designer enough, but that didn't necessarily suit her. Her "power bob" ended at her cheeks, but unfortunately in order to carry off that sort of look you really needed bones beneath the cheeks.

Verity also had several chins which added to the severity of the bob, making her look less Executive Woman and more Executive Hamster, especially when the platinum and copper highlights were freshly done. Who knew if her hairdresser had ever tried to suggest something different or just didn't dare, worried what Verity might start doing with their scissors.....?

Kevin glanced across at Verity. She gave him a cheesy grin and held up her top.

"Very nice." He raised his beer glass. Verity was perturbed that his friends didn't look at her top and wolf whistle like they normally did. What was going on? Why were the boys being so quiet?

"Cheer up!" she shouted annoyingly across the room, and was dutifully ignored. Upset and angry, she told her friends, instead of going over to talk to Kevin.

"Men!" she snorted into her gin and tonic. The girls laughed.

"It's a bit much, isn't it?" said one of Kevin's mates.

"Yeah" Kevin replied, "I don't think she ever watches the news or anything, but she must know what's going on out there. I mean, we talk about it at work all the time."

"But look at her flaunting that" replied another man, "Whaddaya reckon it cost? I mean, it's not Primark, is it?"

The other men nodded and returned to their drinks. None of them had been laid off – yet. But they'd gathered that night in solemn anticipation – a sort of pre-drowning of their sorrows. Didn't Verity and her friends realize that women were even more vulnerable? They were the ones who worked part-time, had kids, were temping – didn't they realize they'd be the first to go? After all , Verity had only cut her own PA's hours the week before.

Or maybe the girls were just ignoring it all, wondering if this might be their last chance to buy glittery tops and fritter the night away. With the company around him unusually quiet, Kevin pondered on his own future. The directors of Mort and Grey had assured him that there would always be a place for him, but what if the world no longer had a place for Mort and Grey....?

The way things were going, that was a very real possibility. Kevin was normally a "glass half full" kind of guy, but tonight, a gloomy mood seemed to have pervaded him. Maybe he was picking up on the feelings of all his mates. For several months they'd been watching images on television of men just like them putting all their office belongings into cardboard boxes and going out on the street.

That was the picture that stuck in their minds – cardboard boxes. The street. Visuals that normally only belonged to down and outs, the homeless. Such media was far more disturbing to everyday normal working folk than any starving Ethiopians or bullet-stricken war-torn children; this was much closer to home.

Verity and Angela had lived and worked through previous recessions, but this was the slightly younger generation, brought up on "me" culture and "having it all". Children of the Thatcher era were actually guided towards saving their money if they wanted luxuries – back then was not a world of credit. Materially speaking, Kevin and his cronies had a lot to show, only ironically – none of it was theirs.

Mortgages wouldn't be paid off for many years and practically everything furnishing their homes still had to be paid for as well. Angela would frequently throw up her hands in horror, regarding the attitudes of her younger colleagues towards making purchases. If she didn't have cash, then she didn't get – they'd get anyway. Worry about paying later.

The office had become more and more like a daily fashion parade, and quite frankly, Angela couldn't keep up. Her salary was a fair average given her job, but these days *everything* seemed to be so expensive. She wondered how all the office "Supermodels" kept up such high maintenance of clothes, highlights, handbags and manicures and a seemingly endless list of body and beauty treatments that had to be constantly upheld. At times like this, she felt thankful that she'd always been such a "plain little thing", to quote her mother and teachers.

Verity had tried to copy the Supermodels and failed. Frittering away money on sparkly tops meant she'd never quite managed to get a mortgage, but that didn't seem to faze her – she loved nothing more than shopping. Each lunch hour Verity would return with bags of luxury goods, "Finest Range" ready meals and shoes. She would quite blatantly display her wares.

Angela enjoyed shopping as much as the next woman, but it seemed no one enjoyed shopping quite as much as Verity. Angela observed how all the colour drained from people's faces when she informed them she didn't actually have any credit cards and paid for things she needed upfront. A frugal person was regarded as somewhat alien and slightly frightening – definitely someone to be wary of.

When she'd first begun her career, secretaries just wore whatever was smart from British Home Stores and definitely didn't need a walk - in wardrobe. They seemed to do their jobs just as well, if not better. For the "Jimmy Choo" buying generation, life was just about to change......

****

Word came quickly and in a flurry of excitement. Mission "Trick or Cheat" was back on. The lights had come back on. Filling the local environment with their heady mix of emotions, The Tunnel Boys ran back into the suburban streets and charged the atmosphere with adrenalin, anticipation and determination.

A group of about six boys knocked on the door of their first target. They chanted in unison, "Trick or Cheat! Trick or Cheat!" A man in his mid-sixties opened the door, chuckling.

"Well – that's a new one, I must say! Haven't heard that before! Can't say I know what you mean, but you'll get your treats alright – stay right there." He put the door on the latch.

"Betcha the arsehole's gone to get some sweets" grumbled a masked Freddy Kruger.

"Yeah, well – we know what to do if he has" replied a witch.

The boys waited a few minutes until the man returned with a large ceramic jar.

"Been putting this away for a while now" he smiled. The boys watched as he took off the lid and tipped a good batch of £1 coins into the waiting carrier bag of Darth Maul. The boys blinked through their masks. There must have been a good £100 or so in there. Darth Maul tied up the handles of the bag before looking directly at the man and saying, "Lucky for you!" as he ran off, leading the others to next door's house.

"I remember when kids used to say thank you" the man shouted after them. He started to push the front door shut, only to see there was still one child left. At least, he thought it was a child. Through the haze of a street light, he glimpsed mottled circles of black and red, until a pair of horns came into focus. Finally, standing only a few yards from him, a devil with a red pitch fork glared directly at him. The man shivered and shut the door.

Next door, number 43 didn't fare as well. Glad with their shiny coins, but a bit disappointed at getting no action, the boys got luckier this time. They wondered if other groups of their comrades had begun "real" Halloween, or if their start had been just as tame. They needn't have worried. Technically speaking, even if they still received a "treat", that wasn't part of the remit, and they'd still go ahead and "cheat" anyway. The scale of the cheat depended on a number of criteria.

Each group had a leader, who would give different signals depending upon the level they deemed suitable to carry out. There had been rigorous drilling about learning these signals correctly – there was absolutely no room for error. Team "A" hadn't expected such a large treat at their very first door – therefore their leader had given them the signal to move on.

Mr Honeywell at number 41 had no idea that by putting away £1 coins for several months, he had probably saved a lot of damage to his property, not to mention his bacon. All the lights were out at number 43. Despite a constant ringing of the doorbell, banging of the knocker and chanting, no one answered. You might actually have believed no one was at home, but for a fatal mistake.

One boy from Team A knew some of the kids who went to the "posh school" and knew this street. He knew the layout of the houses and hauled himself up and over the garden fence, landing on the concrete patio at the back of the house. To his joy, he saw a light and a toddler peering out the window. She'd probably been forbidden to have her light on, but had gotten curious and switched it on herself and climbed up on her bed. Her parents weren't as safe as they thought....

Immediately the Tunnel Boy leapt back over the fence. "They're in!" he yelled. This was it. The time had come. All that training and preparation was for now. Two bigger, bulkier boys smashed bricks through windows in the kitchen and climbed in, after releasing latches. The smaller boys held off until they received a signal and then climbed through as well. Others remained stationed at the front and back of the house.

As soon as they'd broken in, they knew they'd landed on a goldmine. One of the boys flicked the lights on and revealed a chintzy living room filled with an enormous flat-screen television, video games, state of the art music centre and numerous other electrical goodies. No one came running downstairs at the sound of breaking glass, so the team leader figured they were probably too terrified and ordered his team to use this opportunity to act fast.

They'd practised well. Goods were passed out through the broken windows in a chain, until they reached an older Tunnel Boy in a get-away vehicle. The modern age of mobile phones meant that cutting land-lines no longer stopped anyone calling the police. But team A were fast, and if the other teams were doing as well, then lots of people from lots of different streets would also be calling the police and make it confusing for them to know where to head first.

The boys had strict orders that violence was for emergency use only. If a boy felt he needed to act in such a way, he should try and signal his leader. Suddenly, the sound of a child crying ignited panic. That wouldn't have fazed some more experienced boys, but for many this was their first ever mission and startled, two of the younger boys dropped a DVD machine.

"Shit!" gasped one of them.

"Shurrup!" hissed his accomplice. Luckily, the leader was nearby. He raised the signal that meant "drop it" - in other words, it wasn't worth the risk. They'd already got a good hoarding from that particular home and now it was time to leave.

****

The electricity had come back on in their street, but a terrified Beverley begged Mark not to put the lights back on. Instead she lit several more candles and sat huddled on the settee with Mark's arms wrapped around her. She'd managed to persuade him not to call out their doctor, but this didn't make him any less concerned.

Mark had put a large plaster on his chin where Beverley's shoe had cut him. She stroked his face gently.

"Oh baby, I'm so, so sorry – what have I done to you?"

"Doesn't matter. Just a flesh wound." Mark pulled Beverley closer. "I'm more worried about you. Something's really gotten to you. Talk to me, Beverley – please tell me what's wrong. What are you so frightened of?"

Beverley pushed herself off Mark's chest. "Well.....you know how I told you my Grandma lived with us when I was little? And her strange ways and how she tried to cope with life in England? Well, I remember......I must have been only about seven or eight when I had to go to the launderette with her because she had no idea about using machines. I put the money in the slot and showed her how to push it shut and of course the machine came on."

"So – what did Grandma do?" asked Mark.

"She completely freaked! And then of course another customer started a machine and also some of the dryers had been set by the attendant and they all started whirring. Grandma just couldn't handle it! She started waving her arms around and shrieking, shouting 'Voodoo! Voodoo!' I thought it was really funny, but Grandma was so upset. I had to take her out and bring wet washing home because she just wouldn't go back in there. When we eventually got a washer dryer at home, she wouldn't go in the kitchen for days."

Mark started laughing, but then Beverley's memories started to take on a more serious under current.

"Mark.....I know people thought she was just a silly old lady, but....I can't explain. Grandma just *knew* things."

"What do you mean just *knew*?" Mark frowned. He was tolerant of most things, but Beverley's fascination with the supernatural was a sore point between them. Beverley continued.

"She'd make predictions, and she'd always be right. She knew if natural disasters were about to happen and what part of the world they'd be in, and air crashes and presidents about to be assassinated and....stuff like that."

"Didn't she make any *nice* predictions?" asked Mark. Beverley paused.

"She told me I'd be a teacher and that it was just the right path for me. And she said I'd be very comfortable and be successful in my career. And she also told me I would meet my soul-mate when I was in my late twenties and that we'd share a home together and be very much in love." Mark sat up.

"But," continued Beverley, "The last bit hasn't happened yet....." At that, Mark grabbed his girlfriend and tickled her relentlessly until she was helpless with giggles. They both started laughing, but Mark didn't like that last comment. He didn't want to think about whether Grandma got everything right.....

****

Over the other side of town, Team B had been going for the kill. They'd already looted and trashed one house and Callum witnessed Darth Maul grab a young boy about his age, and threaten him. Callum was afraid Darth Maul would do much worse. Even with a mask on, he could tell by the boys' body language and the energy pumping from him. He knew he could be baying for blood.

Callum wanted to pull Darth to one side and remind him of the Tunnel Boys rules about violence, but he feared for his own safety. He stopped to rest in a nearby front garden, adjusting his "Death" mask which was pinching his ears. All the boys had been lightly sewn into their headwear at the back and front to avoid someone grabbing the heads and revealing their identities.

Callum's scythe felt heavy. He swung it to one side, noticing it was cutting through the blades of grass. As he lifted the blade to make a closer examination, he realized why his weapon had been dragging him down so much and seemed so much heavier than when they'd practiced the drill. The blade was real. He'd been given a cold, hard, lethal weapon.

Callum's breathing got faster and shallower. He needed to look up, needed to keep an eye out for the next signal, but he just kept staring down at the scythe with thoughts circulating of what would happen if he received the signal to use it. A creepy monster tapped him on the shoulder and made him jump.

"Watch it, Callum – you missed the signal!"

Callum and the monster leapt over the garden wall. Immediately Callum's head started to spin and he felt sick – he stood back and watched more glass being shattered, heard more screaming and thought he saw a man get punched in the face and fall to the ground.

"Jesus, Callum – don't just stand there – MOVE!!" But Callum was frozen to the spot.

"Fuck it – someone's comin' downstairs – Crissakes, use your bloody scythe, like you've been taught!"

But Callum couldn't move his feet, let alone swing a scythe. Especially now he knew the sharp, metal blade was real. The monster shoved Callum forwards and suddenly boys were running, all running and then car headlights blinded them, but they kept running and Callum got the feeling back in his legs and bolted after them. Monsters and devils and witches, Darth Mauls and vampires – all a blur of black and red and green. Back inside the house from which they had just fled, a man breathed heavily as he held a t-shirt to the gash on his head.

"Tell them – tell them one of them was wearing a Death outfit" he gasped.

****

Fortunately for Angela, she couldn't afford to live in the more salubrious part of town, so "Trick or Cheat" had passed her by, but she was still shocked reading the reports in her local paper. With the paper tucked under her arm, she made her way over to the hospital to see Maggie.

"Coming to see me on a Monday morning, dear? Have you got the day off?"

Angela hung her head. Maggie tried to shift her position, but it was too painful. She winced. Angela dived forward to adjust Maggie's pillow and Maggie seized the opportunity to grab her hand. Angela was surprised by the fact she didn't feel uncomfortable about this – coming to terms with only having half a job was one thing, but explaining to a complete stranger was another.

Only Maggie didn't feel like a stranger. Maggie felt like someone Angela had known a very long time. Angela looked at their entwined fingers and looked down at the pale, papery, blue-veined hands of this woman. Beneath the frail surface, there was something pumping away strong and hard – something that revealed the real strength of Maggie Buxton.

Angela wondered who Maggie really was – she was very well spoken, even though she lived on the Drayton Estate. She must've been a council tenant of old and never moved. Angela could imagine Maggie was involved with all sorts of residents groups and people like the Women's Institute – she imagined her being a powerful speaker and fighting for all kinds of causes.

As Maggie wore no rings, her marital status was impossible to tell –
Angela imagined all her jewellery would have been removed before her
operation, anyway. When Angela finally looked up from their hands, she
was met with the most tender of gazes.

"Oh my dear – tell me, what's happened?" Angela didn't need to reply.
"Oh no – you've lost your job, haven't you? Dear dear, terrible, all this
going on so much." Angela wiped a little trickle of a tear, forming beneath
her right eye socket. She realized she wasn't crying about her job, but
because something was touching her deep inside. Someone was caring
about her very deeply and showing real concern and affection.

"It's not quite that bad," Angela sniffed "I still have half a job. It'll be
hard, but I'll manage. I'll find something else." Maggie examined
Angela's hands.

"Oh my....you're a pianist, aren't you?" Angela pulled her hands away.

"How...how do you know? I mean, that's not really what I do. I trained,
but – well, I teach a bit."

"Hmmmm.....hands like these aren't really made for typing, dear."

"Wait a minute... how do you know I play the piano, and how do you
know I type?"

"No mystery to it, dear. Even I know it's hard to make a living being a
musician....It's such a shame, though. I wish was there was something I
could do....."

A little bolt of lightning shot through Angela. A shame? She'd never
thought of it like that before. It was just a given, that she'd never seriously
try and be a "grown up" musician. She knew she wasn't talented enough –
never put in all the painstaking hours of her fellow students. But maybe
that was a shame. Maybe looking back.....

Looking back, Petra Kapinksy was the one who was going to be a grown
up pianist. After all, Angela Morgan just didn't have quite the same ring to

it. Petra also had blonde hair almost down to her ankles, naturally bee-stung lips and an awful lot of sponsors. Angela just couldn't compete. Discouraged from a professional career, Angela just played these days "for fun". Even though, looking back, she had originally been talented enough to win a scholarship.....

Angela reddened, feeling guilty she'd spent so long talking about herself. Maybe Maggie wanted to talk – after all, she was the one in bed and in pain. Angela tried to second-guess Maggie's life. Maybe it was incredible, unique and inspiring. Maybe it was mundane and uneventful, or just quiet, but happily married. Probably, she was just a lonely old widow. But she didn't seem that way.

Maggie however, was intent on helping Angela. "I'm sorry you've been treated so badly. You certainly don't deserve it." Maggie reached into the bedside cabinet for her handbag, but Angela stopped her.

"My goodness, no! I couldn't possibly! You're on a pension!"

"Quite right there. But I wasn't fishing around for money – don't think I've got a bean in there, anyway. I was actually looking for some business cards – I might know some people who could help you."

Angela frowned. Business cards? Now Maggie was becoming more mysterious. Who did she know? Had she herself been a business woman, or know something about music? Maggie had a rummage.

"Oh no, dearie me. I'm so sorry. Doesn't look like I've got those after all.....lots of tissues...a packet of throat lozenges......wait a minute, what's this......oh, no – that's for the window cleaner.....like I'll be needing that at the moment...."

So, that shattered the fantasy. Maggie wasn't some intriguing local celebrity, but just an ordinary slightly forgetful old lady. Yet, she was kind, warm, funny. It was enough to have her company and friendship. Surely Angela should be concerned more with giving than receiving, anyway? After all, she was young and mobile with many friends, and perhaps Maggie didn't have friends still alive and maybe, maybe......

Maybe Maggie caught the look on Angela's face.

"Oh, please don't be disappointed dear – you have everything ahead of you. I'm so sure better things are about to begin. I know it's hard, but I believe things will improve – I really do. Anyway, you won't have to work so much for that horrible boss of yours!"

Angela couldn't remember telling Maggie about Verity, but suddenly felt a surge of energy through her body and her senses becoming very alive. Even if it would only be in that moment, Angela totally and utterly sensed that Maggie was right.

****

Marisa and Callum sat at opposite ends of his bedroom. The increasing problems with the damp, in turn meant that the electricity wasn't working properly and therefore, Callum only had one poorly lit lamp in his room. He could just about make out his mother as a silhouette, she had become so thin. He watched her fingering his dirty, torn curtains and then curl the bottom of the polyester material around one hand and spread it out and smooth it across the other palm.

She would then cradle a rolled up corner and rock back and forth for ages. That was all she seemed to do these days – she didn't speak any more, but she did hum. Hum and rock. Callum knew the tune – his dad used to play it when he was very young – before he left. The tune was a Beatles song, "Eleanor Rigby" and sometimes Callum's dad would help him pick it out with him on his guitar. Callum remembered very little about his father, except that he was called Andy and that he didn't know where he was now; all he knew was that he was quite a lot older than his mum.

In the days before the flat got so damp, before his mother got so thin and before the Tunnel Boys, Callum would sometimes wonder if he had any new brothers or sisters anywhere. He wondered what they would look like. Lots of the kids on the estate had "half" brothers or sisters – a phrase he always found funny. He told Marisa when he was younger that he hoped she'd get a new boyfriend, so that he could have a "whole" new sibling. She found that funny.

Marisa suddenly stopped humming and shot her son an evil glare. It was as if she knew everything he'd been up to and he felt at once ashamed and vulnerable and afraid. The Tunnel Boys had become his whole raison d'être, but that was when it was all fantasy and now things were happening for real. It was all a bit *too* real.

Callum needed his mother – he was only a boy. He started to sob and she started fingering the curtains again. The woman who'd once made him fish fingers and roly poly pudding, told him off for walking his muddy boots across the hall, made snowmen and pom-poms with him – this woman was now nowhere to be seen.

Instead, a shaking, bony woman had taken her place. A woman with deep, dark circles under her eyes had replaced his beautiful mother. He had to get them both out of there, but how? Where could they go? If he tried to run away, then the Tunnel Boys would find them and then, then.......Callum couldn't allow himself to think that way. He'd find a way – make sure they were both safe, make sure Marisa was well.

****

"Verity – 'fraid it's bad news."

That was all Kevin ever seemed to say these days. Verity took a deep sigh and shuffled some papers, wondering who she was going to have to make redundant next. She wasn't at all prepared for what Kevin was going to say.

"Mort and Grey's Christmas party is cancelled."

You would have thought Kevin had just sacked Verity. All the colour drained from her face and she dropped her pencil.

"Verity....Verity, are you OK?"

"B....but.....my.....top" was all Verity could stutter.

Kevin made Verity a mug of tea with sugar. He'd heard it was good for shock. She drank it, even though she had been dieting into her top and given up sugar.

"Yeah...." Kevin continued, "Sorry, y'know. Nothing I can do about it. It's the Director's decision. We just haven't got the dosh this year. Better to chop the office party, than more staff though, isn't it?"

Verity choked on her tea. "How dare you Kevin – coming into my office to give me news like that. You really should have prepared me first."

"I'm sorry Verity – I just thought I'd cut to the chase. I didn't think you'd mind *that* much..." then he added, "But I'm sorry about your top" before smiling wryly. Kevin had his sense of humour back. If looks could kill however, Kevin would have been dead in an instant. Verity shot back.

"Well, you know what? I'll just have to find a gorgeous man to take me on a date, so I can wear it." Just then, a man who wasn't particularly gorgeous came bounding up the stairs. It was Brian.

"Bugger, just heard about the party" he panted, as he reached the last step. "Say, where's your pretty little assistant today?"

Verity and Kevin looked up. That wasn't normally the way most people described mousey Angela.

"Surely you don't mean Angela?" scoffed Verity.

"Well, um....actually, Verity - could I have a word?" Brian went red. Kevin perked up. This was going to be interesting.

"Um, in *private*?" added Brian.

"Better be good, Brian" laughed Kevin as he got up to leave the room. Brian pulled up a chair to Verity's desk.

"Now....it's just a quick word." Brian appeared to be going very red, although it was quite hard to tell beneath the plethora of beard. He looked up at Kevin, who was lingering.

"Is it safe to leave this lady with you, unaccompanied?" asked Kevin. Verity smiled. Kevin shuffled out of the office before giving her a big wink. Maybe he'd take her out somewhere to show off her top. Yes, he was a dwarf, but times were hard thought Verity....

"Now, I won't beat about the bush" said Brian, nervously fingering his bush of a beard, "But it's about Angela."

"Angela?" This took Verity by surprise.

"Yes – she's single, isn't she? You see, I'd – I'd rather like to ask her out somewhere...."

"Brian! I'm appalled! Angela might be single, but you're not!" Verity shot Brian one of her very hardest Paddington Bear stares. She was angry he hadn't asked *her* out, not about his audacity, as she knew he was married.

"Oh come on, Verity. You know that me and the missus – well, you know...."

"I think you should leave now, Brian. How could you even think of it? Angela deserves much better than you. One move and I'll tell her you tried it on with me as well....."

"But, Verity..." Brian found himself petrified on the receiving end of another stare. He slunk out of the office. As he sheepishly descended the stairs, Verity called after him, "She's *my* P.A and I have a duty to protect her!" Then she angrily bit into one polished fingernail and tore it off to the quick.

****

The tension between Mark and Beverley grew palpable. As far as he was concerned, he'd been supportive and comforting and she was moody and irritable and would rather constantly read her pack of Tarot cards than watch crap tv with him. As far as Beverley was concerned, Mark was narrow-minded and unaware and wouldn't let her be herself. There was a huge shift going on in their once cosy intimacy, which seemed to have begun on Halloween evening. They were both feeling the brunt of it.

The simple truth was, Mark did not have or understand "The Knowing". Beverley had tried hard to ignore the fact that she had inherited hers from Grandma, but now she had to confront it and deal with it. Vivid dreams, night terror – she had a constant feeling of dread and didn't know why. She wondered about visiting a psychic.

Mark sat at the breakfast table.

"The Doctor's coming over later."

"The Doctor? Why? What's the matter with you?"

"It's not for me – it's for *you*."

Beverley was furious. "Why on earth are you wasting our Doctor's time? I'm not ill! What made you do such a thing?"

"Beverley......" Mark took a deep breath. "You just haven't been yourself. For quite some time. I'm worried about you. You're jumpy and on edge all the time and God forbid if I tell you not to get so obsessed with that stupid pack of cards..." Beverley shot Mark an evil glare.

"How dare you! This is important to me Mark, do you understand? Important! I'm trying to work out what's going on and you just want a doctor to come and give me some pills to make me all soporific so that you don't have to deal with it. Well, I'm not taking any bloody pills, even if he does prescribe them. Anyway, maybe he won't have a wasted journey. He can look at your chin, seeing as you've been going on about it."

Mark grabbed his coat off the door hook.

"Wait, where are you - ?" The front door slammed shut. Beverley realized she had no idea when the doctor was coming. What if she also needed to go out? Now Mark had just ruined their long weekend – the one they'd planned to sit down together with each other and talk things through. Now Beverley thought that maybe Mark had engineered the time, just to get Beverley medical help.

She needed to "evoke the ancestors", not see a doctor. A doctor wouldn't have answers. Shaking with fury, she automatically made herself a coffee before realizing coffee would be the worst thing. She emptied the cup and rooted around the cupboards for something decaffeinated, but there wasn't anything. She immediately blamed Mark. He drank even more coffee than she did.

No wonder he was so tense all the time. In her frustration, Beverley flung packets onto the floor. How dare he just go out? Where was he going and how long would he be? She urgently needed to do some marking, but couldn't get her head around it. A knock at the door stopped her pacing. Obviously Mark hadn't taken a key.

When she opened the door, a policewoman and a policeman were standing there. Beverley's heart leapt to her mouth. He could only have been gone for fifteen minutes at the most. She knew the neighbourhood had been getting rougher of late, but surely not in that time....Police only knocked on doors to deliver terrible news, didn't they?

"Oh my God, no." This was it. This was the terror. What Grandma had been trying to tell her. Beverley crumpled to her knees, but the policewoman grabbed her before she hit the floor.

"Are you unwell Miss? I'm sorry if this is a bad time. We're just asking local residents if they can help us with our enquiries about the Halloween looting. We could come back later if it's inconvenient. We just wanted to know if you heard or saw anything." Beverley's relief was palpable.

"Ah, no – sorry. Of course. Do come in. God knows I've got plenty of coffee....."

****

Mark parked his backside on a long, damp log. He felt the wetness seeping through his jeans and the uncomfortable crunch of soggy wood dig into his buttocks. But he didn't get up – this felt like the place where he needed to sit. The sky was grey and there was a faint mist in the air that made everything feel damp, but not quite full-on enough for proper rain. Mark let the wetness of the grass seep through his trainers and deliberately pointed his toes downwards so that the thin material absorbed more.

The comfort of home had become a fallacy and now he needed a sort of pleasurable physical suffering. He also wanted a cigarette. It had been a while since he'd smoked – Beverley didn't like it. He rustled around in a blue plastic bag and pulled out a pack of Silk Cut. Mark twirled the pack around in his hand and chuckled. About time he did something decadent. He pulled his socks off and immersed his feet in the cold wetness.

A small, young voice suddenly appeared from out of nowhere.

"Got a spare one, mister?" Mark swung his head round to see a short, half-caste boy with unruly hair staring up at him. Benji had run into the park ahead of Daz.

"Hmm...well, I might do" replied Mark, "But surely it's not for you?"

"Might be" said Benji cheekily, "I have a quick drag sometimes."

"Well you *shouldn't*" said Mark. "It's really not good for you!"

"So – why's you doin' it then?" Mark couldn't reply. Benji looked curiously at Mark's bare feet. Tentatively he asked, "Are you a hippy?"

"A what?"

"There's this lady that sometimes comes and sits here and she has bare feet. My mum says she's a hippy. If she is, then she's cool. She chats to us sometimes and gives us apples off her own tree. I told her I don't like school and asked her why she's got no shoes – she said she likes to feel the earth beneath her feet. Is that what you're doing?"

"The earth beneath my feet?" replied Mark. "Well. I guess so. Just trying to find it again...."

****

"Tell me, is there a young man in your life?" Angela hated being asked that question, but this was Maggie asking and straight-talking, straight-asking Maggie would always receive honesty in return.

"No – there isn't a man of any kind, young or old." She waited for Maggie to say something like, "Oh, what a shame" or "Don't worry, I'm sure you'll meet someone soon", or even a question she found rather strange – "How come?" Well – because she hadn't met anyone she wanted to be with, that's how come. But Maggie's response surprised her.

Maggie clapped her hands together and then replied, "Excellent! Good thing too!" What sort of reaction was that? Was Maggie a lesbian? An ardent feminist? Angela took on a shocked expression.

"What I mean, my dear, is that there are some things in life you just have to do. And I'm not saying it's a bad thing to have a supportive partner, but – well, there are times when you're just better off not to have those attachments.....I just feel like your life is about to take off, change for the better......once you've achieved those things then it would be the right time to meet someone, but for now......enjoy the freedom, my dear."

Angela felt like a huge weight had been lifted off her. No one had actually acknowledged how she felt about being single. But it wasn't entirely from a place of enlightenment that Maggie spoke. It transpired she had been in an unhappy marriage, but you just didn't divorce in her day.

"All I can say is" chuckled Maggie, "He was hopeless with anything mechanical, even worse with money and I had to manage everything by myself anyway, after he drank himself to death."

"Oh my gosh! I'm so sorry!" gasped Angela.

"Don't be – it was a blessed relief, in a way. Meant I could really get on with things I felt I needed to do. Not have that old soak in the way to mop up after. Oh, don't get me wrong – it wasn't always awful between us. He just got worse as he got older. And I do count myself very lucky – I suppose you might say I've always been surrounded by the right kind of people."

Angela took that to mean Maggie meant people like solicitors and lawyers or anyone who could help her cope financially. She couldn't have ended up with much – the widow of a drunk, on the Drayton Estate......

Just as Angela was leaving the ward, the young woman with the sandy coloured dreadlocks who Angela remembered seeing when she first visited Maggie, arrived.

"Oh, hello there!" called out the woman. "You come to see Maggie a lot, don't you? I have to say, that's very good of you."

"*Good* of me?" replied Angela, "It's because of me she ended up in here in the first place!" The young woman looked taken aback.

"What do you mean, because of *you?*"

"Oh....I was having some stupid fantasy about buying this dress that I could no way afford and so I wasn't concentrating on my handbag and it got snatched, and...."

Chrissie, the woman with the dreadlocks laughed. She knew the story.

"Yeah, sure it's your fault. Maggie really appreciates you coming, you know."

"Does she?" Angela beamed. Someone appreciated her. Someone she really liked, as well. Angela explained how her handbag had miraculously been returned, with everything intact. She said she thought that was amazing.

"Well, I think *you're* pretty amazing" said Chrissie. Angela looked at her, quizzically. "Maggie told me you ran straight to her, without a second thought for your belongings. Not many people would have done that – they'd only think about themselves. They'd be far more worried about their keys and credit cards than an old woman falling in the road."

"B .. but I couldn't just leave her!" said Angela. Then she laughed, "Besides, I don't have any credit cards!" Chrissie searched Angela's features before a broad smile spread across her face.

"I'm Chrissie" she said, holding out her hand. "I do hope we see each other again."

"Yes, I hope so too" said Angela as she walked off suddenly remembering where she'd last seen Chrissie. It was out the bus window, on the same day she'd seen Daz.

Chrissie pulled up a chair besides Maggie's bed. "I've just met Angela" she said.

"I hoped you would" said Maggie.

****

Angela was trying to find some very important papers and Brian was irritating her. Sheepishly, he pulled up a chair and twiddled his thumbs before nervously tugging at his beard. That really made her cringe – what did he want? Brian smiled and then went bright red.

"Angie....."

Angie? Only her mother called her that. That really annoyed her.

"Look, I'm really rather busy, Brian – what do you want?"

"Well....." Brian moved uncomfortably too far into Angela's personal body space. Then he placed his palms flat on Angela's desk and leaned towards her as she recoiled.

"I was just wondering if......maybe you'd like to go for a drink with me...?" You could just about make out Brian's teeth beneath his bush of beard, but in order to see any teeth at all he would have to be grinning very hard.

"What?" Angela tensed up.

"Just you and me. Quiet little place I know. Tomorrow evening."

"Brian, are you....asking me out?"

"Yes. Well, no. Well, sort of. Um – yes."

"But you're married!"

"Indeed, yes – I sort of am, but you see, my wife...."

"Oh for God sakes Brian, please don't be about to tell me that she doesn't understand you!"

"My goodness yes, you are perceptive, Angie. That's exactly it, I..."

"Brian" Angela pointed a finger unmistakably to the door. "Leave."

"But..."

"Leave, or I'll set Verity on you." Brian didn't argue. He may have plucked up the courage to ask Angela out, but at heart he was a real coward. That was definitely not the sort of man for Angela. She felt proud of herself as he left and thought how right Maggie was. She really didn't need a man in her life right now. At least, not one like Brian.

At home that night, Angela started to pull all her clothes out her wardrobe. Buried beneath a pile of neatly folded work blouses was an ancient cheesecloth top – a 1970's original. It was one of those things that she just couldn't chuck out, but didn't know why. God only knows it hadn't been worn since school days.

Angela ran her hands through her hair. It was rarely dressed up in anything other than a scrunchie and a few hairgrips. She wondered how long Chrissie's hair had taken to get into all those dreadlocks. Angela held the top up to her window and saw the little beads shimmering in the winter sunlight. As she did so, she wondered why she only ever wore such dull, drab going-to-work colours. Was it because they somehow seemed –safe?

In that moment, Angela decided not to be mousey "safe" little Angela any more. She didn't know what form that would take, but she could start with some new clothes. Clothes for herself – her *true* self. Not just things that made her look like a P.A. She didn't even stop to consider how considerably reduced her earnings were – the intention was to go out and shop.

From the minute she'd helped Maggie Buxton, seen Daz on the bus and now met Chrissie, Angela couldn't help but feel a "sea change" deep inside. This was a sea she wanted to swim in very much.

****

"I've gotta go – my brother's here" said Benji as Mark pulled his shoes and socks back on.

"Well, nice meeting you" said Mark.

"Ta ra!" said Benji, disappearing as instantly as he'd manifested. As Mark sat up, he caught sight of Daz crossing the brow of the hill in the early afternoon mist. The sun lit the top part of Daz's afro, so that he appeared to have a little halo around him and the winter's light hit the bottom of his combat trousers, showing off the lime green fluorescent laces in his trainers.

No wonder Benji had run off – his brother looked a rather formidable character. Mark couldn't help but stare. Daz was so striking a boy, that anyone who saw him was awestruck. Mark wondered what Daz would grow up to do – he looked like a born leader. Maybe he'd run his own company, be a local M.P, a rap star or front a reality tv show. He looked like he could do anything.

Perhaps he'd even entice the country to revolution. Mark shuddered as he had that thought – there was something about Daz that sensitive beings could sense; an aura of danger, like a beautiful devil in disguise. Was it just by chance that Daz had thought it was hysterical to attach a pair of wings to his Trick or Cheat costume.....?

Daz put a firm hand on Benji's shoulder and stared back hard at Mark. Mark felt the penetrating eyes stab his retinas. He'd never experienced such a painful stare.

"I told you not to go talking to strangers" Daz warned Benji.

"But he ain't a stranger – he's nice" Benji replied.

"Anyone is a suss now – remember?"

"Yeah, I remember – we gotta be....suspicious."

"That's right. Anyone around here could have called the police. You never know what's goin' on with people, so if you don't know 'em, you don't go near 'em. Right?"

"Right" said Benji.

"And what else do you remember?" asked Daz.

"That even if they seem nice, you don't say too much to them."

"You got it" said Daz, "And what else?"

"Be sweet as pie" said Benji, remembering his drilling well. When they'd headed off the path a bit, Benji produced two cigarettes, just to show how clever he was to have sponged them off "the new hippy". Daz frowned as he carefully placed them in the top pocket of his bomber jacket.

****

After the police had left, Beverley relaxed. She'd stayed focussed and calm and actually enjoyed talking to them, by way of distraction. Soon Mark would be home and then they could talk – properly. It surprised her how frequent their fights had become and how Mark would go off on one at the mere mention of Grandma. He used to love hearing about her eccentricities, but now he just didn't want to know.

Beverley had also noticed Mark becoming more uptight and stressed, but she put that down to worry about his job. She thought back to their first kiss. The local pizza house seemed like the most romantic restaurant on earth. Beverley remembered Mark carefully removing the plastic rose from their table vase and scolded him, whilst at the same time secretly loving his daring.

Outside, he placed the rose between his teeth and grabbed her for an impromptu tango. And that was just it – these days they just didn't seem to be dancing in step any more.....But, they'd sort it out. Mark would come back with some flowers, hug her – make love to her; she knew the routine by now.

To the sound of the boiling kettle, Mark put his key in the door, only he didn't have any flowers with him. "Bev, we need to talk."

Beverley reached for Mark's hand, but he withdrew it. This wasn't how it normally went. What should she do now? What should she think? Beverley felt her stomach flip over. Mark didn't even move over to the settee, which was the normal place for settling conflicts. What Mark actually meant, was not that they needed to talk, but that he needed to say something. He'd already decided.

"I.....I think we need a trial separation. I'm going to go back to my parents for a bit."

Beverley's mouth fell open, at the same time the bottom dropped out of her world.

"Mark, you need to think this through, *we* need to....."

"I've thought, Beverley. This is the conclusion I've reached." With that, he sombrely walked into the bedroom and came out seconds later with an already packed suitcase. "I'll sort some time to come back for some more stuff" he said dryly.

"My God!" said Beverley, "You'd *already* decided! Before you even walked out this afternoon, you already knew that's what you were going to do! Couldn't you at least have talked to me about it first?"

Mark glanced downwards full of sadness, before looking at Beverley with tears in his eyes.

"Beverley – how much talking can we do.....?" And then he was gone.

****

Operation "Trick or Cheat" had been an undoubted success. The Tunnel Boys weren't just a regular boy gang, but a massive organisation. Their Halloween rampage was planned and executed with military precision, and not one single boy had failed to please. Except for maybe one.....

Daz and Spencer had been dispatched to "sound down" Callum, which basically consisted of a very severe warning. For their next mission, Callum would be put out as a "Strike One" – a boy who would carry out one of the most dangerous tasks. If he failed, a terrible fate awaited him. Daz had severe reservations about this. He didn't think Callum was ready, and if he failed, it could damn them all.

But The Chiefs were adamant. Three of the eldest boys had now self-selected themselves to lead the whole gang and began further structuring, naming various positions within, as well as types of tasks. Daz and Spencer had been selected as "Seconders" – that is, they reported to the Chiefs.

Whilst Spencer waxed lyrical about the huge success of the Tunnel Boys and their amazing leaders, Daz was getting very edgy about the ever increasing size of the gang. He didn't like to say so, but he preferred it when it was smaller and he'd had more control. He enjoyed being at the forefront of movements, being a pioneer and absorbing all the thrilling buzz of newness.

This gang was a beacon of light in his otherwise grey little world – grey school uniform, grey concrete of the Drayton Estate.....grey future. He was far too bright and special for such an empty existence and desperately needed something to fuel his fertile, active brain. Something more promising than equations and algebra and essays, all handed back with "D" grades.

Daz struggled with school English grammar and discouraged by his teacher, eventually gave up. He was much better at talking than writing things down and he was never afraid of addressing groups or "public speaking". He was eloquent and clear, and that was exactly what the Tunnel Boys needed. Now that he was just a Seconder, he really missed that.

Callum's demeanour and appearance really worried Daz. He seemed to have lost a lot of weight and looked pale and anxious. He hadn't always been like that – Callum had seemed like a real find; intelligent, raw talent and hungry for action. Daz had cultivated him and initiated him himself. Beneath the foreboding surface, Daz was extremely loyal to those he took a shine to.

He thought he might try and talk the Chiefs out of putting Callum forward as a Strike One, but first he had to speak to Callum himself. Seconders had to work in twos and Daz wasn't best pleased that Spencer would have to be present during this conversation. The Chiefs made this a rule, lest an individual might have their own agenda and bias opinion.

If truth be told, Daz did have his own agenda. His continually active brain was formulating how he would work this one out. Callum was found at the entrance to the main tunnel; he was exactly on time.

"Awright Cal?" Daz waved.

"Guess" shrugged Callum, aware this wasn't a social visit.

"Yeah...." Daz sighed. "I know mate – not easy.....but we gotta do our job, y'know?" Daz thought he'd just get to the point, but unfortunately Spencer cut in.

"You loser, Callum. When it came down to it, you just couldn't hack it, could you? You're bloody yellow, you are. Well, we don't want any yellow-coloured Tunnel boys. So you're gonna have to prove you're a different colour....like red. Like you're gunnin' for it and you're hungry and you want it! Like the rest of us. Go ahead and show us you're glowing red, Callum."

Callum sadly looked up at Spencer as Daz looked over at him. Never mind hungry – Callum looked absolutely starving. Daz's cogs continued to tick. He let Spencer impart the Strike One instructions and decided once Callum was briefed that they'd all head off. Then he'd pull Callum quietly over somewhere on his own.

Spencer pulled a flick knife from his pocket and flicked and shut it several times.

"You know what it's about, don't you Cal?" Spencer gave an evil leer.

"Yeah, Spencer. I know. I know Strike Ones have to use knives."

"Too right. And you gotta do a Nip Tuck on a Goldie." Translated from Tunnel Boy speak, that meant cutting the first stranger, unfortunate enough to cross their path. They were called "Goldies" because hurting an innocent bystander was known as "Going for Gold" – something one of the chiefs had heard on television and then borrowed the phrase.

"I know" croaked Callum, "I got drilled. I know what I have to do."

"Good." Spencer nodded. "When you arrive, you'll get your weapon." Daz tried hard to catch Callum's eye as he and Spencer climbed up the hill again, but.......he couldn't. As they walked in opposite directions, some fresh graffiti glowed in the lamplight at the side of the tunnel. It read, "All You Need is Blood – It's Easy."

****

Angela eventually sat down with a calculator and underwent the painstaking task of working out exactly what she had to live on. She was pleasantly surprised to work out the rent would be ok, travel to work and some food, although there wouldn't be much left after her basics. She'd have to make a lot of cut backs, but she'd survive. Never having been much of a shoes or handbags type woman, the sacrifices didn't seem too much to make.

A holiday would be out of the question, but that seemed small fry, anyway. As for clothes, there was certainly no need for sparkly tops, now that Christmas was cancelled. Angela sniggered as she thought of Verity's purchase, but then she also thought about the Celine Dion dress and how she'd really liked it.......Unwittingly, she had found something far better than the dress – Maggie Buxton. A reason to feel good about life again. As she thought of Maggie, Angela felt compelled to completely scrutinize her looks and her appearance. She stood in front of the three quarter length mirror on the front of her wardrobe and took off her glasses. Then she unpinned her hair.

Angela never spent very long looking in mirrors – she felt pretty certain what she looked like and unlike Verity, never saw Jennifer Lopez staring back. Instead, she now saw a woman she had denied for a very long time. This woman seemed to be separate from her reflection. Then, it seemed to start telling her what to do.

The reflection said that she needed new clothes that represented who she was now. Before Angela could protest about lack of funds, the reflection said she needed to remember her Aunt's old sewing machine shoved up in the attic, markets, charity shops and car boots for yards of cheap cut offs.....

More curiously, the reflection then instructed her to "go down the hill she never dared go up." What on earth was that supposed to mean? What hill? Angela sometimes had a repetitive dream about a long, winding hill that had a unique and inviting array of shops. These weren't just any shops – they were the shops of childhood dreams; shops filled with toy animals and fairy cakes and bright candles – colours, smells and textures of things you had never seen, touched or smelt.

During the dreams, Angela would be desperate to know where this hill was – she was sure it really existed, but she knew she only ever visited it when asleep. Near the bottom of the hill was a particularly magical looking tea shop. In the window there was a three-tiered cake with pink and blue and lime green icing and a smiling fairy doll on top ,who would lift a finger and beckon.....

But Angela always woke up before she could push the door open. The frustration of awaking from these kind of dreams was indescribable. It was a searing pain – knowing that what you wanted was out of reach - maybe not even real. And that pain never went away, but Angela never stopped dreaming......

****

Beverley cried a lot. Mark worried about her, but didn't call. Guilty as he felt about leaving her in such a fragile state, he also knew he just couldn't stay. He'd tried so hard to help her, but she just seemed to throw it all back in his face and wave around leaflets with homeopaths' and aromatherapists' numbers, saying she didn't need conventional medicine.

Her behaviour at home may have become more and more erratic, but ironically she now seemed to be coping better than ever with her work, as if she needed an outside focus to divert from her inner turmoil. Mark therefore felt justified in relinquishing the role of carer – he wanted to be someone's partner – an equal. That was how they'd started out. Now he felt like he just couldn't get through to Beverley. Maybe a little time apart would be just what they'd need. He would call her – soon....

Beverley pulled off the duvet cover which was wet and salty from her tears and mingled with the smell of Mark. She tugged off the pillow cases and sheet and bundled all the linen into the washing basket, even though it had just been changed a day ago. No more tears would come now – even if

Beverley had wanted to cry, she was right out of tears and now she knew it was time to let go.

After she'd changed the bedding, Beverley lifted onto the bed a sea grass storage box in which she'd kept old photos and knick knacks. She took out a withered picture of Grandma and gently stroked the frame.

"He might not be able to handle it Grandma, but I know you'll always be there for me, won't you?" Beverley smiled as toothless Grandma smiled back.

* * * * * * * * *

Angela watched as Chrissie only just slightly introduced a tea bag to a polystyrene cup of hot water and then drank it without adding any milk or sugar. She didn't know what she was drinking, but it certainly wasn't a cup of tea. Angela was exceedingly "British" in her own tea drinking and it had to be served properly. That meant in china, steeped for two and a half minutes, a dash of milk and preferably with some finger sandwiches and scones on the side.

One of her favourite pastimes was going to London hotels and being served afternoon tea on old fashioned cake stands, which was also something her mother loved doing. Whenever she was in town, they'd always make a point of "taking afternoon tea". Chrissie's cup of tea-stained water wouldn't even make it past a first audition.

"Don't you find that too hot, without milk?" Angela enquired.

"Eh? No – not really. Anyway, I never touch dairy products. Sometimes I just drink the hot water and don't even bother with the tea."

"Eww!" said Angela. She'd never been into "New Age" brews.

"Gives you a good old clear out" said Chrissie.

"Too much information!" retorted Angela, curling her lip. Chrissie laughed, but then turned more serious. She explained that Maggie had a bit of an infection which might have gone to her chest. They were going to put her on antibiotics, but it was delaying her recovery. She tried not to register worry as she explained. Chrissie then steered the conversation in another direction.

"Maggie tells me you play the piano?"

"Blimey, well, I *did* play, but it's been a while."

"It's just that, well.....I was wondering if you'd be interested in a job....do you sight read?"

"Again" said Angela, "I *did* sight read! Bit rusty, but I'm sure I could do a bit of a refresher." Chrissie explained how a friend of Maggie's ran a dance school and needed a pianist for a couple of afternoons a week. Not many hours, but good pay. She could give Angela the number, if she wanted to follow it up.

Before answering, Angela found herself gazing into Chrissie's large green eyes. There was not a hint of ulterior motive here – nothing defensive. Instead, this woman radiated only warmth and honesty and Angela wasn't used to that. She was used to office colleagues always wanting something in return, bickering, back-stabbing – a sort of ambient school playground type bullying, that never seemed to advance much beyond that level.

In the space of one conversation, Chrissie had presented a whole new world to Angela. Job that wasn't office work? Get paid for it? Having abandoned the piano years back for not being as "decorative" as Petra Kapinsky, Angela occasionally dabbled and had a clunky old keyboard at her mother's, which usually only came out for a sing song at Christmas time.

She'd never really tried to make any serious money as a musician, talented and qualified as she might be. In truth, all her confidence had been zapped years ago, and she imagined that secretarial work was all she *could* do.

Someone had muttered that it was OK, because secretaries didn't need to be as pretty as concert pianists and that had stuck with her.

"Did I say something wrong?" Chrissie's eyebrows formed into a worried upward arrow, as Angela realized she must have been staring at her longer than she thought. Angela apologised, said she would love to take the contact details and retrieved a pen and the back of an old envelope from her handbag.

"Maggie thinks a lot of you, you know" said Chrissie. Her green eyes twinkled again with such warmth and sincerity, that Angela felt hers severely welling up.

****

Things weren't looking good for Mort and Grey. Kevin sat in at an executive meeting where they were talking about laying off more staff and he knew just who would be in the firing line. But it wasn't for him to say anything. He felt he should be grateful for the fact he was still working and that his skills were still required, but he felt for his colleagues – many of whom were also long term friends. He wasn't sure whether he wished he could be the one who would break the news to them, or whether it was kinder for them to feel one swift blow from the brutal axe of his superiors.

Either way, it was an untimely death. Kevin had been made redundant himself before, but it was at a time when he'd virtually get re-employed the next day. Jobs were plentiful for someone with his experience and salaries were excellent. He sat back, twiddling his thumbs and staring at an empty space on the wall, where a poster had been taken down.

There was still work to do and he was still sat at the same desk, with the same window and same over-head light that needed its bulb changed. But everything around him was different. Kevin pondered on how life might change and how the shape of his and everyone else's future might start to be looking very different from how they had originally imagined....

****

There was no milk. Milk was something Mark always got. It was dark and cold, but seeing as she'd hit the caffeine again, milk was something Beverley needed. She'd prepared herself to sit in on that chilly evening, papers spread about the coffee table for an intensive preparation for parents evening. She shivered as she pulled her coat over her pyjamas – it wouldn't really matter just to pop out to the corner shop.

Beverley thought about the Halloween decorations and the mask and then she thought about Mark, but she pushed him out of her mind, surprised to find him being replaced by a thought of Callum. It was a long time since she'd seen him.

Occasionally, boys still hung round the Tunnels, but only small groups and not him. Maybe he'd found other friends now – she hoped so, anyway. She thought about what a promising student he was and how she'd helped him with role play and drama games when he got stuck with his English. She remembered how they'd play "Pretend".

With things other than milk on her mind, Beverley unlocked her front door. There were eight Tunnel boys out that night, five "Fronters" and four behind. The Fronters would consist of at least one Strike One and this evening's Strike One was a pale, tired-looking Callum. Daz requested that he be a Fronter so that he could support Callum, but he was told that as one of the most respected Seconders, he was needed at the back end.

The Drayton Estate had its own shops and even a Post Office, but they had been vandalised to such an extent, shop keepers were refusing to work there. Instead, not so very far away, most locals used a little corner shop round the back of the estate, especially to pick up bits and bobs of things that they had forgotten from their main shopping, just as Beverley had.

Sometimes boys would approach adults with a handful of pound coins and ask them to go and buy cigarettes for them. Sometimes people would oblige, sometimes they'd tell them where to go. Beverley didn't really think about what she'd do either way that night.

The corner shop wasn't really on a corner – it was more like "round the corner" from a corner, standing in the middle of a wide, paved concrete area, with big steps at either side like a sort of amphitheatre. Graffiti was scrawled on the front face of the shop – some obscene drawing with the words "Get your lollipops here". Beverley shook her head as she started to descend one end of the stairs. The Tunnel boys were descending the other.

They almost reached the exact equivalent step at the same moment and it was there that they clocked each other. Normally she wouldn't have worried – kids always hung out there, but it was the way this particular group slowed down and watched her. They appeared to be listening to orders from each other. Two lines moved towards her in the darkness.

The bottom of the "amphitheatre" was poorly lit and got darker the closer to the bottom step you came. In the front line was the shape of a small, skinny boy – barely visible. But what was visible in the patchy light was the glistening blade of a knife.

Before she'd even had a second to think which direction to run in, Beverley was surrounded by the boys. Some had run back up both ends of the steps, giving her no escape route. It was all horribly well choreographed. The skinny boy got close enough for Beverley to see him.

"Callum!" gasped Beverley, knowing immediately by the terrified look in his eyes that he recognised her as well. He didn't dare hesitate as he raised the blade, but before he could plunge it, he heard an order from the back line – "Morgan!" Callum froze up.

"Morgan, Morgan!" the voice shouted again. "Morgan" in Tunnel Boy speak meant major organ – in other words, rather than a "Nip Tuck" or painful but almost harmless flesh wound, this was the real McCoy. There was no time for Callum to decide – it was stab, or be stabbed. If he turned and ran, he'd be chased and at the very least horrifically maimed. The other boys would hurt Beverley as well, so his personal refusal to hurt her wouldn't mean she'd escape injury.

As he pulled the knife up higher, Callum realized no boys were actually close enough to see where the entry wound was being made. As he plunged the knife into the fleshy part of Beverley's upper arm, he hissed, "*Pretend*, Miss!" She understood. Pain seared through her arm, but she immediately clutched her hand to her chest, as if she had been stabbed in the heart and fell to the ground.

The boys scattered and Callum didn't dare look back. No one was around – there were no witnesses unless someone had seen something from a window, and even then they couldn't identify anyone in the darkness. No one ran outside either, although that was hardly surprising as there was no commotion, no kerfuffle -the act was carried out in virtual silence.

Beverley hadn't even screamed as she was stabbed, too petrified and shocked to even let out a whimper. The law of averages dictated that it wouldn't be too long before someone remembered they had forgotten some shopping and none of the Tunnel Boys wanted to be in the vicinity when they did. Beverley lay low until it seemed quiet, then sat up dazed, shaking and bleeding.

By that time, the boys were nearer to The Tunnels and Callum realized it was Spencer who'd given the "Morgan" command. Spencer patted him on the back.

"Well done, Cal – I didn't think you had it in you." Callum immediately vomited into the nearest bush.

* * * * * * * * *

Beverley managed to stumble half a block before being overcome by shock and the heavy bleeding from her arm. The shock was worse than the wound, but she was dazed and confused. She'd cheated death – been protected somehow. Had it been any boy other than Callum, she would surely be lying in a pool of blood now, gasping her very last breaths.

Grandma had saved her. Grandma was watching over her, looking out for her – preventing her coming to harm. One moment she'd been staring death in the face, the next she'd gotten away with only a flesh wound. Who else could it be, but Grandma?

Chrissie was on her way to the corner shop when she suddenly saw Beverley stagger and then collapse in a doorway. She ran over to help the woman, but heard her muttering only "Grandma, Grandma." Was another woman injured as well? Chrissie pulled her jacket off and pressed it onto Beverley's arm to stem the flow of bleeding – she asked her gently; where was her Grandma? Was she with her? Had she been hurt?

"Grandma at home" was all Beverley could utter weakly, leaving Chrissie to deduce that the woman was trying to get home.

"I'll call Grandma for you, but first we need to get you to hospital." Chrissie pulled her mobile out, but Beverley stopped her. "No police, no."

"I'm getting you an ambulance" said Chrissie insistently, then she added "Do you know who did this?" Beverley didn't answer. "You know you'll have to speak to the police sometime, don't you?" Beverley nodded. Chrissie kept her warm until the air was filled with the stomach churning sound of ambulance sirens and a flashing blue light – only too familiar a sight and sound for the residents and the surrounding area of the Drayton Estate.

****

When Callum got home, Marisa had passed out on her bed. He saw an empty wine bottle on the floor and he knew something about alcohol being bad to mix with the medication she was taking, but she seemed to be snoring so peacefully he didn't want to disturb her. He was feeling very light-headed and the events of the evening kept churning in his mind – he hoped the other boys had disposed of the knife by now. He hoped Beverley was ok. Callum unloaded his school bags tipping the books out on his bedroom floor. Then he pulled some sweatshirts and jeans out of his wardrobe, as well as packing his toothbrush. He rummaged through the kitchen, just to see if there were any last vestiges of food, but there was nothing. Marisa had obviously just bought the bottle of wine and no food for them. Callum's stomach rumbled loudly, but he was used to that.

He knew when he pulled his jeans on that they fell below his hips and almost completely slid past his knees, but he had belts and long fleeces to cover up the fact that his clothes were hanging off him. School had been a bit more of a problem. Callum knew that if he neglected his school work someone would be onto it – someone would call his mother, and that was the very last thing he wanted.

Calling in the Social Services would have been the worst possible thing. He knew his mother was in no fit state to look after him – hell, she couldn't even feed herself any more. But being taken into care would have destroyed her. And him. Callum absolutely couldn't let that happen. He'd managed to deflect the teacher who'd noticed the dark circles under his eyes and worsening condition of his skin.

Callum managed to blag it by saying he was worried about his end of year tests and that he'd been staying up late to study. By getting constant good marks, Callum had managed to keep his teacher off his back, but he now looked so awful that it would only be a matter of time before the inquisitions began.

He knew he had to simultaneously run away whilst at the same time get help for his mother. He found her address book and rifled through for numbers of relatives, neighbours – anyone he thought he could trust. Ironically the name that stood out was someone he knew could help; someone reliable and knowledgeable and discreet. The woman he had just stabbed.

****

Daz yelled at Spencer. "Jesus bruvver, how the hell could you?"

"Aw, C'mon Daz. It was just a bit of fun."

"Fun? *Fun?* Callum might've killed someone for all we know! How could you make a Strike One do a Morgan? He wasn't even trained properly!"

"Well, he did it, didn't he?" Spencer shrugged and started to walk off, but Daz grabbed his jacket collar and swung him round. Benji was just reaching the crest of the hill and realized an ugly situation was breaking out. He saw Daz push Spencer up against a tree and hold his fist up to his face. They were meant to be friends. He yelled out.

"Yo! What's goin' on?" Hearing Benji's voice, Daz released his grip. He didn't want Benji to have anything to do with this. He shouted out to some boys at the bottom of the hill to take Benji back home, but Benji was reluctant to leave with them.

"You alright, Daz?"

"I'm sorting it, Benj. Just head back, will you?" But the tone in Daz's voice betrayed anything being "sorted". Benji lingered. Spencer seized the opportunity to leg it back down the hill and for now there was nothing Daz could do. He glared at Benji, but Benji knew Daz wasn't angry with *him*. He knew that his fearless, big brave older brother was afraid.

Benji knew Daz would be glad that he would look out for him and protect him, but he didn't understand *why* Daz was afraid. After all, it was Daz who had Spencer in a head lock – not the other way round. Besides, if it came down to sheer physical blows, Daz would have beaten Spencer hands down any day.

Benji knew that he should obey Daz and head back, but he looked at him quizzically as another boy grabbed his arm and started leading him off. Little did Benji know that his older brother had murder on his mind.

****

It was certainly busy in A & E that night. There was a man in striped pyjamas holding padding on a bleeding head wound, a young girl howling with her arm already in a sling and people being rushed in on stretchers with neck braces from a recent road accident. Chrissie was reluctant to leave until Beverley had been seen.

"Look.....I know it's none of my business, but...you must still really be in a lot of shock. I know you think your arm will only need a few stitches, but the trauma could take a while to heal. If you don't want me to stay, will you at least take my phone number and let me know you're ok?"

Beverley was amazed at Chrissie's warmth and concern. Not many people offered the "kindness of strangers" these days. As Chrissie scribbled her number down on the back of a bus ticket, Beverley was struck by her compassion and knew she genuinely wanted her to call. She watched Chrissie head down the corridor and through the double doors. Chrissie sighed – it was too late to visit Maggie.

A nurse beckoned Beverley into a cubicle and examined the wound. They'd patch her up and she was sure it wasn't serious, but it was obvious it was a knife wound. How long before anyone started asking questions....?

****

It was really too early in the morning for tea, but seeing as they always got woken so early anyway, Maggie drank hers. Chrissie sat by her side.

"I brought a woman in here last night – she'd been stabbed. I'm seeing it more and more, Maggie. Violence. 'Specially round here. Unprovoked. Unwarranted. What can we do?" Maggie shook her head.

"Just carry on doing what we're doing. One little bit towards the cause, every individual adding a little piece. That's all we can do – you can't save the world in a day!"

Chrissie looked pensive. It was what Maggie had always told her. If every single person worldwide did a little bit, day by day, whether it was for better or worse, then eventually there would be an accumulation. If only she could still believe she was doing the right things.

She liked to think she never faltered, always held true to her values. But Chrissie also knew she was human and that sometimes she would give in to dark moods – depression or anger would occasionally overwhelm her and then she felt completely helpless. But Maggie would never chastise her for this.

"Remember what I told you when you were younger?" said Maggie. "It's like surfing. You'll be having the most marvellous time, riding high on that foam, when suddenly – whoomph! Life knocks you off. And you remember the other things I've said – haven't you.....?" Chrissie could never forget anything that Maggie, the wisest of teachers said. In fact, she'd held onto her every word.

Even in hospital in her late eighties, Maggie was articulate and focussed and her voice clear and unwavering. Her mind was still extremely sharp, even if her body was betraying her. Chrissie remembered how in the last few years Maggie was so frustrated that she'd been forced to slow down due to increasingly bad arthritis, but she still seemed to rush around mentally, making phone calls, preparing papers – even asking Chrissie's partner Andy to show her how to use a computer.

There was no stopping the indefatigable Maggie Buxton – until now. How hard for her to have to lie there in that hospital bed, when she'd always been such an active woman. But she never grumbled, never complained, and Chrissie knew that whilst Maggie was "holed up", they all needed to carry on regardless.

Besides, there was an interesting new - comer on the scene and a buzz was going around. Chrissie wanted to ask Maggie if she thought that now was the right time to introduce Angela to some of "The Family". A familiar face appeared at the end of the bed. Well, talk of the devil, thought Chrissie to herself.

"Ooo, sorry – hope I'm not disturbing?" said Angela. Chrissie smiled.

"Of course not" said Maggie getting Chrissie to pull up another chair, "You're always welcome. I was just telling Christina about my riding the crest of a wave theory." Angela listened intently and then added her own comment.

"Personally", she said, "I think life is like the Monty Python foot." Chrissie and Maggie looked at her quizzically. "You know, you're walking along going dee dum de diddly dum dee dum and then – BAM! Down comes that foot!" Angela had always thought that this was very philosophical, but for some reason it sent Chrissie and Maggie into near hysteria.

So much so, that a nurse had to come and ask them to pipe down.

"I didn't think it was *that* funny" said Angela, but she was laughing too. It was fun hanging out with "the girls". Angela radiated a lovely subtle, warm sense of humour. Someone with that was just what The Family needed.

****

It took Angela a while to find the ballet school. First of all, the bus stop seemed miles away and when she walked up a street she thought was adjacent, she discovered it was a cul-de-sac and had to turn round. After turning her A-Z upside down several times and a few enquiries to strangers, Angela eventually saw the battered old road sign, "Hangtree Road."

The road was long and steep – winter trees stood useless and rather fed-up looking. For now, they were redundant – like everyone else. Angela had no idea which end of the road St Peter's was in – good job she'd left plenty of time to get there. Eventually, in the distance, there appeared to be the edge of a beige-tinted turret – surely a sign of a church ahead.

When Angela got closer however, the church seemed to be as dead as the trees. At the back of the decrepit building, a little path twisted through a graveyard which Angela followed until she found what appeared to be the church hall. Pushing the slightly ajar, creaky wooden door fully open, Angela was relieved to see a "live" notice board, displaying meetings with current dates.

"Barbara's Ballet" was clearly displayed in pink font on a sheet of A4 paper that had slightly curled up at the bottom. The poster detailed classes for different age groups and times of lessons. People had pinned notices for slimming classes, bible reading groups and yoga on top of the ballet school, but somehow the lurid pink writing stood out above everything else.

Now Angela just had to find Barbara. Across the corridor were some rooms that looked like they may have housed offices. Perhaps someone in one of them would lead her to Barbara. It seemed a curious set-up for a job interview – Angela was used to glass-fronted buildings with several floors and stand-offish receptionists.

She was used to being looked up and down by smartly dressed, tight-lipped men and woman who would open doors to her to people in suits who would then look down on her, even though they were seated. It seemed funny to have to search for Barbara, even though on the phone she was told the interview would be "informal". Never mind informal, thought Angela – she now had to play hide and seek, as well.

Angela peeped into one room, saw it was empty and swung round into an on-coming vicar.

"Oh!" They were both shocked as they knocked into each other.

"Oh my God – eek, I mean...I'm so sorry – did I hurt you?" asked Angela. Knocking out the vicar wasn't a very good start to an interview. The vicar rubbed his head and then straightened his jacket.

"Nothing broken – I don't think so, anyway. Can I help you?"

"Yes, I mean I hope so. I'm looking for Barbara."

"Barbara?" The vicar rubbed his chin. "Well, we do have rather a lot of Barbara's here. Would that be Barbara who had her triplets christened last week, or maybe Barbara who runs the Saturday school, or...."

"Barbara....Barbara who does *ballet*" said Angela.

"Oh, *that* Barbara. With a bit of luck, she's just up those stairs, but that's anyone's guess. She does rather dart about, so. Try second door on the left, my dear" motioned the vicar before heading back down the corridor. Angela tried the second door on the left, but ballet Barbara wasn't there. There *was* a lady called Barbara, but she appeared to be very deaf and making things out of empty ready meal packs for a nativity play. Angela declined to ask this Barbara if she knew ballet Barbara – she thought she might be there a rather long time if she did...

Obviously ballet Barbara was a law unto herself. She'd asked Angela to meet her at midday in St Peter's, but she hadn't said exactly *where* in St Peter's. "Just pop in and ask for Barbara" were the only instructions.

****

Angela wandered around aimlessly for at least another ten minutes before getting frustrated and on the verge of heading home.

Then, she heard the unmistakable sounds of a ballet class coming from around the corner.

"And arabesque! Plié, plié, en point! NO! How many times must I tell you? *Point* the toes! Don't just flop your foot around like a dirty old sock! Oh dear dear me. Dearie dearie me."

There appeared to be the sound of a plonky old piano playing over Barbara's teaching, but then Angela heard a clunk and the playing immediately stopped.

"Oh, bother bother bother" muttered Barbara, trying to re-start the CD player. "I must have a pianist, I really must." Before Angela could say then I might be just what you need, a long crooked finger with fuchsia coloured nail varnish pointed at her.

"How many times must I tell you!" yelled the person at the end of the finger, "This class finishes at 12.30! 12.30! Kindly wait for your daughter outside!" Angela took in the petite pink form that was Ballet Barbara. Exactly how old Barbara was, it was hard to tell, under umpteen layers of pink make-up. Her dyed auburn hair clashed horribly with the varying shades of pink.

Barbara could have been about eighty. Her face was lined and wrinkly and the deep grooves around her mouth suggested a heavy smoker. Then again, she was erect and toned and flexible and graceful, so maybe she was a forty year old who'd had a very hard life. Whatever her age, Angela decided there would be no point in trying to argue with this particular fingernail.

****

Beverley tried to think up all kinds of accidents. A household tripping up – falling down on the blade of a kitchen knife didn't seem plausible, so she decided to say she'd tried to break up a fight, but got in the way. When the police asked if she could give any description of her attacker, she just said it was too dark, but that the boy was quite tall and maybe about fourteen or fifteen with a skinhead. She was slightly perturbed when one of the officers said that that particular boy might be known to them, completely unaware that she had just incriminated Spencer.

****

Mark tossed and turned uneasily in his parent's spare room that night. In his dream that was rapidly morphing into a nightmare, an elderly lady was pointing at him, wagging her finger. She was insisting he had done some grave wrong-doing, whereas Mark was adamant that he hadn't. The woman had grown in stature and loomed high above his head. Now she was frowning, frightening and growing horrible long brown and spiky teeth.

Suddenly a spear was grasped in her right hand and she was dancing and her foot stomping became quicker and louder and she started to chant, "Voodoo, voodoo!"

"Grandma!" Mark woke up dripping with sweat. He'd called out in his sleep, unaware that he'd woken his mother. She moved to get out of bed but his father stopped her.

"Martha, he isn't a little boy any more."

"But he's crying!"

"He's just split up with Beverley and he's thirty-two. He doesn't need you to go in there." As Mark's mother fell back into an uneasy sleep, so Mark did too. This time his dreams were filled with a glowing boy on the brow of a hill. As Daz came closer into view, Mark felt a powerful surge of energy through his body.

This young boy was urging him to rebel, to follow his instincts instead of always doing the right thing. Mark knew that just seeing Daz that day had been the catalyst in deciding to leave Beverley. He was overwhelmed with guilt and whilst his head was urging him to leave, being a naturally compassionate man, he didn't know he could leave someone so vulnerable.

He still had feelings for Beverley, but her behaviour had become too much. Mark felt shut out. He was a young man with a lot to live for and a promising career ahead of him which demanded a lot. He didn't have the energy to do that and prop up his unstable partner as well.

The straw that broke the camel's back was when Beverley started waving a picture of her wretched Grandma at him. He began to curse it, but felt a sharp stabbing pain in his stomach whenever he did so. This made him curse more and he'd feel intense pins and needles all over his body. It seemed that Grandma could hurt him, but he couldn't hurt Grandma and that made him even more angry.

Mark would never admit this to Beverley. That would be tantamount to agreeing with her about spirits and the supernatural world and divert her from getting the help he thought she needed. At first he'd been gentle, appealed to the down to earth, rational school-teacher in her.

But scared, saucer-eyed Beverley started taking over more and more and it was as if this personality was urging her towards witch craft and charms and the laws of her ancient ancestors. He was interested in her family background, sure, but not when it was freaking her out and intruding in their relationship.

The Daz dream-child glowed large in his dream. When he had first set eyes upon Daz, Mark thought how much he'd reminded him of himself as a boy. Bold, brave, cocky and full of plans and hopes for the future, only Mark had grown up in a very different environment. When he was at school, he thought he might go into politics or something where he was going to "save the world."

He was full of twinkling eyes and glowing ambition and got into a top university. In Daz, there was something darker. An intensity. Just catching a glimpse of him had stirred a part of Mark he had always repressed. He didn't want to be "such a good boy" any more. Now he wanted to join anarchists and street kids, march on protests and throw bottles.

This was all completely out of character and where the feeling had originated he couldn't say, but it had obviously started bubbling under the surface the more he and Beverley pulled apart. No wonder Grandma had been cursing him in his dreams.

****

"Oh my goodness Christina – you didn't really let poor old Angela go and visit Barbara all by herself, did you? My dear, it must have been quite awful for you."

"Well, actually......do you know what? I quite like her. She chucked me out at first, but once she discovered who I was she couldn't have been nicer." Chrissie and Maggie exchanged astonished looks.

"I have to say" continued Angela, "I'm amazed at how well she seems to be doing. You'd think people in that area wouldn't have a lot of money, but she seems to have very full classes. I guess little girls still harbour dreams of being a ballerina – I know I used to."

"I can see you doing ballet" said Maggie "You're the right build." Angela was transported back to her pre-pubescent years. She told how a girl in her class had boobs and curves at the age of eleven, and whilst a lovely dancer, she was always put at the back and yelled at. Some years later, Angela had heard she had become anorexic.

"You know, when that girl left, I went as well" said Angela.

"Goodness, I imagine you were very good friends then" said Maggie. Angela explained that she hardly knew the girl. She was just incensed, even at such a young age that this beautiful girl had been treated like that. Angela knew that the girl had far more of a feel for ballet than she ever had, and that she really listened to the music. Angela loved watching her.

When she'd told the teacher she was leaving, the ballet mistress expressed great disappointment, saying how promising she thought Angela was. Angela thought she just wanted the money. And so, at eleven years old, she told the ballet teacher exactly she what she thought of her. She hated injustice.

Chrissie sat bolt upright and Maggie would have done too if her leg hadn't held her back. So...mousey, funny, slightly self-effacing Angela had been a bold and feisty child with her own mind. Maggie knew there were hidden depths to Angela from the moment she had met her – someone who abandons their belongings to help a stranger is quite special, after all.

Before Maggie could ask any more, Angela started fishing in her handbag and took out two £50 notes.

"I'm a bit confused, you see – Barbara and I didn't actually discuss money. I played for about an hour and half and she just handed me an envelope afterwards. I'm not sure how many lessons this is for. I didn't look in the envelope until I got home. Chrissie, will you be seeing Barbara? Shall I give you one of these to give back to her?"

Maggie smiled. "Oh, just keep it dear. Our Barbara is scatty as hell and anyway – she can afford it. She'll probably call you about half an hour before she next needs you – it's a bit like that with her. The thing is, if you can, I suggest you stick with it. You see, I know she does pay rather well....."

Angela didn't know what to say. Barbara was undoubtedly one of the great British eccentrics, but apparently she was also a very wealthy eccentric, so what was she doing teaching in a run down church hall? Maybe Barbara's Ballet was a veritable gold mine for anyone who could sight read and half play the piano – that was, if they could cope with Barbara.

Fortunately, Angela enjoyed the chaos. She preferred the natural smell of the musty wooden floors to toxic foam office chairs, tiled carpeting and air fresheners. Besides, the church had character and all the modern offices she'd worked in had none. She thought how bizarre it was that such a colourless place as Mort and Grey should be peppered with characters – Verity, Brian, Kevin......but not even Verity could compete on the character front with Barbara.

Angela glanced down at her watch – how time flew when she was with Maggie and Chrissie. Realizing she'd stayed much longer than intended, she bade her farewells. When she'd left, Maggie gave Chrissie the affirmative nod.

"Well Christina, I think it might be time to start introducing that young lady to a little more of The Family....."

****

Verity gazed into space whilst simultaneously twirling a pencil in her right hand. Her work load had dwindled to nothing and she didn't know what to do with herself. She didn't even have anything to give to Angela. Verity had ceased to be angry that Angela was so nonchalant about work, and started to become increasingly curious instead.

Angela was so carefree, so full of joie de vivre, that there could only have been one thing for it. She was in love. Having nothing better to do, Verity thought it was about time she interrogated her P.A.

"So – are we going to meet him then?" Verity asked.

"What? Who?" Angela didn't have a clue what Verity was asking.

"Your new beau. C'mon – I want details, the lot."

"My new...?" Angela caught on. She thought it might be fun to play along for a while. Somehow, she automatically found herself blushing which pleased her, realising what a good actress she was.

"Oh well Verity, you know – it's early days."

"Angela! You little dark horse!" Then Verity took a deep gulp. "Oh my God – it's not – not.....Brian.....is it?" Angela said nothing, but to her delight felt her face turning hotter. Verity collapsed in her chair.

"How could you? A married man! You realize there's going to be nothing but trouble, don't you?" Angela just shrugged, smiled sweetly and returned to her empty in tray. Dark thoughts entered Verity's mind. Did

Angela no longer care about work, because Brian was paying her to be his mistress? She couldn't bear not knowing.

"Listen to me, Angela ...." before Verity could say any more, Brian came in carrying a large collection of box files. As he clocked Angela he coloured, and then looked away. This only added fuel to the fire as far as Verity was concerned. Angela simply carried on in her own sweet way.

"Um, hope you don't mind me popping up here Verity" said Brian, "But I heard you were a bit quiet and if Angela's at a lose end, I – well, I mean there's a bit of typing for me she could do. You know my own secretary got laid off last week, and I've got a massive backlog." Verity glared at Brian with a face like thunder. "B...but, only if it's ok with you," Brian added.

Verity then did something most unusual for her. She faltered. She realized she couldn't really burst forth saying she knew all about their sordid little affair and she couldn't really refuse "loaning" out Angela whilst she had no work for her. Begrudgingly, Verity indicated that Brian could use Angela.

Brian blushed again as he handed Angela the box files, and Angela smiled, knowing that Verity would have to play all day on the internet to amuse herself, all the while practically wetting herself to know about Angela and Brian. Before Angela went downstairs, Verity called out after her.

"Say, Ange – how about we go for a little drink after work – just you and me?"

"Oh..." Angela hesitated. "You know, that sounds lovely, but I've got something on."

"Can't you just make it a quick one? *I really need to talk to you.*"

"Can't you just tell me now?" said Angela, trying not to giggle. Verity lowered her voice.

"You know I like to be very discreet. *People keep coming in and out of this office.*" Highly amused, Angela spoke out loudly, well aware that even though he was halfway down the stairs, Brian would hear her.

"Discreet, eh? Well, when you put it like that I think it definitely calls for a Pinot Grigio! *I can't wait to hear what you've got to tell me!!*"

****

Daz thumped on Callum's door whilst simultaneously ringing the doorbell. At first he thought someone was in and wasn't answering, because he could see a faint light through the drawn, dusty curtains. He started yelling through the letterbox.

"Cal! It's me – Daz! Please come out Cal – I really need to see you!" Callum's neighbour came out and told Daz to stop making such a racket. He said it was obvious no one was there, so why didn't he just leave. Daz looked the man up and down. He was unshaven and pot bellied and wore a most fetching string vest. He was flicking his lighter on and off, trying to get a flame.

Much to the man's surprise, Daz pulled a lighter from his own pocket and lit the neighbour's cigarette. Daz always knew how to get what he wanted.

"Sorry if I woke you" said Daz, "It's just I'm looking for Callum Brown – urgent. Don't s'pose you know if he's gone away, or something?" The man took a long drag whilst giving Daz the once over.

"They don't go away. Between you and me, that mother of his...." The man pulled himself up short. He liked a bit of gossip, but he didn't know Daz from Adam, nor did he trust this sleek young boy who'd so politely given him a light.

"What's up with Mrs B?" asked Daz "I'm really concerned. Callum is a really good mate of mine. He's not been at school the last few days and I just wanted to make sure he was ok." Daz sensed he shouldn't linger. The last thing he needed right now was anyone getting suspicious. He smiled and walked back along the concrete balcony to the staircase with its smashed windows and overwhelming odour of urine. One day, he promised himself he would leave this grim and awful hell hole, but for now there was so much to do and sort out. Far too much.

****

Beverley did her best to make tea with one arm. Reluctant to tell her own school principal exactly how she got her injury, she made up a domestic accident and said she'd need a few days off. The police had suggested she went for trauma counselling, but she declined. She wanted to draw as little attention to things as she possibly could, but the dark shadow of Callum's face haunted her.

This wasn't because he was her attacker, but because he was a vulnerable, innocent, little boy. A gifted student she'd once known. She remembered how his face would light up when he saw her face through the cracked glass of his front door panel. How she might have been the one redeeming feature in this child's life – the one adult to encourage and guide him and give him a sense of worth. Now, where had that all gone....?

Callum had fallen into a place where the only way to prove his worth was by stabbing someone. What a senseless waste. Beverley found herself getting angry as she thought of all the young boys that had passed through her classroom and wondered if they would also end up with no better future than to run riot in the back of beyond, leaving blood on their hands as their only legacy.

The phone rang making Beverley jump and also spilling her tea and hence scalding her good arm. She cursed and decided her arm was more important than the call, so went to run it under cold water, letting the answer phone kick in. The voice at the other end couldn't be heard over the sound of running water and Beverley's swearing.

"B ... Bev. It's Mark here. I'm, er....just checking to see how you are, really. Thought maybe we could, well. Have a bit of a chat. Anyway you've got my parents' number and my mobile, so....give me a call when you can, ok? Hope everything's ok....."

Pre-occupied with one stitched arm and the other scalded, Beverley tried to attend to the new injury with an arm which was already bandaged – it was no mean feat. She let the cold tap soothe the burn and took deep breaths. Just for a little time out of the chaos and commotion. Just for a few moments of peace. The doorbell rang. No such luck.

****

Neighbours started hanging over their balconies, watching Spencer's mother pummelling at a policeman with her fists and the policeman threatening to drive her away as well, as another bundled Spencer into the back seat of a police car. She'd done with swearing, so tried another tact, just repeating over and over "what a good boy" her Spencer was and how he "ain't done nuffin". Her pleading fell on deaf ears.

Spencer didn't know why he was being arrested or why or how someone might have implicated him, but all the police would say was that he "fitted their description". As his head was pushed down under the car door, he yelled to his mother to get Daz and Benji's mother – if news of this filtered through to her, then Daz would know what to do.

****

"Tell me more about the gardens, Maggie."

Maggie was tired, but she loved Angela's company and she loved how much Angela also wanted to know about her. Many elderly people like herself had little contact with the outside world and just as many were lonely and isolated. That certainly wasn't the case with Maggie. She seemed to have an endless stream of visitors of all ages and her bedside was surrounded by an unusual mix of get-well gifts. Angela picked one up. It was a card with some kind of material that Angela didn't recognise. She fingered the green strips, and opened the card to read a child's wonky handwriting.

"Christina's little boy made that for me" Maggie smiled.

"Chrissie's boy?" Then the memory filled Angela's head. That day on the bus when she'd seen Daz – been so anxious about the woman with dreadlocks and the little boy with her.....what a small world it was.

"He's a funny little thing" continued Maggie, "Absolute sweetheart, but a bit unruly – so like his father." Angela wanted to know more. It turned out Chrissie's partner, Andy, was a musician – a bit of a wayward soul. "I have to admit, I was rather concerned when they first got together" said Maggie, "He seemed a bit of a drifter and had at least one other child, from what I know. I did worry for Christina when she fell pregnant, but she seemed so – happy. And Andrew has always stuck right by her. I can see he genuinely adores her, but most of all he really dotes on little Christian."

Maggie watched Angela forming the name with her lips and knew what she was thinking. She said she was glad he'd been named after his mother and not with some strange "hippy" name like Moondance, or such like. "I do confess, I feared the worst!" laughed Maggie. Angela reflected. Chrissie may have had the matted dreadlocks, flowing clothes and unmade up features of a New Age child, but she couldn't have been less dreamy – she was focussed, down to earth and seemed very, very caring. Sometimes she wished she had the courage to be more like her – an utter free spirit. Maggie's kind eyes studied Angela's grey-blue ones and she leaned forwards, gesturing Angela to remove her glasses. Angela did so and allowed herself to be studied.

"There's a whole world behind there" said Maggie, looking deep into Angela's eyes. Angela gazed back. No one had ever spoken to her like that before, but how she had longed for that kind of contact – to be truly understood, for someone to really see the Angela behind the spectacles. She felt herself welling up.

"Now," said Maggie passing a tissue and placing Angela's glasses on the side cabinet. "Do you really need these?"

"God, yes" Angela replied, "I'm so short-sighted.....you're all blurry, Maggie...."

"I mean" said Maggie, "Have you ever thought about contact lenses? Such a pretty face – seems such a shame to hide it with these great big frames." Angela didn't want to admit she'd never been that keen on inserting bits of plastic in her eye sockets, but she'd certainly consider more flattering frames. Maggie then signalled that she wanted Angela to unpin her hair. Angela did so, and realized how long it had been since she'd had it cut. She felt embarrassed about how much grey hair was exposed when it was shaken lose, although God only knows why, in front of an elderly lady.

Angela realized she just didn't like this kind of exposure and felt a pressing urge to grab her glasses and hairclip and hide once more. But Maggie was having none of that. She pushed Angela's hair back over her face and sighed. "Time for a cut, don't you think?" Maggie didn't mince her words.

"I, I really don't have time" mumbled Angela. She was desperate for her glasses.

"Oh Tosh!" said Maggie "I'm not talking about spending a fortune on it, or having these strange highlight things. I'm not even suggesting I'm being so shallow to tell you as a woman, you need to take more care of your appearance. You've seen how Christina dresses – all that raggedy hair, not a stroke of make- up. Why, if this wasn't a hospital, she'd even have bare feet in here! But, but......it's *her*, isn't it? That's really who she is – my brave little earth warrior..." Angela perched on the side of the bed.

"Now you, Angela.....I don't think you really know who you are yet. Or maybe you do, but you're too afraid to let her out in public. I don't know why that is – there is so much you have to offer, so much...."

Angela felt Maggie's words reverberate deep in her stomach. Surely things in life were safer, calmer, more certain if she donned a "mask" and looked the part? She was a secretary. She needed a job. Secretaries were expected to look a certain way. She tried to imagine Verity's face if she had walked in one day with Chrissie's hairstyle...but things were changing.

Now Angela wasn't just a secretary, but also a pianist working for a potty old ballet teacher in a musty old church hall, watching flashes of rose pink and pimply flesh flash before her eyes as little girls twirled round and round, dreaming of the Royal Festival Hall or Covent Garden. She felt her stomach contract tightly again, not wanting to accept what was happening to her – not wanting to take in what Maggie could clearly see, but wouldn't reveal.

Angela's breathing became faster and faster. This was one of those moments when if she hadn't been under "surveillance", she would have retreated into denial and curled up like a little hedgehog. But she couldn't hide from Maggie, because Maggie always seemed to know everything, anyway.

Suddenly, Angela saw a get-out clause. She felt deeply foolish coming out with mentioning that visiting hours must be over, but she couldn't bare the intensity. Besides, she had to get back to real life – had to meet Verity. Maggie chuckled "Ah, the lovely Verity." That really unnerved Angela.

She'd never said that much about Verity, and yet Maggie seemed to know exactly what she was like. Perhaps Verity was a sort of generic boss and in all her long life perhaps Maggie had come across quite a few Veritys. Maggie's insight had made Angela feel very uncomfortable, but she thought she had it sussed when it came to Verity. Only how would Verity react to a new Angela in a completely different form?

****

Beverley unlocked the front door and was shocked to see Callum standing in front of her, shaking, nervous, dark eyes staring into hers with an alarming honesty. Behind him was a woman only half recognisable as his mother. She was also shaking and her normally skinny frame now bore hardly any flesh at all. Her eyes were little more than sunken hollows and her lips were dry and cracked.

Empty caverns seemed to fill the spaces where her cheek-bones had once presided and she gazed down at the floor, clutching a large hold all in one hand and what looked like a packet of pills in the other. Beverley put her hand to her mouth as she gasped in horror. Callum stuck one foot through the door.

"Please – please, Miss. I didn't mean to hurt you. They made me – forced me. Please...we've got nowhere else to go." Beverley's head told her to push him back out the door and call the police. This was the boy who'd stabbed her. But he was also the boy who'd saved her life, risking his own if a vicious boy gang found out what he'd actually done.

And he was still little bright-as-a-button Callum, wide-eyed and innocent.....the boy who'd invented such wonderful stories, hung onto her every word – the boy with such a big future ahead of him, if only he hadn't been born into the wrong time and place. Beverley's heart told her to pull her assailant close and hug him.

"Oh God, Oh God, Callum. I'm so glad you've come here. How did you find me? Get my address?"

Through sobs of relief, Callum gestured towards Marisa. "Mum's address book" he blubbed, "I didn't know where else to go – I just knew we had to get away from the estate – before anyone would find me." Beverley led him gently towards the settee.

"Don't worry – I didn't tell anyone. My arm still hurts a bit, but its fine – it'll heal. You must've been terrified of those boys, though." Beverley wanted to question Callum as much as possible, but first she was conscious of getting Marisa settled. Gently, she reached out her hand which Marisa took, but not before gazing at Beverley's heavily bandaged arm.

She looked at it with deep, saddened eyes, almost as if she was well aware of how the injury had been caused. Then Marisa released Beverley's hand and held her own hand so that it hovered over Beverley's injured arm. It was as if she were "scanning" it to feel the extent of the damage.

Beverley shuddered because this was exactly what Grandma used to do. Grandma told Beverley she was a healer and that she could heal the body without touching it or applying any medications. When she was little and might fall over and graze a knee, instead of rushing her up to the bathroom and applying stingy antiseptic to the wound like her mother would do, Grandma would tell Beverley to sit very still as she did her "healing".

Beverley was never quite sure if this helped the wounds or not, but somehow it made her feel a lot better. She felt special, being comforted and soothed and cared for. No doubt, someone else's loving concern speeded wounds in their healing process, but now Beverley felt a deep emotion stirring.

The combined childhood memory, mixed with the fact that it was Marisa's own child who had injured her, meant that Beverley felt so many tears welling that they were hard to fight back. Luckily Callum broke the awkwardness.

"She learnt that from my Dad" he interjected, "He used to be into doing funny healing stuff. I'm surprised she remembers it though, because she's not exactly been looking after herself." Beverley moved next to Callum on the settee and looked at him directly.

"Callum.....your mother is very ill. We need to get her to hospital." It wasn't the first time Beverley had seen the signs of drug dependency. Callum pulled back, alarmed.

"Oh God, please Miss – no! I'll get put in care!" Beverley sighed deeply. Callum had probably seen this happen to so many kids around him. He'd come to her because he trusted her and she needed to show him that was the case.

"Nothing like that is going to happen, Callum. You're going to stay here with me – just until your mother's better and then we can find both of you a new place to live." Beverley said that with such conviction that for a split second Callum honestly believed that everything was going to be fine, but then images of the Tunnel Boys and school rooms whirled through his mind.

Beverley registered the sheer look of panic on his face and knew what he was thinking. She'd been a teacher long enough.

"And we'll sort that as well. Maybe I can get you registered at my school." That was it then. This boy was now in her care – for as long as she could persuade the authorities it was the best place for him to be....

****

Daz was quite relieved that Spencer was being questioned at the station because he really didn't want to enlist his help. Instead, he went to a couple of the Chiefs about his concern for Callum and told them he needed protection. He desperately wanted to implicate Spencer – implore that there was no way a fresh Strike One should ever be ordered to carry out a Morgan.

But to his horror, it seemed that the Chiefs approved and had been spending several evenings in self- congratulatory celebrations; all of them involving alcohol and whatever drugs they could lay their hands on. Daz knew he had to tread carefully. If he showed any outward signs of disapproval, then he would immediately be a "suss" himself and he could ill afford being held up with inquisition when he desperately needed to find Callum.

On the other hand, if the Chiefs were so proud of what Callum had done, then surely they should be doing everything they could to make sure he was OK. Daz was angry that this seemed to be secondary. He was also angry with Spencer and he was frustrated at what was happening with the Tunnel Boys in general. This wasn't Daz's vision at all.

He may have appeared quite formidable, but in truth Daz deplored violence and felt that things were now going too far. Theft, the odd bit of vandalism, putting the high and mighty in their place – all this blended well with Daz's naturally anarchic and rebellious tendencies, but his nature also unusually veered towards......subtlety.

With his looks, charisma and articulation, Daz usually won most people round and up until very recently he had this all under control. Goddamn Spencer for what he'd done. Just as another shudder of anger hit him, so did the thought of exactly why the police had come after Spencer.

Had someone actually witnessed what had happened? Had the "Goldie" that Callum stabbed survived? A torrent of thoughts tumbled through his mind, one in particular which he tried to suppress. Just suppose Callum *had* killed someone. He was only eleven years old and yet effectively, that would be the end of his life.

There'd be no future for this intelligent bright spark of a boy, all because he'd tried to *get* himself a future, be somebody, move forward. But for the grace of God and a few years difference in ages, it could have been Daz who'd been forced into such a heinous crime. He took a long deep gulp before another, more logical thought entered his head.

Callum was clever. Far more clever than any of the brutish, bullying Chiefs had ever given him credit for. Just suppose he'd somehow found a way *not* to stab the Goldie.....?

****

Verity was getting more and more frustrated. That was three glasses of red she'd bought Angela now, and still Angela wasn't even offering a morsel of gossip about Brian. Verity was quite happy to keep buying rounds provided Angela's tongue started to loosen – it did, but not in a very helpful way.

When Verity returned from the loo, she realized Angela wasn't at their table. Instead, she was sliding all over a man that Verity recognised as a friend of Kevin's. Angrily, Verity went to rescue the friend – she needed Angela to start talking and she needed her to talk fast; she certainly didn't want to waste any more time or money. Goddamit – she needed the gossip.

Gossip was Verity's life blood and without it, she was an anaemic and uninteresting office manager. The power of hidden information about her colleagues attracted people from all departments and at all levels. Verity knew that sometimes gossip was the only thread that held entire companies together and she badly needed to have as much control of that as possible.

She dragged Angela off the man she'd draped herself over, and started to apologise profusely for Angela's behaviour.

"Oh no, don't apologise" said the man " Your mate is a real laugh. Let me get you two lovely ladies a tipple. What'll it be?" Before Angela could say "reddish wineshhh pleeeshhh", Verity was hoiking her up under her armpits and saying they really had to go.

"But the night is young!" protested the man.

"Yes, but *she's* not" scowled Verity. The man looked shocked.

"That's not a very nice thing to say about your mate. She's a nice-looking girl and I don't care how old she is. And like I said – she's a laugh. So why don't *you* go home and er.....I'll look after her." Great. This, Verity really didn't need. It should have been far simpler – take Angela out, get her a bit tipsy, get as much sordid information as she possibly could about her and Brian.

She knew Angela was hardly the Lee Marvin of town, but she honestly had no idea what little ability Angela had to hold her drink. After the same amount as Angela had just had, Verity wouldn't even be feeling the effects. It would be tantamount to sipping an orange juice, to her. Of course, Verity would never think of attributing this to the fact that she had a great deal more "body mass index", nor that many years of after work meetings and socializing in pubs and bars, meant that her alcohol tolerance was extremely high.

Unfortunately, Angela seemed positively paralytic. Verity decided she wasn't going to take no for an answer and started to drag Angela away, dismayed that Angela had now flung her arms around the man's neck and wouldn't let go. Having also had a few too many himself, things started to get nasty.

"Why don't you push off? It's pretty obvious who she wants to go home with." Verity wouldn't stand for that. Before anyone really knew what was happening, a full on fisticuffs broke out and continued outside as a screaming landlady told them to "break it up" in a high pitched roar, worthy of the Queen Vic.

Verity swung a chubby left hook, just as the man made a grab for her skirt, ripping the hemline. Verity screeched, as a good quantity of material tore and made a swing at the man's chin with her other hand, but was suddenly stopped in her tracks by the feeling of her feet becoming warm and wet.

She looked down upon her best stilettos to see that Angela was vomiting heavily all over them. Verity's "pulling" stilettos. Her crème de la crème of footwear. It was bad enough that she had nowhere to wear her sparkly top to. Surely she didn't deserve this.

****

Maggie seemed to be drifting in and out of an uncomfortable afternoon snooze as Chrissie sat beside her, scanning a big folder of typed up notes. It was important that she had them all, but Chrissie just couldn't concentrate – all her focus was on Maggie. What if.....? She stopped herself. She couldn't allow herself to think that way, but the grim reality of the run-down hospital ward made that difficult.

Whilst all the nurses seemed very pleasant, they were obviously run off their feet and sometimes Chrissie noticed that Maggie didn't have any water or that the line on her drip was beeping and no one was coming to change it. She wished she could have taken her out of there and back home, but......

Chrissie turned some pages of the file to see some notes on Ballet Barbara and registered surprise. Those were certainly unexpected figures. Maggie started to rouse.

"Mornin' Sleeping Beauty" said Chrissie.

"Oh, Christina – oh my goodness, did I nod off for long?"

"No idea" said Chrissie, "I just got here. I'm just looking at this stuff on Barbara."

"Oh, Barbara....yes, well, never mind her. I really do need to speak to you about Angela."

"How do you want me to do this, Maggie?"

Maggie looked at Chrissie intensely. "Gently. Gradually. I don't want her not to trust us. Think I need a bit more background on her admin skills, though."

"Not a problem, Maggie – I can ask Andy to look into that. You know I'm not much of an I.T person."

Maggie looked agitated. "I'm afraid we may need to press on a bit quicker with this than we thought."

"But, Barbara ...."

"It's nothing to do with Barbara, it's about – me." Maggie's watery hazel eyes met Chrissie's fear, in the middle of both their emotions. Maggie held her stoical gaze. "Oh, for goodness sake Christina, don't cry. After all, I am eighty-seven – it's somewhat inevitable." Chrissie wiped her eye.

"Please Maggie, Please. Not yet. You've still got at least a decade in you, I'm sure. You can't. We need you. Why won't you let us get you somewhere else and pay for..." Maggie put her finger to Chrissie's lips. Such a thought was out of the question.

"Well, I certainly don't intend popping my clogs today. We've got that massive file to go through, after all." Chrissie gently placed the file on the floor beside her.

"I can handle that. What I need to know from you is the next step. Should I be making some...introductions?" Maggie gazed straight ahead and focussed hard.

"Yes....I think it's about time. Perhaps just the allotment for now and maybe take her to Andy. I'd be interested to see what he thinks she can do, as well."

"Right you are" said Chrissie, then she added, "You do look awfully tired. Shall I come back later?" Maggie wasn't having that.

"Later is not part of our vocabulary! You do remember that, don't you? Right now, procrastination would be absolutely the worst thing for us."

"I thought you told me to go easy."

"I told you to go easy – I didn't tell you to stop!" Chrissie heaved the file back on her lap. Maggie Buxton was not a woman to argue with.

****

When Angela arrived at the Queen Mary ward later that day, she was startled to find Maggie's bed empty. All kinds of worst case scenarios started running through her head before a nurse who recognised her told her that Maggie had been moved down to the physiotherapy ward. Angela's relief was clearly visible. It was unthinkable that she could lose Maggie – not now, not at this time in her life.

All she was learning from and about this remarkable woman, how her own life was changing, and how deeply she was feeling. It seemed like this was the Angela she had always wanted to show the world, but had hidden her behind her glasses and tucked her behind her ears. She was afraid she wouldn't be employed if managers witnessed her real boldness and so she presented the perfect, mousey little secretary who had long forgotten just what a talented pianist she was.

Maggie would be so proud that "Little Miss Prim" had gotten completely wrecked and then heaved over her boss's shoes. As Angela entered the new ward, she was in for another shock. Sat bolt upright in bed, Maggie had a pair of wartime style pince-nez balanced at the end of her nose and perched in a similar fashion at the end of her bed was Ballet Barbara.

For a moment, Maggie didn't look like herself. Instead of the welcoming geriatric with the twinkly eyes, she looked like a stern schoolmistress. She peered at Angela down the length of her nose.

"Ah, hello dear. Glad you've popped along today – we were just talking about you." For the first time since they'd met, Angela started to feel a little afraid of Maggie. Maybe it was the unexpected presence of Barbara, maybe it was Maggie's glasses, or maybe it was just the fact that they'd been discussing her in a way that appeared to be more than a friendly interest.....

She approached the bed with some trepidation. Meeting Maggie had been a little bit like falling in love; you're minding your own business when a sudden chance meeting changes your life and everything in the world looks bright and sunny and all the clouds look fluffy and there are bouncy little bunnies everywhere.....for a few months.

It seemed a little too early for the blinkers to be removed. Maggie saw the look on Angela's face and gently nudged Barbara from beneath her blankets. Barbara shuffled uncomfortably. Sensing Angela's wariness, Maggie removed her glasses.

"Goodness, please don't look so worried! Can't read a damn thing without them, and I just wanted to make sure Barbara wasn't ripping you off!" Barbara coughed.

"Maggie tells me you're a secretary."

"P.A" Angela corrected. She knew it was always best to be firm with Barbara, even if she wasn't really listening.

Well, anyway," continued Barbara, "We've had a little bit of an opportunity come up. I don't know if it would be something that would interest you, but basically it's some administration for the ballet school – at least to start with." Angela relaxed. This offer seemed innocent enough and with things approaching an ongoing downwards sliding scale at Mort and Grey, she appreciated any information about any work on offer.

"Are you interested?" asked Barbara, "I can let you know more about it after the Thursday afternoon class. It does mean working in the vicar's office though, which as you've probably seen is a bit of a tip. Still, I'm sure you're used to tidying up these sort of things." This time, Maggie scowled at Barbara. Angela smiled.

"That's what P.A s do" Then, thinking of Verity she added, "Sort out everyone else's mess."

****

Beverley did her best to try and calm Callum down as he chewed endlessly at his raw fingernails. "Don't worry – your mum's going to be just fine. She might need to stay in for a bit, but it'll just be temporary." Callum stared up at Beverley with big round eyes. He was still a child and so full of innocence, but he'd carried a knife and plunged it into an adult and from that moment his childhood had been removed. Even though she'd been a teacher for many years, Beverley didn't know if childhood could ever come back. She tried to swallow down a hard lump in her throat.

Callum rose his hand to his mouth again, but Beverley slapped it back down in his lap. "Stop that Callum – it isn't going to help. You'll have nothing left but bloody stumps." Callum's wide eyes met hers again – he was shocked.

"That's what mum used to say to me."

"So – have you always been a nail nibbler?"

"I don't know....I know mum always slapped my fingers away, just like you did. One time she painted this stuff onto my nails that tasted so disgusting, it was s'pose to stop you biting them."

"Hmm .. guess that didn't work then" said Beverley.

"I just used to breathe through my mouth, so I couldn't taste the stuff, then carry on biting" Beverley laughed.

"Nothing stops you Callum does it?" Her eyes met the boy's as she realised just how loaded with meaning that statement was. He was so afraid and pleading and – young. Beverley realised that maybe, just maybe, for a moment or two.....childhood does return in that time when a child really needs an adult. In that split second, she promised herself that she would look after Callum, no matter what.

Finally, after what seemed like an age, far too many coffees for herself and far too many cans of Coke for Callum, a doctor came out. He appeared to want to speak to Beverley alone, but Callum looked at him squarely. Beverley indicated that he was strong enough to hear whatever needed to be said. The doctor spoke gently.

"Ms Brown is really quite ill at the moment. We're concerned that she's rather underweight and anxious and we'd like to keep her in for a while, but – don't worry. She is going to get better. I do need to speak to her G.P – I don't suppose you know who that might be?"

Callum piped up, "Yes, it's Dr Feris at the Beech Street clinic."

"Well, thank you young man, that's very helpful. Don't you worry now – we'll look after her." He glanced anxiously across at Beverley, indicating that there were still things he needed to say out of Callum's earshot. He hastily scribbled a number and his name on a card, which Beverley took and pocketed, fully understanding the intention.

"Come on Callum, it's been a long evening. Let's get you home." Callum seemed struck with a sudden realisation. Where was home? If his mum couldn't look after him, then Callum didn't want to be with any adult other than Beverley. They both knew it wasn't a given that he could stay, but for now her home was home to him. Callum had told the hospital staff quite convincingly that Beverley was his mum's "best friend" and in turn she had said the mother and son were staying with her whilst some repair work was carried out on their own home. The one thing both Beverley and Callum needed to work out was the problem of going back to school....

****

Mark drove round and round the outer road of the park. Beverley hadn't called him back. If anything had happened to her then someone would have contacted him, but he was agonising about whether to try her again or just leave her alone and hope she'd eventually respond. Despite the heavy rain, Mark opted to turn into a parking bay and retrieve a big golfing umbrella from the boot.

He'd found the umbrella on the tube and felt a bit guilty for not handing it in to lost property, but couldn't understand why anyone would have forgotten to pick up something that size. He remembered Beverley had laughed at it when he'd gotten it home, saying it was bigger than he was. He also remembered how they'd cosied beneath it on a humid April day and held hands crossing that very same park......Today it was nowhere near as warm.

It was blustery late November with the kind of heavy showers suitable for sobering up anyone or bringing you out of a reverent daydream. Mark felt the stinging water hit his face, before opening the umbrella and making his way up the hill to the moist bench. Huddled out of the rain, a little further off in the distance, Spencer and Daz sat at the entrance to one of the tunnels.

"The stupid bastard stabbed her arm!" yelled Spencer far too loudly. Daz tried to shush him. Spencer was angry at having spent hours being interrogated at the police station before being let go on the grounds of insufficient evidence. Daz resisted letting any signs of relief show on his face. He listened carefully, intently – totally aware that he needed to be on full alert.

Information Spencer had might give him clues as to where he could find Callum. "What more did the police say to you?" Daz asked. Spencer started to calm down and become a little more rational.

"They said they interviewed this woman at the hospital who'd been stabbed in a random attack and apparently described – me. She also said she couldn't really see her attacker properly in the dark, but the police came for me, didn't they? They came for me 'cos of my brother. 'Cos they think I'm the same as him. S'aright for you Daz – you just manage to duck and dive and somehow always keep your nose very clean. How do you do it?"

"Never mind that" said Daz, "So this Goldie is still alive. I'm just trying to figure out how much the police know about the Tunnel Boys. What did they make you say? Do they know you're part of a gang?"

"All they know is, I was with a few mates at the scene of the crime. There's nothing much that makes me stand out more than any other boy – hoodie, crew cut, average height – she could've described someone else. The police only have a pretty sketchy description."

This gave Daz food for thought. How come the Goldie hadn't given the police a description of Callum? She'd have seen him close up and he looked nothing like Spencer. It may have been dark, but there was enough street light to see features, close to. Did she know him? Was that why Callum didn't actually carry out a full Morgan?

A million thoughts crossed Daz's mind, but again he couldn't let on his true feelings to Spencer. He continued with his more subtle line of questioning. "So, it's only this woman's description of someone who vaguely looks like you that the police kind of have. Not much for them to go on."

"I hope not brother, I hope not" said Spencer. He was still agitated, despite Daz's calm presence. "I'm wondering if they're gonna start linking stuff – y'know, what with Trick or Cheat n'all that." Daz didn't want to admit he hadn't exactly been happy about the sloppy management of The Tunnel Boys in the last few months, but he needed to keep Spencer off his case.

"There's loadsa gangs these days round this area Spence – I can't think we've got anything to needlessly worry about. But let me have a word with the Chiefs will you?" Spencer trusted Daz, but deep down Daz knew there was huge cause for concern. Callum hadn't been at school for nearly two weeks, so it could only be a matter of time before people started asking questions. Daz needed to find Callum and he needed to find him fast.

****

Mark couldn't believe he was trembling as he dialled Beverley's number. It was early Saturday afternoon and he mentally went through the chances of her being in, or otherwise where she'd most likely be. She was actually just on her way back from the hospital with Callum and the answer phone kicked in. Mark hung up and decided to text, but what?

He was the one who'd walked out, after all. Should he say sorry? Should he just say, please get in touch? Eventually he called back and left a voice message, expressing his deepest regret. If she didn't reply to a second message, then he'd have to send her a more formal email about collecting the rest of his stuff.

His heart raced – he hadn't anticipated how much he would miss her or be sorely sorry about his actions. Now that reality had kicked in, practicalities also started to come to light. What would they do about the flat? Would they still be friends? Would they have another chance? Mark realized he'd have to sit on that bench a lot longer to figure out what it was he really wanted, but it was so soggy and damp, that he decided he needed to walk to resume quiet contemplation.

Daz rushed out of the tunnel and immediately caught Mark's eye. Mark remembered the boy – he couldn't forget him. He'd even featured in his dreams. Only there was something different now about his demeanour. He looked distracted, anxious, stressed. And he was most definitely in a hurry.

Mark felt an overwhelming urge to approach Daz, but he knew the boy was on a mission and unlikely to stop and talk to a stranger. Besides, he was obviously up to something and would be very suspicious if approached by a random adult. To this end, Mark decided to follow him.

****

"Do please make yourself at home" said the vicar "And please do call me Anthony. Vicar is so formal, don't you think?" Angela immediately warmed to this affable man with the twinkly blue eyes and thick white hair. He was calm and collected and whilst his office seemed to be a rather jumbled collection of box files and a highly dusty computer keyboard, Angela found working in there to be a welcome contrast to Barbara's frenetic and erratic energy. She started to clear a space to sit in and then asked where best to begin.

"Begin?" said Anthony looking surprised, "My dear – you don't even have a cup of tea. We don't do anything here without having tea first. And you'd like a few biscuits to go with that, I'm sure."

"That's very kind of you" replied Angela, "But, um – I don't know where the kitchen is." Anthony looked at her quizzically.

"Well, it's just across the corridor, but *I'm* the one who always makes the tea, so don't you worry yourself about that. Be sure to let me know if we're out of jammy dodgers, though." Angela pressed the small of her back into the wooden chair. She wasn't exactly used to this laid back kind of attitude in her work environment.

She was used to being the dogsbody, the one who ran around making hot drinks for everyone else, the one who'd be admonished for forgetting to add the correct amount of sugars or too much milk. She'd once worked in a small office for a sales firm and shared a room with three managers. She counted that she'd made thirty cups of coffee in one day and seeing as she didn't drink any herself at that time, that averaged ten cups per manager. No wonder they were all so wired.

Angela started to go through the paperwork and found to her surprise that it was extremely well ordered and classified, thereby making her job quite simple. Barbara may have been the scattiest of teachers, but her accounts were in impeccable order. She started to make notes on expenditure for the ballet school – new floor slats, sheet music, ballet shoes; all outgoings and any items that Barbara purchased for re-sale to parents, directly from her stock cupboard.

Anthony seemed to be having rather a lot to be getting on with so didn't stick around to make small talk – it was shame; there was so much Angela wanted to ask him, although not about the church. He seemed such a sparkling and likeable man that regardless of her many non-church going years, Angela just wanted to get to know him better.

Barbara was supposed to be giving her some kind of "induction", but Barbara never even made an appearance. She'd made it clear to Anthony that if Angela could make sense of everything then just to leave her to it. Those were also Maggie's instructions, after all.....Angela was also being paid a not unreasonable rate – almost as much as she earned being Verity's P.A.

Maggie and Barbara had casually mentioned that if all went well, there may well be more hours available. A sudden, shocking realization hit

Angela. Without going out and looking for it, work had landed in her lap just when she needed it. She may not need to be Verity's little part-time slave for the rest of her working life.

It was completely inconceivable, but it was the truth – could it really be that maybe, just maybe in the midst of a recession she would be able to hand in her notice? Maybe there was something about working in the presence of God, after all.....

****

Once Angela had packed up for the day and left, Chrissie and her partner Andy unlocked Anthony's office. Andy opened up the computer details Angela had been working on and quickly started to transfer data. Barbara's ballet wraps were converted into allotment expenses and numerous other items including school books, cooking utensils, camper van petrol and a curious folder that Andy had labelled "Drayton Upkeep".

"Looks like your new chum has done an excellent job" muttered Andy as he continued processing the information.

"Maggie has a hunch she's the one" said Chrissie. "I think it's time you met." She shook lose her dreadlocks from a hessian headband and started scanning the shelves for some folders as Andy typed. Thanks to Angela, their evening wasn't going to be quite as long as anticipated.

****

Daz plonked himself down at the end of West Hill with a notebook and mini A-Z. He mentally went through all the places and people that Callum may have known. He knew Callum had an aunt only a few miles away, but he also knew he didn't like her, so it was hardly likely he would have gone there.

Callum had often spoken about his unknown father – he'd just come of an age when he'd started to be curious about him and his background, but his mother never told him much. Maybe he'd gone to try and find him – found some info at home and thought he could at least make a trace.

Daz figured that as Callum had been involved in something extraordinarily awful and his mother was a complete mess, then there'd be an adult he'd want to turn to. Daz also toyed again with the idea that Callum might have known his victim, but who on earth could that be? Desperate as he was to find him, Daz needed to bide some thinking time.

There was a slim chance Callum might've returned to the flat to collect some stuff. Perhaps he'd bypass the C block on his way back home and just see. That was until he saw the police outside Callum's front door, talking to the slobby, portly neighbour.

"Half-caste lad, early teens you say?" Daz heard the officer as another P.C whipped out a notebook and hastily scribbled. Daz ducked behind a flower pot and made himself as small as possible in one of the very few decorated balconies on the Drayton Estate, managing to conceal himself behind some evergreens in the cold winter drizzle.

To his horror, Daz heard the neighbour give the police a further description of Daz. He debated scarpering, but then heard the rest of the conversation about occupants previously in the next door flat leaving the premises.

"So...you say you saw the lad leaving with his mother and quite a few bags....Hmmm...going away for quite some time, would you say?"

The neighbour paused. "I couldn't really say. All I know is, I've not seen either of 'em since. Gotta be a reason people do a runner, 'int there, officer?" Daz took a deep gulp. Even though it was dangerous to hang around, when he heard the policeman say they'd need to search the flat and asked the neighbour if he might have a spare key, Daz thought he would linger a little bit longer – there might be valuable information to be had.

Mark peered around the side of the block, having followed Daz back to the Drayton Estate. Seeing the police and then clocking a crouched down Daz, he became extremely curious. He pressed his back to the wall and tried to hear more. But he didn't account for being spotted. Benji was out on the square, a couple of floors below. He saw Mark and shouted up and waved.

"Hey there! Mister!" Mark waved back, but pressed a finger to his lips. Benji looked puzzled, but just carried on waving. Even though it was only a little yell, Daz recognised the voice of his own brother and wondered how Benji could see him, concealed as he was. Then he realised Benji's voice was coming from around the other side of the block, so he must have been shouting up at one of his friends. At any rate, now was the best time to move it before the police came out and try and find somewhere safe to continue watching.

Eventually the officers came out of the Brown's flat coughing and waving their hands across their noses.

"No wonder they left" wheezed one P.C "Completely addled with mould and rising damp in there. Got any problems like this in your flat, sir?" The unprepossessing neighbour just stared blankly. The officer figured that a man like that probably wouldn't notice, if he had. He couldn't believe he was just standing there on a cold winter's day in only a string vest, his belly flopping over the top of his stained trousers and a comb-over pressed flat against his forehead.

This man probably just grew out of his couch whilst the television continued its own tirade and he allowed the damp to escalate without even realizing it, seeing as the rest of his property probably smelt just as bad as he did.....

"Anyway – thank you for your time, sir. I trust we can call on you again if we need to follow anything further." The neighbour seemed to be annoyed that the police weren't shaking his hand and giving him a reward. He was missing "Deal Or No Deal" for this. Daz darted directly across from the flowerpots to the glass door that led straight down the staircase.

He needed to bound down the steps three at a time to be well ahead of the police – something he was well used to doing down all the stairwells of the estate, escaping marauding gang members, older boys and people like Callum's neighbour. Mark waited until the police had left then headed down the stairs himself. All the glass was smashed and the stairs stunk of urine.

Obscene graffiti was plastered on any spare bit of wall and used condoms and litter were strewn across the steps. Mark could only breathe through his nose as he descended – he nearly heaved as he passed one step and a delightful graffiti painting of a man vomiting the words "Welcome to C Block". The stench was awful.

Mark worked in the Youth sector, but it was usually in comfortable community centres where the "youth" were engaged in drama workshops and discussion groups, not tearing around with lethal weapons. He began to imagine Daz a few years older, attending one of these workshops.

A kid like that would immediately be talent-spotted by one of the visiting casting directors; he'd get a part in "The Bill" or "Casualty" and then gain a purpose in life. Instead of ending up behind bars, he'd be a proper actor. Through one of the smashed glass panels, Mark watched Daz disappear through a bush-covered path, but decided he would try and follow him further.

Without really being conscious of his obsession, Mark knew he now had pieces of Daz's "story" – he was looking for a friend who had fled the estate, assumedly before the police found him. What had the friend done?

****

Beverley did her best to hold back tears as Callum sat holding the hand of his deeply sedated mother. She thanked God that Marisa had her eyes closed and wasn't just lying there staring in a half-zombie, half-human kind of way as various other occupants of the ward seemed to do. She thought a ward like this might be too hard for Callum to handle, but he'd begged to see his mother.

As he spoke , Beverley thought her heart would break. "Everything's gonna be alright, Mum. You'll see. Miss, I mean Beverley is gonna find us a home that's warm and dry and where we don't get any bother from people like Mr Pontis and no more 'bad letters' like you always chucked away. And you're gonna get a really really good job so that we can both buy new shoes."

Beverley cast her attention down to Callum's shoes where she could see his toes were almost breaking out of the scuffed nylon trainers. "Who's Mr Pontis?" she asked.

"Our neighbour" Callum replied. "Nasty bully. Always sticking his nose in. He used to tell everyone in the block if he hadn't seen Mum leave for work at the usual time, or me go to school and once he stitched us up to the DSS, although Mum was only getting her usual child benefits. Whenever he saw Mum, he'd always ask if she was ok, but not in a friendly way, y'know? It was more like a sort of, sort of...nosy way. Kind of like he always wanted information, or something. Well, he's not gonna get any now, is he?"

Beverley shook her head. It didn't even occur to her that Mr Pontis was at that very moment, rubbing his hands with glee – he felt all important now that the police wanted to speak to him and he thought he might have some juicy gossip. No one thought that Daz might desperately be looking for Callum or that Marisa's disappearing act was the talk of the estate.

"Sounds like you're well away from him, Callum" said Beverley, "Not to mention that awful flat. You must be missing your school friends, though - maybe there are some people you should just let know that you're ok?" Callum trembled at the thought. All his friends were Tunnel Boys and the fact he'd done a runner was very bad news indeed. His expression told Beverley a lot.

"Your friends.......it's the gang, isn't it?" Callum just sunk his head low. Marisa started to groan. Callum changed the subject. His mum couldn't know what he'd done – what he'd been involved in. Beverley gripped Callum's left hand as his right one tightened his grip on Marisa. Tears started to trickle down his cheeks.

"I'm gonna make you so proud of me mum, you'll see. I'm gonna work really hard and Beverley will teach me, 'cos she knows everything. Then I'll be like a really big manager and work in the city and we'll have lots of money and our own home, Mum....jus' you an' me in our own home." Beverley couldn't stop her own tears. This poor broken woman and her son shouldn't have to fight to have a decent roof over their heads.

But what Callum had just said planted a seed of thought in her own mind. Perhaps she could try and get Callum a place at her school, but she knew the both of them would need to talk to the police and authorities and come clean. It was the best course of action. "Come on now" she said, "Mum needs a rest. We'll come back tomorrow."

As they turned at the end of the corridor, so Chrissie came up the other end with some more files for Maggie. She thought she recognised Beverley and then seeing her heavily bandaged arm, realised who she was. "Hi there! How's your arm?"

Callum froze. Who was this woman? A teacher Beverley knew? She didn't look like a teacher. What had Beverley told her? He looked at her, hard. She had lose, unruly hair, flowing cotton clothes and a warm and engaging smile. Callum didn't know she'd started out in life from the same place as him.....

Beverley felt embarrassed. She coloured and waved hello back – and felt guilty. Chrissie had gone out of her way to help her and yet here she was, sheltering and protecting her attacker. She knew Chrissie would want to ask her questions and didn't know what to do. Fortunately, Chrissie turned her attention to Callum.

"Hello there, young man. Do you belong to this lady?" Callum gazed up at her.

"My mum's on a ward here" he said.

"Oh, I'm sorry" said Chrissie bending down to him, "I hope she gets better very soon." She took in his wariness, his hardened attitude, but his soft heart. There was something rather special about him, in a strange sort of way. He must have been just a little younger than she was when her own mum was rushed into hospital from a heroin overdose.

She'd been ushered into other rooms by strangers and doctors and had to grow up very fast and .....she could have had a completely different life, but she was one of the lucky ones. She had met Maggie. "She's definitely going to get better" said Callum. Then he looked Chrissie directly in the eye and said "And she's going to come home very soon." His eyes bored through her, although he was convincing himself that this was the truth.

"Well, I'm glad to hear that" said Chrissie. "You look after your friend, now. She's had a bad arm injury." That's a good place to leave it, thought Beverley, but then Chrissie continued. "I'm sorry, I don't even know your name – it was all a bit of a blur that evening, what with the ambulance and everything."

Callum's heart started thumping. Chrissie was there? Did she know it was him?

"I'm Beverley and this is Callum" said Beverley as she made movements towards the exit. Chrissie went to shake hands, but nearly dropped her files. "Oops! I'm Chrissie. Good to see you again."

Beverley wanted to thank Chrissie, tell her more, but with Callum in tow, all she could hope was that they'd meet again. She knew that once home, Callum was going to want answers. She tried to think of some in advance, but as they pushed open the exit doors, Chrissie shouted after them, "By the way – how's Grandma?"

****

As Beverley stirred some hot milk into some chocolate powder, Callum sat on her settee, staring at the photo of Grandma. He was intrigued by the wrinkly old woman with the darkest skin he'd ever seen and missing teeth. "Is this who that lady was asking about?" he asked.

"Yes. Yes, that's Grandma" said Beverley.

"How come she knew her?" he asked. Beverley knew she was going to have to tell Callum everything. She knew this would make him very anxious, but she assured him that if he told the truth then everything would be ok. There suddenly seemed to be an insurmountable amount to cope with. Events had shaped up in such a dramatic way since Mark had walked out that she'd barely had time to think about him and now she had a child to take care of, his mother to worry about and possibly finding out as much as she could about a boy gang.

Callum seemed temporarily placated as he blew on his hot drink, but then she saw him quizzically turning the picture of Grandma as if he already knew about her. "She knew lots of things, didn't she?" he said.

"Yes she....how do you know that, Callum?"

"I can just tell – by her eyes, I mean. I know when people just know things. Like that lady at the hospital – she knows things. An' also, Grandma's really old an' old people know lots of things, don't they? My Grandma died before I was born, but I think I might have another one, somewhere. Only to find her, I'd need to find my Dad first." He placed the picture of Grandma back on the shelf then asked, "Miss – I mean Beverley ....would you help me find my Dad?"

Beverley didn't know how she could possibly deny such a request. In all the chaos of this very young life this was probably the only hope he had to cling to. But there was so much to wade through first.

"I know it's very important to you Callum, but don't you think we should wait until your Mum's out of hospital? We might need to do quite a bit of running back and forth for a while and we've got to get your schooling sorted out as well." Maybe he'd feel safe at her school, knowing her presence was always there. But what did Callum mean when he said he knew when people "knew things?" The only other person who'd ever said that was Grandma. She pushed the thought aside and wondered what reasons she could use for Callum needing a transfer. She'd been mulling over that for the last few days.

Callum's eyes which had previously registered only despair, terror and sadness, suddenly seemed to light up with hope. At last it seemed he might have a future. He looked at Beverley with his still child's soul, fully trusting of an adult and holding an innocence that might otherwise forever have been lost.

"I know it'll all be ok" he smiled. "Grandma told me so."

* * * * * * * * *

Both Angela and Verity stared at the phone, almost willing it to ring. It was frightening how few people were ordering custom made paperclips these days. Verity had started chewing her nails – something she had never previously done and she'd sort of been almost nice to Angela – something she'd never previously done , either.

The "sea change" was turbulent and drastic and now coming in tidal waves that even Verity could no longer ignore. Distracted and nervous, Verity was also losing weight and as Angela stared out the window, she wondered if her thoughts were along the same lines.

"Bit of a worry, isn't it, Angela?"

"What?"

"Y'know – I mean how quiet it's been."

"Oh – that. Mmm." Verity couldn't understand Angela's lack of concern. Surely she didn't have some kind of secret trust fund somewhere or a massive amount of savings or some other source of income that meant she could be so laid back about the recession. Verity didn't want to admit that she felt a bit shame-faced about thinking Brian had become Angela's Sugar Daddy – even Angela would have gone for a man with a higher earning capacity and no ex-wife to support, if that was what she wanted.

In a weird kind of way, Verity had almost come to respect her mousey little P.A, whom she thought no one would even give a second glance. The office staff on the whole seemed to have a great respect for Angela. In the light of all the anxieties and tensions, Angela somehow seemed to retain a calm and dignified silence and simply got on with as much as there was of her job left to do.

Angela had practically set up her own practice, becoming "Office Counsellor" for the regular stream of colleagues who would now filter through, simply wanting to be placated by her gentle "aura" or soothing words. Work had not become a pleasant environment to be in. Mutterings and rumours of who would be next up for the chop always seemed to be circulating and there was a constant atmosphere of tension. Worst of all was the back-stabbing and bullying. Kevin reported back how inhumane his direct bosses had become.

Kevin had learnt to cope by keeping his head down and keeping a low profile, but this wasn't at all in keeping with his personality. Kevin was the office joker, the chap with the cute grin – the flirt and easy-going one who'd always lighten things up. Now he seemed morose and quiet and with many of his friends laid off, nights at the pub had gone into decline as well.

These emotions saturating the Mort and Grey office were felt deeply by Angela, but not absorbed by her. She hadn't told anyone about her new friends or unexpected job offers, save for a few people close to her. Various colleagues would come and perch on the corner of her desk and it was so quiet, that even Verity didn't seem to mind if they stayed to chat a while. It gave her something to do, as well.

They'd hear about how so and so had gone into the manager's room one day and never returned. Angela was told how one girl wasn't even allowed back in to get her coat and another colleague had to bring it out for her. Any of the usual cheerful banter and camaraderie had been destroyed by echoes of fear.

It seemed to many that the only way to cling onto the last vestiges of hope was to kill off the competition by whatever means possible. Angela came to grasp that the term "constructive dismissal" really meant being bullied so severely, you felt you had to leave.

On another plane, still somewhere on earth, Callum Brown had been forced into "resigning". He thought he had nothing else much in his life other than the Tunnel Boys, but now his eyes had been opened to another existence. In the grey-coloured light of the Drayton Estate, there shone a few beacons of colour.

When he'd been tutored by Beverley, he'd actually enjoyed learning. He was bright, but his class teacher was dull, tired and un-inspiring and Callum found what was going on outside the window more interesting than her lessons. Beverley wasn't a teacher like that. She had a genuine desire to help children learn and she seemed to love her life and the world around her.

She was enthusiastic about everything she did and her energy would penetrate you and make you feel good. She made Callum feel like he had some kind of hope.

Angela had found some of her own shining beacons of light in her friendship with Maggie and Chrissie and the job opportunities that had led to. But she did feel sorry for some of her colleagues. Several of them had young children and their husbands had already been made redundant. They felt they'd already been swept up by worse case scenarios of losing their homes and not being able to provide for their families.

In the morning, they'd sat in a room where no one even dared get up for coffee, lest their desk had been taken over by the time they returned. They barely dared to breathe in case their supervisors accused them of taking a break and anyone who walked past was eyed up nervously.

Angela surprisingly got the go-ahead from Verity to light incense sticks and have Radio 3 playing gently in the background. The small room at the top of the stairs became a refuge and a place where people could air their woes and just "be" for a half a moment.

No one asked Angela how she managed to retain her unruffled air – they were all too wrapped up in their own stuff to even care about a barely-known colleague. That is, until Brian came in. Brian dared to ask. He couldn't help himself, but he knew he was falling in love with this new "guru" Angela, even though she'd rejected him.

Now he didn't care if she could be his friend or mentor, that would be enough – as long as she was still there. "How do you do it, Angela?" Brian asked her in front of Verity. "You're a little shining light in an otherwise dull grey little world." Verity grimaced as Brian did the same, only his was under several layers of beard.

"Well, thank you Brian, but I'm sure you have plenty of lights in your life" said Angela.

Brian gazed out onto an imaginary horizon, trying to think if there was anything he felt was a "light". Verity really didn't want to get into anybody's deep existential angst and was quick to move the conversation on.

"Did you want something Brian?"

"Yes, yes I did. I wanted to come and talk to Ange. Bit quiet over in I.T and by the look of things it's the same here. Ange gives us all hope, you know." Brian pulled up a chair opposite Angela's desk and sat with his elbows propped on it, whilst gazing into her eyes. Verity slammed shut a big box file which made Angela jump, but didn't even shake Brian from his reverie.

Angela was glad for the distraction – she was beginning to feel distinctly uncomfortable with the love-struck Brian and exactly how much he was now invading her desk space. Verity started. "Really Brian, don't you have anything better to.....?" She trailed off, realising how foolish that sounded. Of course he had nothing better to do. He had nothing to do at all, just like the rest of Mort and Grey and Verity knew that she was becoming more and more frustrated as to why her formerly mousey P.A was behaving like some aloof Goddess.

Honestly, she didn't know what the world was coming to. "Hrrum" Verity growled. "I'm going to make some coffee. Anybody want some? Or maybe you'd like some nectar or disgusting herby tea type stuff, Ange?"

"Nah, just a coffee thanks" said Angela.

"Good to see Verity's back to her old self" laughed Brian. Then he turned more serious. "What you gonna do, Angie?" She shifted uneasily backwards banging her head on the filing cabinet behind.

"Oh, oh I'm so sorry, I didn't mean you to get so worried." Brian stood up, meaning to reach out and rub Angela's head, but as she retreated back further, virtually trying to crawl inside the filing cabinet, so Brian stretched further across the desk, finally falling on it with one arm outstretched towards Angela's right breast. Enter Verity to what appeared to be a very uncompromising position.

"Brian! I think it's time you left, don't you?" Gingerly Brian hauled himself up, reddened and nodded at both the women before leaving the office. Angela resumed her seat whilst rubbing the back of her head. Verity frowned but said nothing.

"Never thought I'd hear myself say this" said Angela, "But Verity – I'm glad you were here."

****

Beverley had replayed her answer phone and felt she really should call Mark back, but that was definitely a "should" and not because she wanted to. It was more of a courtesy call, a response. There were practical things to sort and then the thought crossed her mind – he didn't want to come back, did he? He couldn't.

She needed the room for Callum and Marisa. Besides, he'd disappeared and left her with the financial worry – he hadn't even spoken about paying his half of the rent. As far as Beverley was concerned, this wasn't his home any more. Her eyes flickered across the room towards Grandma and she saw the half-smile, half-frown which partly approved of how Beverley was handling things and yet came with an added warning.

Being a philanthropist was all very well, but it didn't pay the rent. If she was intent on housing these people then there were more legal things to put in place. Then there was Mark. Did she even want him back? That was the question that toyed with her mind the most, pulling her emotions in many different directions.

On the one hand she'd been devastated that he'd packed up and gone. Yes, they were arguing more and yes they hadn't been seeing eye to eye of late, but wasn't that what happened with most couples? Surely after the honeymoon period, everybody's rose-tinted spectacles came off and another view was seen. Beverley didn't feel that was a bad thing.

It made for a clearer reality and opened the path to real love and understanding. Made each half of the couple see their partner as a whole person – where they were similar, how they differed and other opinions; light and shade. But this had not brought her and Mark closer.

She couldn't deny that her burgeoning interest in the esoteric was something Mark couldn't and didn't seem to want to understand. Beverley couldn't explain that it wasn't really a choice – her very being was rooted in folklore, magic and ancestral ritual, even if both her parents were down to earth and living in a nice semi-detached.

Beverley thought that if you had that kind of heritage, then up-bringing made no difference; one day the ancestors would find you and bring you their knowledge. Whenever she thought of this, a soft warmth seemed to surge through her as though she knew that somewhere on another realm she was deeply loved and thought of highly enough to have ancient family secrets passed onto her.

Mark didn't quite see it the same way. He'd told her she was "possessed" whenever she wanted to sit down quietly and do some meditation. He didn't like her chanting or even flicking through packs of Angel cards. For her, this wasn't something evil or occult – it was a benevolent thing, something opening up to her and making her a better person – not one who wanted to practise black magic on her partner.

For some reason Mark felt threatened by Grandma. She might have been a formidable force, but she had never harmed anyone. Perhaps she had been involved in Voodoo which had frightening connotations, but this was part of her land – her life; merely something she was exposed to from a very young age.

In truth, Mark was also changing and that was why he felt threatened. Whilst all that was giving and spiritual was growing in Beverley, his darker, nastier and more repressed soul was pushing forward, pushing Mark to rebel and virtually destroy all the good in his life. Beverley hadn't seen this yet – she'd only seen his aversion to her own activities.

This part of Mark hadn't really ignited until he'd seen Daz and that had triggered a lot of childhood issues. Whether or not he and Beverley were completely pulling apart or could find some place they could meet in the middle remained to be seen. Tentatively, she dialled his number.

****

Angela waited just outside the front of the supermarket, but Chrissie was nowhere to be seen. She was sure she was in the right place. Eventually, a rickety old Volkswagen camper van pulled up and a young boy jumped out, followed by the swish of Chrissie's dreadlocks.

"Sorry I'm late" Chrissie grinned, "Had a bit of trouble with this one – been playing where he knows he's not supposed to!"

"Mum....." Christian started to protest, but his muddy trousers only heightened the fact that he was in the wrong. Chrissie got the formalities out the way.

"Right now, Christian – I'd like you to say hello to my friend Angela; Angela, this is my son, Christian." Christian's eyes sparkled and his lovely big smile spread across his face. He held out his hand.

"Hiya Angela!"

"Well, hello!" said Angela "Aren't you polite?"

"You betcha" said Chrissie, ""We don't tolerate rudeness, do we Christian?"

"I appreciate that" said Angela "Most little boys I know are nowhere near as polite as you." Spontaneously and unexpectedly, Christian threw his arms around Angela's waist. Surprised, but also deeply touched, Angela looked over at Chrissie - she wasn't sure how to react. Chrissie smiled.

"Looks like you're an instant hit. I've told Christian you've been working for Barbara – some of his friends go to her ballet classes." Again, Christian came out with the unexpected.

"I really like ballet" he said.

"Really?" said Angela.

"Yes" said Christian "But what I'd love most is to go and see a proper really big show. Have you seen any?"

"My mother used to take me when I was a child. I like ballet too" said Angela.

"Is that why you want to work for Barbara? She's a funny old lady!"

"Christian!" scolded Chrissie.

"Out of the mouths of babes!" laughed Angela. "You're absolutely right, Christian – she is quite funny, although it would be more polite to call her eccentric." She watched Christian grapple with the word.

"Eccsen.....exsentrik......"

"It means you have lots of quirky ideas and a very original way of looking at the world", said Angela.

Christian's broad smile stretched to the end of his cheeks. He seemed to really like that. It struck Angela at once that he was a child brought up in a very unusual way – she didn't know where he and his mother lived, but she was shortly to discover more about their lives.

Chrissie had invited Angela to meet Andy and see their allotment where they grew most of what they ate. There wouldn't be a lot there to see this time of year, but Chrissie thought it would be good for them all to get out into some grass and fields, even though there was a definite nip in the air.

The back end of the supermarket led directly onto some rural roads and Chrissie drove a little way out of town, past some small villages and then further along some farmland, until forking off onto a gravel road to reach the allotment.

"Is Mum letting you take the day off school then?" Angela asked Christian.

"Nah. I don't go to school."

"What – ever?"

"No. At least, not a big one. Mum teaches me at home, mostly. Sometimes Dad. And sometimes, me and my friends, we have our own school altogether." Once again, Angela looked over at Chrissie for an explanation.

"He's home-schooled" Chrissie explained "And then there are also some little groups he goes to. As long as he gets an education he doesn't need to be institutionalized. Hated school, myself. Anyway, I'd rather this than send him to Rook Hill."

Angela had heard of Rook Hill. It was the breeding ground for the Tunnel Boys and most of the kids from the Drayton Estate. It had a reputation for turning out young offenders rather than university entrants and it was becoming increasingly hard to find teachers who would stay there any length of time.

"I'll probably send him somewhere when he's older" said Chrissie "There's a limit to what Andy and I can do. But he's not deprived of playmates his own age. We think play is very important, that's why we...." Chrissie suddenly realised she was saying too much too soon. "We.....well. It's sort of like Maggie said. We have our own little family."

Angela was delighted to be integrated as part of this "family". For the first time in many years she felt excited and enthusiastic about something and had suddenly seen a light at the end of the tunnel of endless filing. She felt like The Family liked her and wanted her to be part of them. Whoever *they* were.....

She now counted Maggie and Chrissie as friends and Barbara and Anthony as employers and acquaintances, but what was this part of something bigger that they all belonged to? As Christian leaped out of the vehicle and bolted ahead, Chrissie led Angela down the gravel path and over a stile which led to a rapeseed field. Angela breathed in the crisp air. It felt so good to get out of town.

"I really like painting that field when it's all a-glow" said Christian.

Painting. All the children Angela knew these days would never say that. They seemed to have permanent attachments to electrical software which was more real to them than the actual world around them. Angela thought future generations would evolve without limbs and only space- hopper like little protrusions growing out of their heads, as these would be all they'd need for pressing endless buttons.

She could imagine Christian propped up at a long wooden kitchen table as she once was, with a box of poster paints, licking his lips at the lusciousness of the colours and wondering which one to use first.

Angela drifted into a childhood reverie of all the things she liked to do before school and adulthood and real life took over. She remembered her mother was very house proud and particular and always wore an apron in the kitchen which meant that if Angela was painting or making things from modelling clay, then she had to wear one too.

Her mother's apron had tiny bright orange and brown flowers against a cream background, so beloved of the designs of the 1970's. The flowers were so garish and so bright that if Angela stared at them for long enough she could actually induce her own psychedelic trip, but would usually tell her mum she had a headache, which came in handy for several days off school.

She wondered if staring at the apron was the reason she had always worn glasses. A small hand grasping hers shook her out of her moment of nostalgia. "Come on!" urged Christian, forcing Angela to run through the long grass with him, excited to show something to his new friend. After running uphill for what seemed like a very long time, they reached the allotment where a man with shaggy grey hair was digging.

He had a craggy kind of ageing rock - star face with a broad Mick Jagger type smile and very twinkly eyes behind all the wrinkles and sun-weathered complexion. Christian ran towards him and the man scooped him up in his arms.

"Wotcha little 'un! Hey look out – it's a bit muddy here!"

"Dad, Dad – did you find me anything?" Andy stopped digging.

"Not really the right time of year mate, but I'm turning the earth over a bit to check on stuff...hang on, what's this?" Andy appeared to bend down and retrieve a small, muddy potato, but Angela actually saw him cleverly palm it and produce it from his pocket "Well, I never! You knew I'd find you something, didn't you?"

Angela knew in this moment, this was the most important potato in the world. Christian's dad had found it and now he was holding it and the pride on Christian's face was something to behold. Angela felt as if she were watching some mystic ritual, something symbolic as Christian held the potato up to the fading sun, twirling it in his fingers. Andy saw Angela hovering in the distance.

Christian ran to grab her hand. "Dad! This is Angela." As the "rock star" grinned, Angela could see where Christian got his smile from. Andy extended a muddy hand towards Angela, apologised and wiped it on his jacket before offering it again. She could see he had muscular arms and strong, artistic hands. They looked like the sort of hands that toyed with stuff all day – not puny unused hands that only touched computer keypads. Angela guessed that Andy must have been around the same age as Brian, but what different stories they had. It seemed like Andy had a light switched on inside, whereas Brian's had gone out years ago.

Brian had lived his life in a linear fashion and worked at Mort and Grey even longer than Verity, working his way up to a managerial position and a respectable marriage with two sons. Both his work and his marriage gradually became stultified, but he made no effort to change either. Life after Mort and Grey looked like being one long void – he hadn't planned on retiring this early.

Angela was the only little bit of horizon in Brian's life, and he clung to that like a limpet, terrified that if he didn't, he would be washed away forever. This was in stark contrast to the man who stood before Angela now. Andy's face showed that a lot of living had been done and the "inner spark" showed there was a lot more to do. He radiated passion and enthusiasm.

"Pleasure to meet you, Angela" said Andy "Chrissie's told me a lot about you – in fact, she doesn't stop talking about you." Angela hoped this was in a good way. Andy intrigued her, but he said no more. He'd been instructed not to – at least, not at this stage. He beckoned Angela over to a little shed and started rummaging around the shelves." Got some tea bags, but don't think there's much to eat – Chris, did you remember to bring any milk with you?"

In a broken little shack on the allotment, in the middle of nowhere, Andy made Angela the best cup of tea she had ever had.

****

Benji just came out with it on the school bus. "The Hippy's back."

"The Hippy?" queried Daz, "You mean that lady with dreadlocks?"

"Nah" said Benji, "The *man* hippy." Daz sat up and gulped.

"When? Where?"

"He was up the balcony where you were when you went to see if you could find Callum. I waved at him and he put his fingers to his lips, like telling me to shhh, y'know?" Daz was aghast. Exactly who was the Hippy? Undercover police? A nutter? He paled as he questioned Benji.

"Did you see where he followed me from? D'ya think he knows where we live?" Benji shrugged.

"Dunno. I just saw him on the balcony. I reckon he's alright though – maybe he'll give us some more ciggies." Daz smiled, but couldn't hide his anxiety. "Wassa matter, bro?" asked Benji. "Is it that you don't think that really he is that nice?"

"I don't – look. We don't *know* him Benj. We just have to be careful, that's all. You know that."

"Do you think he knows something about Callum?" Benji caught on. Daz didn't know what the Hippy might know. Maybe he was trying to get some more general information on the Tunnel Boys, seeing as he'd been hanging around the park. Daz fished in the pocket of his bomber jacket and pulled out a stick of gum, which he handed to his brother.

"So, Benj.....tell me what else you noticed.....did the Hippy look happy when he waved, or like – what?"

"He had shoes on" was all Benji said before happily taking the gum.

****

They really could have waited until after Christmas, couldn't they? On the 19th December, Mort and Grey officially went into liquidation. Angela was glad she hadn't needed to go in to retrieve any stuff. She had visions of a bleary-eyed Verity packing at least fifteen years of her life into a cardboard box – photos of cuddly kittens and Valentine's day teddies that totally belied the Verity Angela knew – being stuffed in head first.

On the floor below, Brian would be wondering whether to take home the picture of Mrs Brian or just leave it there, sneakily fixing in the frame a picture of Angela. Angela could imagine nothing worse than the funereal mood that must have pervaded the place and as she sat at home watching the news, she couldn't believe her luck in finding all these new friends and work at just the right time.

A very cold wind was howling around her old flat windows and it was definitely starting to feel cold enough to snow. That's the way it always was – the country would be covered in white, either just before or after Christmas and never on Christmas day. Angela was making arrangements to visit her mother, but wanted to go and see Maggie before Christmas.

She started feeling grateful that she was still young and healthy at this time of year and not holed up in a grotty hospital bed, unable to get out in the daylight. But the elderly lady was always cheerful. And chatty. And also, it seemed, she was always occupied, busy making notes in folders and files. Now that she had a little time to sit and think to herself, Angela did start to wonder about all the connections between Maggie and Chrissie and Barbara.

She'd learned that Maggie had virtually adopted a surly teenage Chrissie when she'd run away from a broken home and a barrage of abuse. They'd met where Maggie was volunteering at a refuge. Yet, it was more than just a chance meeting – the two women seemed to share an incredible bond and shared some kind of deep knowledge that went beyond any blood connections.

Barbara was a very good friend of Maggie's, but Angela didn't know how she and Maggie had met. A poor widow from the Drayton Estate meets an eccentric, wealthy ballet mistress – an odd combination, if ever there was. Angela knew Maggie was into all sorts of "causes" and had helped Chrissie and Andy get the allotment, but she didn't know much about any of her new friends, really. She was waiting for Chrissie to invite her round. Then it occurred to Angela, that why didn't she invite Chrissie to her own place? What was she waiting for? Chrissie and Andy hardly struck her as the sort of people who'd stick their noses up at her pokey one bed flat, or the fact that she didn't have matching tea cups.

She couldn't believe she'd once had people round who did that. When she'd first stumbled across her little place to rent, after years of bedsits it seemed like a palace. A place of her own that wasn't sharing with people who always left the sink full of dishes or a dirty bathroom or had arguments over the bills.

Finally she could live on her own, and that was bliss. She shuddered as she became aware it might not be her home for much longer. Income was now a tenuous thing and landlords needed money. Angela had moved so many times, forced out by the property developers who would turn her bedsits into luxury flats, pricing her right out of the market.

Maybe in the recession the landlord would be grateful for whatever she could pay, as selling up might be difficult. Still, moving on was always at the back of her mind. She had become used to "home" just being a temporary place – she wondered if it were the same for Chrissie and Andy. She'd now been in Linden Crescent four years, which seemed like a lifetime.

Nothing Angela now owned was anything that couldn't be rolled up, packed down or stuffed into anything much larger than a Renault Clio. In the bedroom were paintings of jolly fat ladies by Beryl Cook; not exactly high culture, but they always made Angela chuckle. Had Verity been brought up elsewhere, then she might have been one of these women, prostituting on the high road in one of her little skirts, baring acres of wobbling, pimply flesh.

Angela had few pictures in the living room, largely because that space wasn't so personal to her. That was where visitors sat in two wicker chairs and where she sat on a sofa that had seen better days to watch telly. Nothing really matched, but everything was functional and she didn't really want for anything else. Angela thought about what she'd make Chrissie and Andy to eat and then cast her mind back to previous visitors.

When she'd first moved in, she finally felt that she could invite back Sharon, a secretary she'd befriended at work. Sharon had bought her own flat and had a rather nice car. She'd come up the stairs and walked in displaying a look of disdain.

"So...this is your *little* place...." She plonked her Prada bag down on the coffee table and pulled out a beautifully wrapped box. "Just a little something for your....housewarming." Tentatively Angela took the box and stared at it, unsure whether to open it then and there, offer a coffee first, or just try and ignore that it was there, and hope it would go away.

Both she and Sharon were obviously embarrassed. Sharon was expecting a far more salubrious pad and Angela wasn't expecting anything at all, let alone something that she feared was from Harvey Nics. "That's very sweet – why don't you – oh no, thank you ..." Both women spoke nervously over each other.

Angela carefully pulled off the wrapping paper, as though she were carrying out delicate surgery. Sharon started pacing "Oh – just rip it off." She felt increasingly anxious about buying the wrong gift now – had she known Angela lived somewhere like...this....well. She would have saved the voucher.

Angela's hands shook and she knocked over her coffee. "Oh!" Oh! Cloth!" she muttered jumping up, then realizing coffee was trickling down the leg of the table onto her cream coloured rug and spreading across some important work papers. Both she and Sharon dabbed frantically with sponges and kitchen roll, but the damage was already done.

"Um....I think I'll open it later" said Angela, carrying the box into the bedroom. She peeled soggy wrapping paper off the coffee table and left it in the kitchen to dry out. She may have ruined her work, but at least she was spared that awkward moment of finding out exactly what Sharon's gift was in front of Sharon.

****

Maggie looked tired, but very happy to see Angela. She was, however, very confused when Angela plonked down what looked like a soufflé making gadget on her bed.

"Oh......is that for me, dear?"

"Well, you're welcome to it Maggie, but actually I was wondering if you thought Andy and Chrissie might like it." Maggie looked even more confused.

"Y'know what?" said Angela "I'd never opened the box. And then the other night I thought of you and I did. And I brought it to show you because it made me laugh so much. This is what someone bought me for a housewarming, Maggie – a soufflé maker." Maggie warily perused the item.

"Tut, really. Don't modern women know how to use measuring jugs anymore? We used to crack eggs and stir things and do it all by hand in my day."

"I think it's a 21st century convenience gadget" said Angela "Although why anyone would think it's convenient to make soufflés beats me!"

"Why, my dear" said Maggie "Just imagine how you missed out on making all those dinner parties with canapés and vol au vents!"

"I have a confession to make" said Angela "I'm an awful cook. I microwave everything. It's not because I can't cook – I'm just so wiped at the end of the day. I've no idea how women like you managed."

"Well, maybe it's because the microwave hadn't been invented" offered Maggie. Then she turned serious. "It's gone, hasn't it?"

"What?"

"The company that you worked for. Stopped, or gone under, or something......something about you....I can just tell."

Angela was shocked into silence. Maggie continued "Dear me. Another casualty. When I can get to watch the telly, I watch the news. Usually I like to know what's going on in the outside world, but now.....Tell me, whatever is that boss of yours going to do now?"

"You mean, Verity? Oh I'm sure she'll find something. She's good at bludgeoning her way in."

Maggie nodded, but her real aim was to find out how Angela was getting on as freelancer. She asked Angela if she was managing – paying the rent and getting by. Angela said how surprised she was to discover that she was – thanks to her.

"Do you know what, Maggie? I'm finding out that there's really so much I used to buy that I don't actually need. I used to get a cappuccino every morning before I got to work and if I had time I'd go shopping in my lunch hour. It's not that I've ever been very materialistic, it's just that work was often so boring, shopping felt like a sort of compensation factor. I felt like I deserved to buy myself nice things, because I'd survived another working week."

Maggie knew this was the way for many young working woman – unless that is, you were a young woman like Chrissie. She didn't want to admit how depressing she found the average working lifestyle. There was no passion behind it, no meaning – just a means of accumulation. Having lived through rationing and other recessions, Maggie couldn't help thinking that the spirit of independence in women had changed.

How many young, single girls had she met with surplus income and no dependents, who didn't use the money to maybe help charities, set up independent businesses or travel – they used the money to buy things they didn't really need, because they hated their jobs. What a sorry state of affairs.

Angela realised how insensitive her own comments must have sounded.

"Gosh, Maggie – I'm sorry; it must sound awful and so selfish with you having to manage on a pension and everything...."

"Don't you worry about me, dear" retorted Maggie. "Never hurt our generation having to live without flat screen TVs! I meet so many women your age who just complain about their weight all the time. At least we didn't have to worry about that with rationing!" Angela laughed and pinched at her non-existent spare tyre.

"Guess I don't have to really worry about that either!" she giggled.

"Well, you have a delightful figure, my dear" said Maggie. "Tell me something.....the day we met......did you ever go back and buy that dress?"

"You mean The Celine Dion? Good lord, no! When on earth would I ever wear something like that? It was just my silly film star fantasy."

"Every girl needs at least one ball gown" said Maggie quite seriously.

"Not me" replied Angela, "I never get invited to balls. Besides, I'd look a bit silly wearing it down the pub."

"If I were you, I'd go and have a look and see if it's still there. It might be reduced." Maggie was adamant.

"Oh, I don't know.......that was ages ago, Maggie and anyway, I think I've gone off the idea now. Besides, I don't hate my job anymore, so I don't need to buy stupid items!" She changed the subject. "I'm thinking of asking Chrissie and Andy round.....thing is, I don't really know what they eat....."

"Ah well, let me see.....mung beans, seaweed – possibly chick peas for starters, but you'll need to boil those for three hours first...." Angela went pale. Maggie chuckled. "Actually, what I think would be really up their street would be a good old Sunday roast. Used to do one myself for all of us."

Angela imagined the little "family" being all cosied up in Maggie's council flat – a really homely smell of slow cooking meat and roast potatoes ...some old black and white film on the telly....she wished she'd been there.

"Will your mother be making Christmas dinner?" asked Maggie. Angela started welling up. Suddenly she felt all nostalgic.

"We'll both be making it. It'll just be me and mum."

"That's nice" said Maggie, "I do like Christmas."

"Mmm" replied Angela. "Its gonna be a bit weird this year – what with what's happened at work and everything. But I can't wait to tell mum about all of you!"

"Ah, yes – talking of work...." said Maggie reaching down for her handbag "Christmas present for your mother...."

"Maggie!" scolded Angela "Put your purse away at once! Don't even think about it. I wouldn't dream of letting you lend me any money!" Pensioner, widow, Drayton Estate Maggie Buxton was always trying to give people loans that Angela was sure she couldn't even afford herself.

This huge-hearted and incredibly generous woman had already given her work, new friends and a new lease of life, which was more than enough. "I'll manage" said Angela, closing her hand over Maggie's purse, "Even if it's hand-made, Mum will get a present."

"You know it's only because I so worry about you all, don't you?" said Maggie. "But – hand-made? How delightful! Do you knit? Embroider?" Angela looked embarrassed.

"I um.....I suppose I could make a Christmas cake." Maggie looked sad. "Please Maggie, please don't be disappointed in me. I was really lousy at needlework. But I can bake."

"It's not that dear, it's just.....not that I'm complaining or anything , but the food in here is sometimes a little bit.....oh, no matter. I'm sure they'll bring us something nice on Christmas Day."

"Maggie.....I can't bear to think of you in here at Christmas. I wish I could take you back home for the weekend. Wouldn't it be great if I could just sneak you out of here, conceal you in a wheelchair and get you back before anyone knew it?"

"That's a very kind thought" said Maggie, "But I'm sure I'll have visitors. Christina isn't so very far away." Angela wanted to think of Maggie wearing a paper party hat, giggling with Christian and gorging on mince pies. She tried the hardest in her mind's eye to see her surrounded by loving friends, because as far as she knew, she had no other family.

But something in Angela's vision just didn't ring true. No one had mentioned when Maggie might be allowed home and she'd developed this perpetual cough – Angela knew what that could mean, but didn't want to let it over-ride her joyous thoughts – not now it was Christmas. Even though she only went near a church to work for Barbara and Anthony, Angela held the time of year very dear. She asked Maggie to tell her about Christmases past – the good old-fashioned kind.

"Well, let me see...." Maggie began. "Christmas dinner was usually me making cheese sandwiches, because my good-for-nothing husband had forgotten to take the turkey out the freezer! So we'd have our sandwiches with stuffing, sprouts and roast potatoes! Thank goodness he couldn't do much damage to mince pies! I'd heat a couple up whilst waiting for the Queen's speech and take them into the living room, only to find him already snoring loudly, where he'd remain until Morecambe and Wise would come on. There's a good old-fashioned Christmas for you."

Angela looked disappointed. "B...but, before you got married, Maggie. Tell me about Christmas then."

"Ah" said Maggie "Now you're talking...." But as Maggie closed her eyes to remember those days, almost instantaneously she drifted off to sleep, leaving Angela to imagine a big gathering with all the trimmings and everyone believing in Father Christmas.

****

It didn't take Daz as long as he thought to find Callum. He saw him one day coming out of Woodfield Prep, wearing their school uniform. That was enough to satisfy Daz for the time being – he knew if he pounced that Callum would run and he needed to approach very carefully and think about exactly what he wanted to say. That was always Daz's way – slow, careful and calculated.

But Spencer and the Tunnel Boys weren't going to allow Daz to go at his own pace for much longer. In fact, the Chiefs had summoned Spencer to a meeting, with strict instructions that he shouldn't tell Daz where he was going. A tall, black boy spoke first, letting his hood fall from his head.

"Gotta tell ya Spencer – we're worried about Daz, man. Real worried."

"Why's that, brother'?" said Spencer, unconvincingly.

"C'mon – I know you've noticed it as well. He's not as dedicated anymore. Ain't got the motivation. You got any idea why?" Spencer knew he was going to be treading dangerous ground.

"I think Daz is just a bit obsessed with Callum" replied Spencer, "But only like he was his younger brother, like Benji or something, y'know? He just looks out for him. Nothin' to be concerned about." That didn't wash.

"Whaddaya mean nothin' to be concerned about? It's got everything to do with us. Callum stabbed someone and now we don't even know where he is. We don't know what he's saying about us. He must've told his mother, mustn't he? Otherwise she wouldn't have moved them both away. You know we need to find Callum just as much as Daz wants to look after him. So, got any clues for hiding places, Spencer my friend?"

"Why the hell do you expect me to know?" spat Spencer. "Daz is clueless about Cal's whereabouts, and he's the one that knows him really well." Spencer felt a shadow circling his presence, as the Chiefs closed in around him.

"You'd better not be lying to us." Spencer gulped. He used to love the danger and the tension, but now he was being treated like an enemy, not one of the gang. His eyes widened. "Hell, bruvver! If I knew where Callum was, don't you think I'd tell you? I know it puts us *all* in danger." The tallest of the Chiefs looked down at Spencer. Spencer was hardly a midget, but the boy towered above him. This boy also carried a knife – everywhere.

Knowing that, Spencer wondered if he should also get a knife – just in case....After all, these were unsettled times. It seemed like the Chief knew just what Spencer was thinking.

"Right. Well. Keep a close eye on Daz" he said. "And make sure you're up at the Tunnels 6pm next Thursday. We've got a Christmas swoop to plan." Spencer shook the Chief's hand, but now an iciness permeated his body that seemed to have nothing to do with the frosty evening.

Another day, another looting. Only before, he hadn't seen heads spouting blood or toddlers howling as their mothers fell to the ground, whilst boys covering their own faces with hoods just laughed. And whereas once it seemed like fun, now he wasn't sure if he wanted to see it any more....

****

Mark toyed nervously with his coffee. He kept checking the clock and the waitress kept looking at him as though she knew the exact circumstances behind his waiting. He tried not to catch her eye, but it was hard not to, whilst glancing up at the wall behind the counter. Instead, Mark occupied himself by making careful observations of the cafe. It was still in most of its original 1950's Formica format – one of the few left.

At that time of morning it was mostly filled with construction workers from over the road, ordering full English breakfasts that arrived at their tables dripping with grease. The men seemed to relish this and wolfed down the food, washing it all down with copious mugs of tea.

Mark circled his sloppily washed up coffee cup with his finger. There appeared to be a large oil mark around the rim, but he didn't want to ask for another as they were probably all the same. He looked across the room at some oily sausages and bacon, fried eggs and bread and chips piled on top. The waitress came over and asked Mark if he wanted to order some food. Just the sight of it was making him feel ill. He shook his head and said he was still waiting for someone.

The waitress shook her head back. She didn't say anything, but Mark could tell she was disapproving. It was a busy time and she was dashing between the kitchen and tables. Mark stared at the milky sludge in his mug. It was now stone cold and whilst he knew he'd ordered a coffee, it was more like a cup of hot milk with one coffee granule stirred in. So, he certainly didn't want another one.

He put the cup down, looked briefly up and saw – her. Beverley came in and placed an order at the counter. Mark's heart started thumping as she clocked him and came towards his table. He didn't know how to feel – on the one hand he was excited and on the other he'd taken the decision to walk out on her. It wasn't one he'd taken lightly. He hoped the woman he'd be meeting that morning was the bright, bubbly school teacher he'd originally fallen for – the woman with a spring in her step and a steely determination in her heart.

As Beverley pulled up a chair, Mark could see that the determination was still very much rooted within, but everything else about her seemed to have changed. Mark couldn't sense any trace of warmth towards him, but that was hardly surprising. He searched her eyes looking for coldness and hurt, but that didn't seem to be there either. Instead there was nothing.

No spurned or angry lover, no glowing thank-goodness-you've-come-back rejoicing and no animosity. Just a sort of black empty space in between Beverley's look and her emotions. She pulled forward a plastic chair and then tucked it under the table.

"Hiya....sorry I'm a bit late. Took a bit of time to sort my papers. Still, luckily I don't need to be in until later today. So....how are you....?" The way Mark looked at her gave her an immediate answer. He may have left her, but he still loved her. And he wanted her back. She could see that, only Beverley had other ideas.

Mark thought he'd meet with Beverley that day to tell her how he felt, but he couldn't answer the question about how he was. How the hell did she think he was? He was confused, anxious, guilty, but she – she didn't seem to be anything.

"I'm fine" replied Mark eventually, almost taking a chunk out of his tongue as he bit down hard on it to prevent himself saying everything else he really wanted to say. He grimaced with the pain.

"Is your coffee too hot?" asked Beverley.

"On the contrary" said Mark "Stone cold." She looked at him quizzically which was the only sign of humanity in her.

"Let me get you another."

"Thanks Beverley, I..." Mark wanted to say so much, but all he could manage was "Actually, I'll have a tea instead, please." Beverley raised her hand to catch the waitress's eye and the waitress took her order, smiling at Mark knowingly. When the tea arrived, Beverley put a plastic wallet of papers on the table and told Mark how such and such a bill needed paying etc and if he could pop the keys back to her, they'd be handy for her new housemates.

New housemates? So that was it. She'd already decided. There was no compromise, no negotiation. Beverley didn't want Mark to move back in. Who were the new tenants that had suddenly appeared from out of nowhere? The waitress arrived with a plateful of bacon, sausages, beans and mushrooms and plonked it down in front of Beverley. She tucked in with relish.

"Like any sauce with that?" asked the waitress.

"Yes please – ketchup."

"Bread and butter?"

"Yes, thank you – both" said Beverley. Mark stared at her.

"What's wrong?" Beverley asked.

"It's just that – you don't eat offal" said Mark. Beverley stabbed one of the sausages and bit down hard on it halfway.

"Do now" she said chomping whilst looking directly at her ex.

****

"Now take this and don't argue" said Maggie, handing a blank cheque to Chrissie. "Anyway, it's not for you, it's for Angela." Reluctantly, Chrissie put out her hand.

"It's not that I don't want you to get Angela nice things Maggie, it's just that – don't you think it's a bit of a futile purchase?"

"Don't question me dear, I know what I'm doing! Just go and see if it's still there and if it is, buy it." Chrissie knew that when Maggie had made her mind up about something, she didn't say no. She tucked the cheque inside her rucksack pocket, kissed Maggie lightly on the forehead and promised she'd do her best.

Meanwhile, Angela dragged herself up from a very uneasy sleep. Many jumbled dreams had filled her head and there was one recurring dream in particular she was always trying to decipher. She was in that street again – the one where she'd heard the voice telling her to "go down the hill" she always tried to climb up. This time, Angela could clearly see the street and bottom end of the shops. She looked uphill and the street was winding and very steep. The more interesting shops were closer to the top of the hill – they looked like they'd be worth the climb.

She'd put one foot after the other, but hadn't gone anywhere and just found herself puffing and panting and exhausted, her legs desperately trying to reach....what? Angela had woken up in a sweat - no doubt she'd been trying to climb that hill in her sleep. The first ballet class of the day didn't start until after school hours and there was no admin work to do that day.

Angela could have had a lie in, but she didn't want to fall asleep again to be further troubled by exhausting dreams, so she decided to head towards the shopping centre, purely to do a bit of window shopping. Immediately a guilty thought filled her head. Only the day before, she'd told Maggie she felt no need to stock up on material goods, yet she was heading to one of the most expensive places in town.

Then Angela remembered it was almost Christmas; what an excellent excuse. She could get things for other people, couldn't she? Yes – surely just *looking* for yourself whilst buying for others wasn't hedonistic. Angela determined that she would get something especially beautiful for Maggie. After hours spent trawling discount stores and horrible yet expensive specialist shops, Angela felt weary.

There was nothing befitting a woman like Maggie Buxton on the High Street. Maybe she should take a bus up to the organic farm centre and look around there. She headed towards the bus depot, when suddenly – she saw it. There, still on a front store mannequin was the Celine Dion dress. It may not have had a head, but the mannequin upon which the dress was draped had Angela's exact proportions and figure.

She stared hard. Bad times. No one had wanted to buy a ball gown. And yet.....no. Don't be so silly, she told herself. Just because it was still there didn't mean she had to buy it. There then ensued a little argument that Angela had with herself, almost as though a little angel figure was sitting on one shoulder and a devil on the other.

She deserved to treat herself to something nice, didn't she? After all, it was Christmas. But the only place she was going for Christmas was Littlehampton-By-Sea and they didn't have many balls there. Besides, her mother would faint if she turned up wearing that. But.....hadn't Maggie said that every girl deserves at least one dress like that.....?

No – NO. Who the hell did she think she was? Liz Hurley? Oh, for sure she'd get invited to a ball at the church. She ought to go into that department store and buy herself a tweed skirt and jacket – that would suit her new lifestyle much better. Frightening images of Women's Institutes flashed through Angela's mind. There were a lot at the church....

She shook herself out of her reverie and tried to focus on the image of a large cappuccino instead. That's what she'd do. Go and have a coffee and sit down and think about it. Walk away from the dress, she told herself, walk away from the dress......

****

Callum picked the breadcrumbs off a fish finger and toyed with the fish innards. "What's wrong?" asked Beverley "I thought you liked fish fingers?"

"Yeah, I do" said Callum, "It's just that......"

"You're thinking about your mum, aren't you?" said Beverley. She'd sensed he was anxious about her coming out of hospital, even though he longed to have her with him. He put down his knife and fork.

"Do you....do you think she'll be able to come back properly? I mean, might she go all funny again and have to go back onto the ward?"

"Your mummy's going to be an Outpatient" said Beverley gently. "You remember what that means, don't you? It means that she has to go back and visit every week whilst they monitor her medication, but in the meanwhile she can come back and stay with us – all the time." Callum flinched and Beverley noticed he was fixated on Grandma's photo. "What's making you so worried, Callum? You can tell me. You do know your mum is being very well looked after, don't you?"

Callum thought carefully. "I didn't like that man very much."

"You mean the psychiatrist?"

"Yeah. Grandma didn't like him either."

Beverley laughed. "What do you mean Grandma doesn't like him? She's never met him."

Callum continued. "I spoke to her late last night. She said he wears this smart suit n'everything and looks all like a proper Doctor with his posh office n'that, but really he hasn't got mum's best interests at heart." Beverley took a deep gulp.

"Callum....what on earth are you talking about?"

"Grandma said Doctors like him just like giving lots of pills 'cos they get money for it and what mum really needs is the countryside and peace, just like *she* used to have."

"Grandma had a very different life to us" said Beverley, but she couldn't ignore the grain of truth behind the surface. Where had Callum got information like this from? Beverley could only imagine that he'd been sneakily looking on the internet. She tried to pacify him.

"Listen sweetheart.....your mum has been getting much better by taking those pills. So even if the Doctor is getting money, it's still helping her, isn't it? And that's what really matters, surely."

Callum frowned. "You should listen better. She's *your* Grandma, after all." He pushed his dinner plate across the table and ran out the room.

"Callum!" Beverley reasoned that he'd been traumatised and was trying to make sense of everything. After all, look what he'd been through in only a very short period of time. She started to clear away the left-overs, but put a plate back down as her arm started to twinge. She rubbed it and looked up directly at Grandma. She shivered as she could swear she heard Grandma say "Watch that boy."

****

Ok. That was it. Holding her credit card over the brim of her coffee cup, Angela pictured handing it to the shop assistant who would then hand her back her receipt and beautiful laminate carrier bag with string handles, the dress carefully wrapped in layers of pink tissue paper. Maybe there was a very good reduction on the dress, seeing as it hadn't shifted yet and she must be fated to buy it as the first day she saw it had changed her whole life.

Excitedly popping the plastic back into her purse, Angela leapt up, handbag swinging behind her and triumphantly headed straight back to the Celine Dion store. But the dress was gone. Heart thumping, Angela rushed inside, but her worst fears were met.

"Oh, I'm so sorry Madam – we sold it about five minutes ago." Damn that cappuccino. Angela nodded sadly and backed out. She couldn't even bring herself to flick through the other rails to see if there was something similar – she just knew there wouldn't be.

The Celine Dion had stayed and stood proudly waiting for Angela and then finally, now that the day had arrived for her to go and get it, she had hesitated. What a lesson to learn, thought Angela. If you know, deep in your heart that you really want something, then damn well go and get it before someone else does.

****

Mark kicked hopelessly at an empty, crumpled beer can, half angry with Beverley and half with himself. Honestly, what was he expecting? That she'd welcome him back with open arms? Why had he felt that he had pulled so much apart from her in the first place, that he had to leave? More to the point, why did he want her back so much?

Rain started trickling slowly at first then turning into a heavier downpour. People dived into nearby doorways or under bus shelters and the dark skies seemed to make all the tacky, neon Christmas lights look even cheaper.

No girlfriend – no flat. Mark guessed he should be grateful he still had a job, but somehow he just couldn't seem to bring himself to show any gratitude. He really should have been heading into work by now, but he'd also expected to have spent a lot longer with Beverley. That meeting was so short, so terse and over in the amount of time she'd quickly gulped down her huge breakfast.

Mark started thinking about what she'd said. Who were these new tenants that had moved in? Where had she found them? He wasn't satisfied with either her explanations or decisions and was determined to take things further. Beverley had no right to do this – Mark still had a return deposit due, and he'd already paid the rent for several weeks in advance. He trudged into the shopping centre and towards a more expensive cafe. At least they did healthier breakfasts than Beverley's.

Just as he approached the cash machine, he saw a familiar face. Rifling through a school satchel and sitting on a wooden bench opposite the bank, sat Daz. He looked as if he was desperate to find something, but the more he clawed his way through, Daz just couldn't seem to find whatever he was looking for. Mark seized his chance.

"Can I help?" he asked. Daz nearly jumped out of his skin. "It's only me" laughed Mark, "We've met before, remember. The park? Your little brother scrounged some ciggies off me."

"Oh yeah, yeah" Daz ignored Mark and carried on looking through the satchel.

"Looks like you're trying to find something very important."

"Yeah...." Daz thought quickly. He really didn't want to talk to Mark and couldn't abide him being chatty. "It's a letter from my mum......says why I'm off school this morning....."

"So – why are you off school this morning?"

Daz immediately became defensive. "What's it to you?"

"Just being friendly – only asking...."

"What do you want? Why do you keep following me?"

"I'm not, I haven't , I mean....."

"You're lying, Mister. My little bro' saw you. You went up to our flats. What were you doing up there and why me? Why don't you just tell me here and now, seeing as you've got me cornered anyway?"

Mark looked away, shame-faced. "Ok, yeah. I did follow you, but only because I was interested in looking at the Drayton Estate, because I might be moving there." As the words tumbled out his mouth, he realised how implausible they sounded. He didn't look like a typical Drayton resident – he was too clean, for a start. He thought of something that might sound more like the truth.

"I've lost my home....." he told Daz. Daz looked interested for a moment, but then said, "So, what's that to me?"

"Nothing. Absolutely nothing" said Mark. "You know how it is when you're down on your luck and got nothing better to do than hang around the park.....it's just where I like to sit to sort out, you know – stuff. Helps clear my mind." He felt Daz soften a little.

"How come you've lost your home? Have you lost your job?"

"Nah. Girlfriend kicked me out. Seeing you and your brother just reminded me of when I was a kid, and brought back happier times. I've got a little brother as well."

"Trust me" said Daz getting up "It's not so great, being a kid." As Daz walked off, Mark saw a little slip of paper where he'd been sitting. Maybe that was what he'd been looking for. Mark unfolded it and read. Callum Brown, 48 Rochester Road. His......Beverley's flat......

Mark glared at the piece of writing and turned the paper over again and again. So...was Callum Brown, whoever he was, Beverley's new tenant? Was he a new boyfriend? What on earth did he have to do with Daz.....?

****

Chrissie handed Andy a large Alpaca jumper. It was cold in the caravan. "Gonna have a bit more office work for you come winter, Angela – not much we can do outdoors this time of year," said Andy pulling the jumper on. Angela realized she was getting work without even asking for it. She didn't even know what Chrissie and Andy did or how they earned a living themselves. As far as she could see, they sold bits of vegetables from their allotment to local shops and friends and Andy seemed to do a bit of I.T stuff, but on the whole she really knew very little about them.

She was sat shivering in a mobile home in the middle of nowhere and took in her surroundings. The living area had a fold up couch which also seemed to convert into a double bed and there was a small separate section at the back where she assumed Christian slept. There were loads of cushions, throws, draped silky scarves and dangly ornaments that hung down from the ceiling. Chrissie handed Angela a steaming mug of tea.

"Sorry it's so cold in here – didn't have time to pick up an extra gas cylinder. Andy's going to pop out later. Hope this helps warm you up in the meantime." Angela gratefully took the tea in her numb hands and let it thaw her fingers. She flicked at a round silver ornament dangling above her head and noticed feathers attached to it.

"What's this?" she asked.

"That's a Dream Catcher" replied Chrissie. "It's supposed to catch bad dreams."

"Hmm, I could do with one of those" murmured Angela. Chrissie wrinkled up her brow. She moved to sit beside Angela on the fold up couch.

"Tell me.....you've been having bad dreams?"

"No, just a bit disturbing" said Angela. "I feel they're significant, but can't work out the meaning." Angela explained the dream with the hill and the shops as Chrissie listened intently. She asked Angela if she'd ever been to this place in real life. Angela couldn't recall anywhere she'd been that looked like this. Chrissie went very quiet for a moment and stared into her cup of tea. Then she said slowly and deliberately, "Struggling your way up a hill.....I think you may be struggling with your new way of life. I feel guilty. We've thrown you into all this, and just expected you to take it on. But....you're sure you've never been there....?"

Angela shook her head. But she didn't want Chrissie to feel responsible for her dreams. She was excited and enthused about all these new people and new ways of doing things. She was intrigued with this tiny home on wheels which she knew most people would think of as a temporary shack or even a holiday home, but this seemed like a permanent abode.

She knew that if she told her mother about Chrissie and Andy, she'd tell her to "keep away from the gypsies", but they weren't like that. Angela wanted to know more about their work. She discovered that a friend of Andy's kept sheep and Chrissie wove and knitted their wool, making clothes to sell. Pointing to Andy's jumper, Angela asked if Chrissie had knitted it.

Andy stopped warming his hands on the teapot and turned to show that one sleeve hung slightly longer than the other and the neckline was too wide so that it slipped slightly down one shoulder.

"This is a Chrissie Classic" he said "You can tell she made it – slightly asymmetrical is her trademark." Chrissie threw a cushion at him.

"Oy – watch it! I've got hot tea here!" yelled Andy. He stepped backwards and then saw that Angela was fondling the bottom of his jumper.

"Sorry – may I?" asked Angela. Andy's brow turned into a question mark shape as she continued to feel his clothing. He looked across at Chrissie to see if she was also thinking Angela's behaviour was rather odd, but she just gave him a look as if to say "serves you right".

Angela lifted her glasses. "I think it's beautiful."

"Well, thank you" said Chrissie "At least someone appreciates my ....*originality*...."

"I wonder.....I wonder if you'd knit one for me? I mean, of course I'll pay whatever you sell them for normally and the wool and your time and everything...."

Chrissie cut Angela off. "Angela – it would be my absolute pleasure. These are pure wool and will keep you warm in what I gather is forecast to be a pretty nasty winter."

"Gosh" said Angela "Will you be ok? I mean if all you have is that little heater and jumpers, well.....what if it snows?" Andy looked across at Chrissie and she put her finger to her lips as Angela had her back to her.

"We'll manage" Chrissie replied "We always do."

****

7pm. The Tunnels. All the boys were present and correct, including Spencer and Daz. Daz looked distracted and agitated, which only led the Chiefs to suspect him all the more. The boys were briefed over operation "Christmas Presence". One of the Chiefs thought that was a brilliant name – the boys were going to make themselves known they were in town at Christmas and no one should feel safe.

Daz clocked a nasty bit of graffiti pornography on the wall behind where a Chief was giving the briefing. It said "Lock up your daughters" with a rather crude drawing beneath. Daz wondered what had happened to the wit and artistry of whoever it was who had previously covered their local area with graffiti.

This was the Tunnel Boys first Christmas raid and it was laid down in no uncertain terms that if anyone got caught, revealed their identity or liaised with the police, they would be in serious trouble. This was going to be a big operation, but without the precision, tact or united front of Trick or Cheat.

There were already two disparate groups forming within the gang; the bullying brutish Chiefs and those who didn't like the changes, but dare not utter their displeasure. Once, the Tunnel Boy leaders had been charismatic orators, now shoved aside by those with brute force as their chief weapon. Spencer realized that there hadn't been any discussion about disguises for Christmas Presence, and brought it up.

One of the Chief's roared with laughter. "Bruvver – Spencer – that is what hoods is for!"

Spencer protested. They were going to loot shops with fluorescent lighting – hoods weren't going to protect their identity. As a hand gripped his shoulder so tightly, Spencer felt a rapid pain spreading down to his leg, he knew he shouldn't say any more. He went with Daz back through the tunnels, crossing the road at the bottom of the high street.

Whilst both of them thought and felt the same, they didn't discuss it. Daz, at any rate, apparently had more pressing things on his mind. He needed to sound out Spencer.

"Fancy a burger?" asked Daz.

"Yeah – but I ain't got no dosh" Spencer replied.

"Na, it's on me mate" said Daz, "What do you want? Cheeseburger? You can have fries, n'all."

"Where did you get the money?" Spencer looked at Daz suspiciously.

"Don't look at me like that Spence! I washed some cars yesterday, remember?" Spencer was hungry – he felt his stomach rumble at the thought of a large, juicy burger. He accepted Daz's offer as they walked down to "Jimmy's" – a local hang out for the Chiefs. Jimmy hated the noise they made and the litter they left, but the Chiefs were good for business. Besides, they didn't look like the type of boys to whom he should make any complaints...

As they ordered, Spencer realized Daz wasn't buying for philanthropic reasons. The moment he mentioned Callum's name, Spencer realised the ulterior motive.

"Spence – I think I've found him. I think I know where he is." Spencer doused his plate with ketchup, dipped his fries in it, and greedily scoffed them. He spoke excitedly through mouthfuls.

"Yeah? Really? Have you spoken to him? Do you know where he's living Mmmph?"

"Well, I *did* know where he was living, only...."

"Only what?"

"I lost the bloody slip of paper with his address on it." At this news, Spencer banged his fork down on the side of his plate.

"Aw, Daz! I don't believe it, man! But....how did you get hold of it in the first place?"

"Well...." Daz told how he'd seen Callum coming out of Woodfield Prep in their uniform and seen Beverley handing him some lunch money over the course of several mornings. He'd made a wild guess that Callum was living with this woman – whoever she was. He followed Beverley one day and made a note of the street and door number that she went into.

"I know it's Rochester Road, but I can't remember the number" said Daz, frustration making him bite at a nail.

"Nothin' for it then" said Spencer "You'll have to follow her again." Daz sighed deeply. It wasn't like him not to remember stuff. Spencer frowned.

"Daz.....if that woman wasn't Callum's mum, then you don't think......he's been fostered or something?" Daz had no idea. He'd heard a rumour Mrs Brown had gone "a bit funny". Perhaps the police were now involved, and protecting him. All Daz knew was that he hadn't seen Mrs Brown up at the school. Spencer sat forward. He, like Daz, started to worry that the Tunnel Boys or even they as individuals might be in danger.

"D'ya think there's trouble, Daz?"

"Dunno. Depends who Callum's been talking to. Either way – we need to find him. I think you're right Spence – there is only one thing for it. We need to find a good time to hang out around Rochester Road."

****

Angela wrote down meticulous instructions from her mother. She was going to make the best Christmas cake ever. She wanted to make it with all the traditional ingredients and wondered if Chrissie might even know where to source things like organic dried fruit, or if she had any stored herself that Angela might borrow. When Angela told Chrissie that she was making the cake for Maggie, Chrissie clapped her hands in glee, like a little child.

"Oh my God, that's bloody brilliant! Maggie absolutely adores Christmas cake. And she adores Christmas. Andy, me and Christian were thinking of going to the hospital on Christmas day with silly hats and everything, but it depends if she's up to it."

Despite her steadfast determination to carry on working on papers and her endless supply of box files, Maggie was becoming more frail. Angela pushed the thought from her mind. This Christmas with her new friends and new jobs, would be one to celebrate.

"Lots of people will be doing anything but celebrating this year" said Chrissie "Didn't you say your whole firm had gone under?"

"Yep. Mort and Grey is no more."

Chrissie sighed, deeply. "That's a lot of people out of work – and I keep hearing about more and more every day, all over the country." Her green eyes registered deep sadness. Chrissie had more compassion in her than most people had in their little finger and she seemed intrinsically connected to the human race – in a way that seemed to resonate within the very core of the Earth.

Angela looked at Chrissie. "Have you ever had a proper job, Chrissie?"

Chrissie was taken aback. "Proper? What do you mean by that? What I do is proper!"

"No, I'm sorry, I didn't mean it like that, I meant...."

"You mean – have I ever done the 9-5 thing?" asked Chrissie.

"Well, yes. Before, before...."

"Before I was a hippy?" Chrissie cut in. "I've always lived this way. I don't know any other life. I guess I've just done what's suited me and I've always worked. Never claimed any benefits, except ones I was entitled to when I had Christian. Andy did a short spell in the city. He lasted a month. He told me his job was just like going to school and he'd hated school. There was so much bullying and he described his boss as being like a vindictive headmaster."

"I suppose both of you are rather....loose cannons?" ventured Angela.

"Some might use that term" laughed Chrissie. "But it's only because they've never lived our way. As far as we're concerned, they're the loose cannons. They're the people so frustrated with their daily lives that they could implode at any moment. We're gentle souls – we don't harm anyone else and we don't want to. We just try and live our lives respecting the earth and our fellow human beings."

Delivered by a true hippy, thought Angela. Yet she couldn't deny that Chrissie honestly *was* the most gentle soul she'd ever met. Her sad green eyes seemed to carry half the woes of mankind in them, whilst her long fingers and soft touch seemed able to heal the pain. Angela had watched how she'd soothed Christian to sleep or stirred ingredients into huge pudding bowls.

She'd seen her love for Andy and her child, extended to complete strangers – including her. Chrissie really was a very special, rare being. Angela's stomach knotted up as she realised her own pre-conceived notions and prejudices. She knew she'd just been swept up in other people's fears – fears of the afraid, the insecure; judgements made in order to justify their own cowardly actions and protect themselves.

She felt ashamed she'd even said such things as "proper job". She'd hated her own proper jobs. Was *that* proper? Was it right to spend so much of your life ground down, vilified, bored, tired? Was it right that her last, long ago relationship had broken down because both she and her partner spent most of their time being ground down, vilified, bored and tired?

And yet, it was people like Andy and Chrissie who were denigrated by society. They gave unconditional love, they supported, they took and gave back to mother nature. They were a hard-working couple who didn't appear to be scrounging in any shape or form. The means by which they lived were frugal and yet they were two of the happiest people Angela had ever met. These were the people she'd been bought up to regard as the enemy.

She found herself choking back a tear, but unable to flow the stem she had to put her coffee down. Chrissie put a comforting arm around her shoulder.

"Angela – whatever is it?"

"Oh Chrissie.....I feel so stupid. I went back to the shops yesterday to try and find that dress I'd seen. It was there, but I dithered and then when I went back it had gone. I'm frightened Chrissie – frightened that I'm going to spend the rest of my life missing things."

Chrissie knew that Angela was a bit overwhelmed. It took most people a little while to get used to The Family anyway and she had kind of been thrown in the deep end. But only because Maggie thought she could take it.

"You're not going to miss out" Chrissie reassured her. "There will be plenty of opportunities. We miss some – get others. That's how it goes. Besides, you've tackled everything we've offered you with relish. And you've become a really good friend."

That made Angela cry even more. When someone was kind, when something made her happy – that could make her howl like a baby. Chrissie reached up towards a shelf and pulled down a huge tin, saying she knew just what Angela needed. She lifted out a huge Christmas cake and cut a couple of slices.

"But don't you want to save this for a few more weeks?" asked Angela.

"Are you kidding?" said Chrissie "This is one of ten! We make a massive batch every year. Maggie, Barbara, Anthony and most of Christian's friends all come and join us at Christmas and then we make one for all of our ......neighbours."

Angela mentioned how she'd wanted to make a cake for Maggie, but if Chrissie already had so much then she might be a bit overwhelmed. Chrissie laughed. "Angela – a woman can never have too much cake."

****

"That's it" said Daz "Number 48."

"You sure that's the right house?" Spencer was fidgeting. He didn't know what they were supposed to do – just hopefully wait until Callum came out? What about that woman? Daz had reckoned that as it was nearly dark, Callum should have been getting back from school in the next twenty minutes. He and Spencer had bunked off – school was the least important thing in their lives these days.

"So...." said Spencer "We're just supposed to lurk around here, round this street where we don't even live without looking suss?"

"Yeah. That's right" said Daz "For Crissakes, stop fidgeting, will ya?"

"It's a bit dodge, innit?" said Spencer "What if neighbours come out and start asking us stuff?"

"We're just waiting for a mate, aren't we?" replied Daz "That's exactly what we're doing. Just waiting to see if Callum's free to come and kick a bit of football with us."

"What if he doesn't want to talk to us? What if he won't come? What if that woman won't let him?" Daz glared at Spencer. This wasn't the way tough Tunnel Boys spoke and thought.

"I'm really disappointed with you, Spence. Hasn't being a Tunnel Boy taught you anything? What ifs aren't in our vocabulary, remember?"

Spencer sighed deeply. It was all he could do. "Bit posher than the Drayton Estate, innit?"

"Yeah" said Daz " I reckon Cal is being protected, I mean....it's logical, isn't it? I reckon his mum knows what happened and that she's sent him away for a while. I wonder where she is...." Just then, a car pulled up outside the house and three people stepped out. Callum, Beverley and Marisa. Beverley helped Marisa out of the mini cab – she looked a bit unsteady on her feet.

"Isn't that Mrs Brown?" gasped Spencer.

"Uh huh" said Daz "Obviously they're all staying together."

"So – who do you reckon this woman is? A police officer?"

"Nah – people don't go and stay with police. She might be something to do with the social services."

"Right" said Spencer, assuming they'd just seen what they needed to, "What do we do now?"

"Nothing" said Daz . Spencer looked at him open-mouthed.

"Nothing? You make me bunk off, walk all this way and then sit curled up getting pins and needles for an hour for nothing?"

"That's right" said Daz, watching the group go inside. "We definitely know this is the right house now. I need to find out more about who this woman is."

"How you gonna do that Daz?"

"Trust me Spence."

But Spencer was finding it hard to trust anyone these days. Even his best mates.

****

Angela peered over the rim of her glasses, frowned and peered again. Either the computer screen was going fuzzy, or she badly needed another eye test. Anthony came into the office and fiddled with a button at the back of the P.C.

"I've tried that as well" said Angela "But it still won't come into focus."

"Well then, we both need better glasses or to get a new computer....better call it a day. Young Andrew is the one who knows about fixing these things. He'll be here tomorrow." Angela took her glasses off, rubbed her eyes and sighed. The frustration of not being able to get things done. She picked up some papers that looked like they should have been dealt with years ago, but all had recent dates. Angela thumbed through the paperwork to see if there was a better way of organising anything, when a leaflet caught her eye. Cake making. Angela flicked it over. She'd missed the date.

"Oh, what a shame" she said. "That would have been very useful."

"Yes, they're very popular" said Anthony "Charming woman who runs them as well. But I believe she's doing a Christmas special weekend and...." he winked at Angela "I don't think that one's fully booked yet...." How on earth did he know? Angela folded the leaflet into her handbag.

"I'll get the kettle on" said Anthony. Angela noticed he always did that when there were things he didn't want to discuss. Still, she never complained about being brought endless cups of tea, although she had noticed a little roll of flesh appearing around the middle of her otherwise skinny frame, to which all those jammy dodgers must surely have contributed. Angela wondered how she could be loosening her belt at a time when everyone else had to tighten theirs.....

This was something else she didn't understand. She knew people were having to cut back on shopping, but they seemed to be getting fatter. Maybe it was to replace wholemeal things with cheap white loaves and chips. Gillian McKeith must be having a hernia. Also, no one could afford gym membership anymore, so that couldn't be helping. Yet, how come Andy and Chrissie always managed to make delicious food out of nothing? Seemingly they knew something the masses didn't.

Angela pushed the biscuit tin away as Anthony looked astonished.

"During the war...." Angela started "People didn't pile on weight, did they?"

"On the contrary" said Anthony "We only had rations to survive on."

"Well, maybe it's time we brought those back" said Angela. "It would stop people being greedy and evenly distribute healthier food. We could solve the obesity problem easily."

Anthony laughed. "A good idea in theory, but I don't see how the government can possibly enforce it in these times – things have changed. For a start, we don't have the war effort."

Angela sipped at her tea, pensively. She wondered what it must've been like to live in a Britain at war. No doubt it was extremely frightening, but there was that camaraderie – a nation pulling together. Not such a massively disparate society of people ignoring each other, the likes of which she had grown up in. She found herself wishing how everyone would pull together again in hard times, get a National Spirit back. But everyone she knew now was either angry or terrified or both. Except.....except for her new friends. Angela may have had tea on tap, but she was thirsty for knowledge.

"Tell me Anthony...Andy and Chrissie.....I know they knit and grow and make things and Andy does freelance computer stuff and somehow it all kind of seems to work and they survive. They don't live conventional lives at all. They just have that ramshackle caravan – they don't really have a home." Anthony looked uncomfortable, but Angela continued.

"And....they always seem so happy. And so do you. And Maggie is always so upbeat. Are you all on drugs, or something?"

Anthony laughed loudly. "Wouldn't know where to get them from these days, my dear! But you know what? I've just remembered I need to go and unlock the church hall for the Weight Watchers class. Just carry on with those papers and come and find me when you've finished." He always found an excuse to leave when Angela started asking too many questions. Maybe he really was on drugs...

"I might have to join that class myself soon" said Angela pinching her tummy, but Anthony wasn't listening. He was already half way out the door with the biscuit tin. It was unusual for him to take them away when Angela was still there. Suddenly the computer screen flicked back on again. Angela called after Anthony, but he was already at the bottom of the corridor.

A window she didn't recognise flickered into view on the screen. She was about to close it, but what she saw intrigued her. There was a spreadsheet which seemed to cross reference the accountancy figures she had already entered. Only nothing was listed as Barbara's classes or things for the church. She saw expenses for a school room, livestock, vegetable, herb and flower seeds and scrolling down further, something itemized that made her sit bolt upright.

Furnishings for the Grand Hall. What on earth could that be? The church didn't have a Grand Hall. Just a pokey little room that smelt of dust. Was someone pillaging church funds? Was fraud at play? She gasped. Andy was the only other person with access to that computer...

****

Callum frowned as he stared. The framed photo of Grandma seemed to return the same expression. He asked her, what do you mean they're coming after me? Who, Grandma? Who's coming? She didn't reply. Callum felt the coldest of shivers run down his spine as he knew the ancient one spoke the truth. He didn't have any names, but he sensed he was in real danger.

The Tunnel Boys. It had to be. No one else would be looking for him. He knew he should be focussing on his mum, take her a cuppa, but his thoughts were diverted elsewhere. Besides, Beverley could look out for her now. She was safe now. It was him they were after.... Callum started to breathe heavily before telling himself to calm down. No Tunnel Boys knew where he was now living or which school he was at. There, he was just the new boy.

Callum Brown, good at Maths, rubbish at Geography. Quiet, unassuming – made a few new friends. At a new school he could start over, wipe the slate clean. No one need ever know he'd stabbed somebody. But the police knew, and because of this they knew all about the Tunnel Boys. Or, at least they knew as much as Callum and Beverley decided to tell them, which might have been slightly fabricated.

Would they find out? Would they come after him? Or would the boys be following in hot pursuit, determined to do their worst to a grass and deserter? Grandma seemed to glow red as Callum's whole body trembled, like a volcano about to erupt. Involuntarily he let out a loud howl and heard Marisa gasp with shock and come running in from the kitchen.

"My God – Callum- what is it?"

"I...I just fell asleep on the sofa, mum. Had a really bad dream. It was horrible." Marisa pulled her son close to her chest.

"Oh Cal – sweetheart. Mummy's not going to go back into hospital. I feel much better now. I'm going to be just fine – you'll see." And bizarrely enough, it seemed that she was. Whatever Grandma had invoked in Callum to terrorize him so much, seemed to have completely healed Marisa and she was like her old self – the good old mum of days gone by.

****

The thought kept biting into her normal every day routine and churned in and out of her brain, interrupting everything she did. Angela just couldn't get what she had seen on the computer out of her head. The first chomp of thought was whether or not to tell anyone. The second was *who* to tell. The third was trying to decipher what it was all about.

Angela wracked her poor demented brain – if she truly had cause to believe someone was dipping their hand into church funds, then surely the first person she should tell was Anthony. But.....oh no. What if he was the one doing it? She'd heard about things like that before – vicars who embezzled. No wonder the biscuit tin was always full....

Angela tried to replay recent events. Anthony seemed to be completely clueless about computers, but maybe that was a foil. Also, he had seemed rather edgy when Angela had started talking about Chrissie and Andy.... something was undoubtedly going on. She wondered if she could stop the thought annoying her for half an hour whilst she went to purchase the last vestiges of Christmas presents.

****

Mark sat back down in the same Formica cafe. A waitress with a strong East European accent folded her arms and stood in front of him.

"If you don't like our coffee, you don't need to keep coming back." Mark looked up.

"No, no – coffee's delicious....thank you. I'm just a slow drinker, that's all." The waitress scowled.

"Maybe all the time you sit here you make order food?" Mark felt uneasy about that. But then he was trying to be more daring – venture into the new.

"Yeah, why not. Pass us a menu, would you?"

The waitress declined and walked away grumbling, "All food on board". After deliberately taking his time to scan the items, Mark went for the roast chicken with roast potatoes and two vegetables. He wondered what they'd make of that. In the briefcase on the floor beside him sat numerous case studies and files he needed to work on, but his mind had been dangerously diverted from anything to do with work.

Some colleagues had already cleared their desks on Friday and not come back on Monday. Several people did a similar job to Mark, so why should he be so complacent? But unlike most people, Mark's focus wasn't on his job. His brain was completely consumed with Beverley. And Callum Brown....

The roast dinner arrived lukewarm with congealed lumpy gravy. Mark started catastrophising about Callum being Beverley's lover. Where had they met? What did he look like? How long had it been going on? With her hectic schedule, surely Beverley never had much chance to meet anyone, so the mysterious Mr Brown must have been a new teacher, or worse still – maybe he was a single parent.

Maybe he'd noticed the way she was with children and fallen in love with her; the ideal partner for him and his own child. Perhaps they'd all moved in together. Angrily, Mark gulped down the cold chicken in huge pieces, barely chewing. Then, he washed it down with the even colder coffee. His face formed into a grimace as he started tapping his fingers on the table. The waitress came to clear the cutlery.

"So! You like our food after all! Pudding?"

Mark shot her a look. The look was a face full of hatred and intended for Callum Brown. The waitress recoiled and jumped backwards. She was a woman normally scared by no one, but Mark's expression was truly murderous. She trembled slightly, then pulled her lips into as best a smile she could muster around her bright red lipstick.

"So glad you like! Our chef make specially – give you extra gravy, for being our.....re-gu-lar-lar customer!" She spat the words out. Enjoying his new found power over stroppy cafe staff, Mark averted his scowl back towards the board.

"Well....in that case I'll have the jam roly poly and extra custard. I take it pudding is on the house – seeing as I'm a re-gu-lar-lar......?" The waitress tried to smile again, but her bottom lip was trembling too much.

"I check with my boss" was all she said before scurrying off into the kitchen.

Unfortunately, Mark's power over waitresses didn't seem to have the same effect on his own boss. He'd walked back into work twenty minutes late back from lunch, which hadn't gone down well. He'd barely noticed the time as he'd sat plotting new ways to deal with Beverley on his laptop. He shuffled back to his desk after a severe ticking off.

His boss was concerned. Mark looked distracted and unwell. His mental state had appeared to be rather unstable since the break-up of his relationship. In normal circumstances he would have been told to take some time off, but everyone was stressed up to the eyeballs and all hands needed to be on deck. Mark's boss had a tough decision to make.....

****

Twelve days to Christmas. The graffiti in the tunnel read "Get your REAL turkeys here", with arrows pointing downwards towards a makeshift seat. Several Tunnel Boys sat huddled on it. They sang "The Twelve Days of Christmas" in unison, only with altered lyrics. "Five gold rings" was incorporated in a line about smashing into a jewellery store and "Eleven lords a-leaping" seemed to include a lot of head-butting and punching.

Operation Christmas Presence should have had even more adrenalin and thrall than the build up to Trick or Cheat, but the mood was somewhat subdued – sombre even. Lots of the boys were feeling the Christmas pinch themselves with parents who'd lost their jobs and some threatened with losing their homes. Whilst the Drayton Estate housed huge numbers of families on Social Benefits, any that had jobs were looking like being the worst off, either unable to claim anything due to having some meagre savings, or having to wait months before they could get any redundancy payments.

Bailiffs had come round and banged on doors and even sometimes come out with furniture – as if life on the Drayton Estate wasn't hard enough.

Spencer's mother was on benefits and as far as he knew she'd never had a job. She depended on the DSS and hand-outs from his estranged father. A prime candidate for the "Jeremy Kyle" show, Mrs Vaughan looked like someone Verity might have become had she not had a better upbringing.

Mrs Vaughan had lots of missing teeth and the rest were rotten. Some had been lost through decay due to her poor diet and some through punch ups. Her hair was bright auburn with mousey brown roots and scraped back so tightly into a pony tail that she was in danger of being scalped.

She was quite overweight with blotchy skin and let her ample stomach hang over a pair of pale pink leggings with the outline of her underwear showing through. A stereotype of herself, Spencer's mother also swore like a fishwife and didn't suffer policemen gladly. But Spencer had never heard his mother swear so much as when she had some of her benefits cut.

A neighbour had grassed her up: told the DSS they thought she was doing some work on the side. Normally, people on the estate stuck by each other, but the recession had brought out the nastier, even more competitive side of people. Whereas previously it had been dog eat dog, the dogs were now going so hungry that they'd gobble up even the tiniest of goldfish. The Vaughan family were seriously struggling.

Spencer hadn't told any of this to Daz, even though he was a "blud". Daz seemed so distracted these days anyhow with his Callum obsession. Instead, Spencer suffered in silence. He wasn't the only boy with a mother like that and a sibling in prison. He had a diversion in this hard-core boy gang, but even that provided little respite. Still, he would go along with them.

Perhaps once Christmas Presence was over he could help Daz more and get to the bottom of the Callum mystery. That was at least something a little more interesting and not so mindless. What Spencer hadn't been prepared for was the way the Tunnel Boys would use him next. Someone had pointed out that unlike the Trick or Cheat raid which targeted local residents, there would be numerous CCTV cameras in the shops and malls where operation Christmas Presence was planned.

There was also concern over disguises – nothing as elaborate as devil masks or scythes this time – not even so much as a little elf outfit. Instead, all the boys were ordered to wear black "hoodies" and black trousers which took all the excitement out of everything. Instead, it just reflected the mood of a group of youngsters who had no idea when, if or how their lives would have colour in them again. Nonetheless they all agreed to the plans without dispute. There wasn't much else to do.

"Got a main job for you Spencer – our man." One of the Chiefs grinned and came and tapped Spencer on the shoulder. Recognition at last. "You're gonna go check the stores. See where the cameras are and cover 'em." Spencer laughed and nodded and then the realisation sank in.

"What – just me?"

"Yeah. Just you."

Spencer protested. "That's a big job to do on my own. Surely I can get at least one other blud with me?" Several Chiefs started surrounding the unnerved teenager.

"Nuffin' to it. Like we said, you're our main man, right? You don't need no help." Spencer shot a look at Daz but his eyes stayed firmly fixed on the ground. How on earth was he going to get through this one?

****

As the blackness of a bitterly cold evening surrounded a gang of boys now dispersing, Spencer waited by the high wall at the back entrance to the Tunnels. As Daz rounded the corner, he yanked down on the back of Daz's hood, before shoving him hard up against the wall.

"Bloody bastard! This is your fault!"

Shocked, Daz couldn't see Spencer in the darkness, but he knew his voice.

"What the – Spence? What are you doing, brother?"

"You don't care about me. You don't care about the Tunnel Boys. You only care about that bloody Callum Brown. Who the hell is he to you anyway? He's a coward. He ran. He's the reason we're in this knee deep." Daz managed to jab an elbow out intending to try and swing round to reason with Spencer, but instead caught him in the ribs and a very nasty bout of fisticuffs ensued.

Hearing the kerfuffle, a load of the gang came running over to see what was going on. The Chiefs were absolutely delighted to see Spencer and Daz laying into each other – the bond between the both of them was no good thing. Especially when they started keeping secrets from the gang.

The irony was, Daz knew he could have felled Spencer with one swift blow if he'd wanted to, but showing himself as a dominant force in front of the boys was not going to be to his advantage. They were becoming more and more dangerous and ego-led. Conflicting yells of "Go on Spencer!" or "Get 'im Daz!" rang out across the park and eventually Daz tucked himself into a small ball, trying not to flinch too much as Spencer kicked him in the lower back and arms.

"Get up you bloody coward!" Suddenly Daz felt a strong, sharp blow in his kidneys, so painful that he couldn't even yell. He uncovered his eyes to see that Spencer had already been dragged off him, but was shouting obscenities. More pain shot through his back as the most thuggish of the Chiefs pulled him to his feet. Daz clasped his back with one hand and his bloodied nose with the other. He knew at once that the damage was severe.

"That'll teach ya" said the Chief, before letting Daz drop back down on his knees.

****

Angela spent ages wrapping the little silver butterfly necklace in baby blue tissue paper. This present had been selected the most carefully and was now going to receive the ultimate in pampered packaging. This gift was for Maggie. Once Angela was satisfied with the perfection of her handiwork, she completed the package with a gift label and royal blue rosette. For Maggie it needed to be neat and traditional and yet understated. She placed the present on top of the tin, which cased Maggie's Christmas cake.

At the hospital, a nurse said Maggie was tired. Maybe Angela wanted to have a coffee and come back in half an hour or so. The thought of not seeing Maggie was unbearable – it was the last chance Angela would get before she went away at Christmas. Reluctantly, she slowly trudged towards the cafe, but wished she could have sneaked onto the ward, just prodded Maggie gently and then at least have been able to wish her a happy Christmas.

She browsed the plastic sandwiches and slightly pale looking pastries, not really wanting a coffee. She wondered what the patients were getting if the food for visitors was so bad. She took a seat and imagined Maggie drinking tea and eating cake and unwrapping presents. She would love the little delicate necklace, Angela was sure of that.

But it would be the cake that would really make her face light up. Real, homemade food. She thought about the good old days when ready meals hadn't even been invented, barely noticing that nearly forty minutes had passed. She dashed back to the ward where everyone was too busy attending an emergency to notice her draw back the curtain around Maggie's bed.

Maggie still had her eyes closed and a drip in her arm. Her face had thinned and was a grey-ish blue colour, but she was moving her face from side to side and seemed to be stirring. Angela sat beside her and gently took her hand.

"M....Maggie, it's me. Angela. I've brought you a Christmas present." Maggie turned towards her and weakly grasped her hand. "I guess you need to rest a bit longer, so I'll leave this here for you. I'm off to visit Mum for a bit, but I'll be back just after Boxing Day – promise." Maggie managed a faint smile. Then she closed her eyes again, but seemed to fall back into a more peaceful sleep than before and Angela wasn't quite so worried about leaving her.

A nurse came and took Angela to one side of the nursing station.

"You really should have come and checked with someone first. Mrs Buxton isn't allowed any visitors at the moment." Angela protested. She'd been told Maggie was only sleeping. She'd only wanted to drop off a Christmas present after all. She was informed that it might be an idea if she phoned before the next time she wanted to visit.

As Angela exited the huge double doors of the hospital, a great big lump formed in her throat. She knew she would have to face up to the inevitable sooner or later, but please - not now. Please let Maggie make it through Christmas. And please let everyone be there with balloons and party poppers and most of all – cake.

****

Benji held the pack of frozen peas against his brother's lower back as Daz gasped. "I'm really worried about you, you need a Doctor" said a concerned Benji.

"No – no Doctor" yelled Daz.

"Then at least let me tell Mum? Maybe she can get you something from the chemist?"

"Tell Mum I've been in a fight? Yeah, sure. She'll get me something all right...."

Benji shrugged, but he couldn't leave his big brother writhing in agony. Daz tried to tell him he was fine and that the bruising would subside once the ice numbed the area, but he was flinching a lot. Benji knew that Daz couldn't ignore the fact that he was very badly hurt.

"Perhaps....perhaps if you go through Mum's handbag and get the address of our Dr, I can just *talk* to him.....maybe I won't have to go to the surgery and we won't have to say anything to Mum." Daz was relenting and Benji was glad. At least he'd get some medical help. But if the Doctor did suggest that Daz came to the surgery, Benji had no idea how he was going to get there. He could hardly walk.

"Perhaps Dr Feris could do a home visit?" suggested Benji. Daz glared at him. Benji found the number pinned on the kitchen notice board. He was still a little boy, but in the midst of violence and misery was having to grow a much older head, on those very young shoulders. He gasped.

"Daz....whatcha gonna do about Christmas Presence?"

Daz's mouth fell open and his eyebrows formed into an upward arch of worry as he tried to answer Benji, but a voice at the end of the phone and at the Doctor's surgery suddenly said, "Can I help you?"

****

A soft, wet tear fell on the picture of Grandma. Callum told her he was sorry as he wiped it off. Grandma seemed to say that she knew it wasn't his fault. But Callum had bad feelings and signs and he'd talked to Grandma for a number of weeks now. And he knew he didn't want anyone to be in danger – least of all his Mum. And Beverley. When he'd received a "message" that "they" were looking for him, he didn't know that this meant Daz.

Daz – his friend, ally – the boy who was desperately trying to find him in order to protect him. Daz who would be fiercely loyal, come what may. Callum had only heard the word "Tunnel Boys" next and he instinctively knew that he couldn't hang around for much longer. Marisa had gone out to the supermarket to see if she might be able to get her old job back and Beverley was doing shopping errands.

Carefully, Callum pulled down his sports bag from the top of his wardrobe and began packing it with essentials. He rummaged in any coat pocket he could find, just to see if there was any change. He still had his dinner money which he had saved up; Marisa wondered why he was always so ravenous when he got back from school.

A change of clothes, a toothbrush and a total amount of about £30. Callum didn't know where he was going, but he knew he had to go. Trusting in the wisdom of Grandma, the ancestors and his dreams for guidance, he gently pulled the door shut behind him, taking a sharp intake of breath as he left Beverley's house.

****

"We need to be brave and keep on" said Chrissie "Otherwise, how on earth will Maggie be strong if she sees us faltering?" Angela could see that Chrissie wasn't going to accept that Maggie might quietly slip away before Christmas. "Anyway, there's really important work to be done and I don't want her to think we're flagging."

Suddenly, little light bulbs started going off in Angela's head, as she remembered what she'd seen on the computer with the conflicting accounts. No time like now to confront them. She told them what had happened and what she'd found.

"Clearly there's important work. At least someone thinks so, if they're doing something fraudulent...." said Angela. The colour drained from Andy's face. Chrissie looked down.

"Andy......look. Angela's going to have to know sooner or later." Chrissie had only followed Maggie's instructions that Angela should not know any more about the set-up of The Family until later, but now that Angela had accidentally made this discovery, perhaps the time had come. Angela's heart sank. If these people she had grown to love and befriend – people who had given her a livelihood and inspired her were now betraying her then she didn't know how she was going to cope. Had she been used all along?

Chrissie saw Angela's face redden and contort with hurt and anger. She needed to put her straight. Reluctantly, Angela sat down whilst Chrissie explained. Andy sat right on the edge of the sofa bed, ready to add his own details.

"It's like this" said Chrissie "We're looking after a very large sum of money on Maggie's behalf. She's chosen to do something extraordinarily special with it and you might say that the rest of us are, well – Maggie's administrators, if you like. The money was inherited – after her husband died."

Angela had never known what Maggie's husband did for a living. All she knew about him was that he'd been a drunkard. Obviously, Maggie hadn't used the money to better her own life, still living in her widow's flat on the Drayton Estate.

"Maggie's an ardent philanthropist" continued Chrissie "She's been helping a lot of deprived families from the local area and has been funding all kinds of schemes......schooling, housing...we have......well, The Family is really just our very own little community."

"I still don't understand about the accounts" said Angela. At this point, Andy took over. He explained how Barbara's Ballet operated as a sort of profit loss and as a wealthy widow herself, Barbara had originally joined forces with Maggie. Angela discovered how Chrissie had come from one of these deprived families and formed a real bond – a kind of spiritual connection with Maggie.

Maggie and Barbara had a vested interest in keeping quiet about how their money was really being invested – God only knows enough people were trying to get their hands on it. Long-term friends, this was their dream and could only be carried out when they reached pensionable age and financial independence from their late husbands.

Their dream........what a huge dream to have, let alone carry out thought Angela.

"Do you know what, Andy?" said Chrissie, "I think it would be less confusing for Angela if we actually go and show her some of the work we've been doing, rather than just tell her about it. What about we take a drive when you've finished up at the church on Thursday?" Chrissie knew that Maggie didn't want this for Angela yet, but surely if she'd chosen to employ her on account of her compassion, diligence and sharp humour, then she'd also realise that Angela was shrewd and clever and would be taking off the rose-tinted spectacles of a "honeymoon period", to replace them with her own before too long. And surely Maggie would want Angela to see things in her own way, as well.

When Angela looked into Chrissie's eyes, she knew that there was no need for doubt. This gentle soul was one hundred percent genuine. She had to be. She had massive responsibilities to many people. Angela noticed how Chrissie seemed to radiate a rare combination of honesty, humour and determination. It was something she had seen only once before. In the way Maggie looked at her......

****

Mark barely seemed to register what his superior was saying.

"I'm afraid we're going to have to cut your hours." Mark stared blankly. "This is going to happen during an investigation period. You understand what I'm saying, don't you?" Mark nodded slowly. His supervisor continued, a little less harshly.

"I understand you've been having some personal problems, Mark – I hope you've sorted things out now. You do realise however, that we can't give you a full case-load until things have been cleared. It's just temporary.....I hope....."

What disturbed the supervisor most was that Mark didn't seem to react. Faced with this sort of news, most employees protested – at the very least, tried to defend themselves. Not only did Mark appear to be far more pre-occupied with other concerns; he seemed to be in another world entirely. His colleagues were finding it hard to get through to him.

The supervisor got up to open the door for Mark and smiled as he exited. But when Mark had left the room, instead of putting the file away, the supervisor took a large ink stamp from his drawer and put a permanent red mark of "Action" on the top of the folder.

****

Callum had no idea how many miles he'd walked, but he knew he was exhausted and he knew he was hungry. He'd reached some kind of country lane and instead of starting to venture uphill, he sat on a small stile and pulled a flapjack from his rucksack. He'd barely taken a bite, when a football landed by his side.

Callum looked up to see a young boy of about seven or eight, surprised to see him sitting there.

"Oh!" gasped Christian. Callum stopped the ball from rolling forward and picked it up.

"This yours?"

"Yeah, thanks" said Christian. He retrieved the ball sheepishly and looked Callum up and down. He looked at his rucksack and scruffy trainers. Christian was sharp – he twigged immediately. "You runnin' away?"

Callum shuddered. He didn't appreciate such a direct and sudden confrontation with a stranger – especially from a boy younger than himself. He seemed too knowing for someone his age. Callum thought on his feet.

"Nah – school field trip. Got lost." Christian wasn't being taken in.

"Then – how come you've not got school uniform on?"

Callum was irritated by this and took a more defensive tact. "How come you ask so many questions? It's not your field – is it? I'm allowed to walk here."

Christian shrugged "Guess so." Callum thought he might as well try and get the stranger on his side. He was going to need all the friends he could get.

"So..." said Callum "You live round here?"

"Sometimes" replied Christian, annoyingly indirect. He was being deliberately evasive – it was true. Sometimes he slept in the mobile home with his parents and sometimes he shared a room with another boy his age in a house that belonged to The Family. Christian didn't know any other way of life and assumed all children lived in this type of rather unique set up.

Callum started to feel very frustrated. Who the hell did this cocky little kid think he was? Didn't he know better than to speak to someone older like that? Callum was street-wise, alright. He hadn't grown up in a single parent family on one of the roughest estates in town, let alone been a Tunnel Boy not to know how to protect himself.

But this kid had completely thrown him. He observed and queried and answered in unexpected ways. He was exceedingly clever and Callum didn't want to admit that he rather liked that.

"So" he asked Christian, "When you sometimes live around here, where do you live? Bit quiet, innit? I can't even see any houses from here."

"That's 'cos I don't' live in a house when I'm here" replied Christian, "We've got a caravan." Callum's eyes widened. Had he just met a real-life gypsy boy? He'd heard about them, but he'd never met one. Some of the elder gang members had mentioned them and how they travelled around. Callum had heard how these type of kids were sharp, edgy and knew how to steal. The Tunnel Boys liked them.

"I've never seen a caravan" said Callum "Can I come and see it?"

Christian didn't exactly look suspicious, but he seemed unsure. He knew that he needed to run anything like this past an adult, first. He hesitated and said he'd need to ask his mum. He told Callum to wait and he'd let him know the reply. Callum stopped him.

"Wait" he said, "I *have* run away. I'm not sure about letting adults see me right now."

"That's alright" said Christian, already running off, "We meet lots of runaways. Mum likes them. She'll be cool about it."

Callum recoiled. What kind of a mother was this? Yet he was alone and young and it was starting to get dark. What choice did he have? He had to trust this boy, and his mother. The worst that could happen was that they'd send him home and then he'd just have to come clean to Beverley. At least she'd understand about Grandma. But for now, he needed to protect his own mother – he just didn't want her involved when the "sinister forces" came for him....

****

Marisa headed up the street, still shaking as she clutched the piece of paper. She was going back to work. She couldn't believe how supportive her manageress had been; said she was sorry about Marisa's illness, that she'd been a good employee, etc....best of all that she could come back three days a week and possibly extend that to full time depending on how well she was coping.

At last she could pay Beverley with more than gratitude. It was fantastic news and would give her and Callum a real chance. Marisa decided to pick up some shopping on the way back – she'd surprise Beverley by doing a full weeks worth for all of them. She also felt like she and Callum had outstayed their welcome, and she vowed that as soon she was back on her feet, she'd look for a place for her and her son.

A place that was safe and dry and a long way from where they had come...She still didn't know that her son had stabbed the woman who was looking after them.....Laden with shopping bags, Marisa burst through the door to deliver the news, when she heard Beverley scuttling around as though she were urgently looking for something very important. Beverley jumped when she saw Marisa.

"Oh God – Marisa....thank goodness you're back." The tone was serious. Marisa dropped the shopping bags with a heavy thud. Beverley didn't want to beat around the bush. "It's....Callum. I don't want you to worry, you mustn't worry, but....." Beverley stopped herself. How stupid of her. This young woman was still recovering from a breakdown and was very fragile, despite her recent buoyancy. She would already be worried. Beverley needed to be far more sensitive.

"Look......Callum hasn't come back. I'm sure he's just at a friend's house and it was all very spontaneous. I can phone around, if you like." But Marisa just ran into the bedroom and went through Callum's belongings. She knew what her son would take – what clothes, what bags....the nightmare was real. Marisa ran to the phone and said she'd call the police, but Beverley stopped her.

"He can only have been gone a few hours at the most. I'm sure we can find him – at least let me phone some of his friends. If we have no joy, we jump on a bus – see if he's at the late night shops, or something." Marisa agreed to this, but felt herself hyperventilating and reached in her bag for her pills.

It was almost Christmas and it was freezing and any thoughts she'd been having about actually being able to buy her son some presents this year were now replaced with how she might be able to find him.....

****

Mark shovelled down a plateful of over- oily Spaghetti Bolognese in a fit of anger. The waitress stood frowning at him wondering if he were yet another of her many customers who had lost their jobs and were taking it out on her mince. Mark almost gasped as he washed down the gristly meat and barely cooked pasta with a weak, milky coffee. The waitress noticed how he turned over a piece of crumpled up paper again and again, then put his mug down with a thud, before staring vacuously into space.

Suddenly Mark got up, threw some money down on the counter and bolted out the cafe. Woman trouble. It had to be. The waitress had worked as a waitress for long enough....

The bus came almost immediately and Mark leapt on and grabbed a seat, fidgeting until they pulled up at the bottom of Beverley's road. He ran to the front door and repeatedly rang the doorbell and knocked, until a neighbour came out to see what all the commotion was about. Mark started swearing.

"Bloody well open up! I know you're in there!" The neighbour was shocked to see Mark.

"Mark! What are you doing here? I thought you'd moved out. Beverley's not in – saw her leave about half an hour ago."

"Well" spat Mark, "It's not Beverley I want. I need a word with her boyfriend."

"Boyfriend...?"

"That Callum. Callum Brown. He lives here, doesn't he?"

"Yes, but he's not...."

Mark wasn't in the mood to listen. "You just tell him I've got a message for him, OK? Tell him I'm bloody well gonna kill him. Got that?" The neighbour quickly pulled her window up. Benji shuddered in the bush he'd leapt behind when he saw "The Hippy" heading up the road. What had happened? Why did The Hippy want to kill Callum? All Benji knew was that he had to run home as fast as he possibly could and find Daz immediately.

****

Christian ran excitedly towards the mobile home. "Gotta new friend, Mum!" Technically that wasn't true, but Christian was so upbeat, that everyone he met became a "new friend". Chrissie came down the metal steps. She clocked the skinny boy with the bad skin, unwashed hair, rucksack on his back and defensive look on his face and knew the score.

"Hiya!" she shouted down. "Guess you were trying to get to the Crosslands, but got lost, right? Don't worry – people do it all the time and wind up on our doorstep!" Callum tried to take this woman in, in the half shadow. He thought he recognised her voice. It radiated warmth and if he hadn't been in his predicament, or a rough Tunnel Boy, he would have wanted to run straight into her arms and tell her everything and be protected and safe.

The spirit of Grandma seemed to tell him that everything was ok – that he was in the presence of a highly benevolent being. But his real-life background told him to be wary. Chrissie put out her hand.

"Obviously you've met my son. We're doing some work up here tonight, so I've already put a big pot of dinner on. You're welcome to join us." Callum was famished, but this was a bit unexpected.

"Um....I dunno" he said "I mean, I've got to get back."

"Get back where?" asked Chrissie "Where do you live?" Callum didn't need this. He told her he'd got lost from the group on a school field trip – they were camping in a field out here....somewhere.....Chrissie said she thought it was a strange time of year to be out camping....

Callum could smell and feel the December night drawing in and soon it would be pitch black over the fields and he'd been foolish enough not to bring a torch. Chrissie knew that a young, hungry, frightened boy wasn't going to turn down food or even somewhere to crash for the evening, however cocky he might seem.

As he entered the light of the home, he and Chrissie stared at each other as she fried up potatoes, vegetables and herbs, filling the place with an aroma that made his stomach rumble noisily. The hospital. Chrissie had been at the hospital. That evening, he may have stood there defiant and proud and told her his mother was coming home, but in truth he was terrified.

She might have had to stay there forever. She might have died. He told no one, not even Beverley that he'd secretly prayed to Grandma and it was she who had finally pacified him and told him his mother was going to be alright. Callum may not have packed a torch, but he'd put some bubble wrap around the photo of Grandma and taken her with.

Even though the picture didn't belong to him, he felt justified in taking it. It was his guiding light – a protector and comforter. He moved closer to

Chrissie. She smiled. She was beautiful and soft and warm, whilst Grandma had her missing teeth and deep furrowed brow, but it seemed to him that Chrissie had the same gift – that she had a.....Knowing.

"I remember you" said Chrissie. "How's your mum? Is she OK?" Callum said she was. "Well, then – why are you running away?" Callum cast his eyes downwards. And then it all came out – almost involuntarily. The Tunnel Boys, Beverley, his mother's breakdown, the stinking, dangerous flat......

The sadness behind the twinkle in Chrissie's eyes came to the fore. She thought back to when she was Callum's age and her own childhood poverty. Maggie became like the mother she never had. She learnt her values, worked for her and became a best friend.

Chrissie's breathing became more rapid as she thought about Maggie – she thought she should be with her, but Maggie had instructed her to stay with her own family. It was on Maggie's insistence that Chrissie took the last remaining A4 folder with her, after they'd thoroughly gone through all the contents together.

Chrissie instinctively knew what Maggie had meant when she'd asked her to look after the "last folder". Chrissie knew she was going to be responsible for all the children in The Family, including any that just appeared, or were "sent" to them. Somehow, Callum was going to be integrated. He'd come for a reason. She knew instinctively that he also had The Knowing. Feeling overwhelmed, Chrissie needed to get outside and gulp down some fresh air, however cold it was.

Her head was throbbing and her chest ached. "Andy – just stay with the boys for a moment, would you? I forgot, I need to make a call to Angela...Can't get any reception up here, just gonna wander downhill a bit." Andy switched off the hob that was lighting the frying pan and let the other saucepan continue to slow boil. He knew Chrissie didn't need to call Angela. Nonetheless, he complied.

He reached behind a folding wooden screen and the woven Indian cotton throw, pulling out a slightly battered twelve string guitar. Christian clapped. He loved it when his Dad played. But Andy played a mournful, sad ballad, "Eleanor Rigby". Callum immediately knew the tune. He knew he was very young when he first heard it, but he knew his father used to play it. Andy sung softly, "All the lonely people – where do they all come from?" whilst Christian joined in with the bits of lyrics he knew.

Tears welled up in Callum's eyes as father and son sang along. He quickly tried to wipe his eyes, but larger tears started to roll down his cheeks.

"S...sorry" he sniffed, "It's just that - my dad used to play that – before he left us...." Andy's right hand slipped across the strings. Christian continued humming, not noticing that Andy was staring at Callum as his face turned gradually whiter.

"Your – *Dad?*" coughed Andy.

"Yes" sniffed Callum. Andy put the guitar down. Now he was the one who needed to go outside to gulp down some air.....

* * * * * * * * *

Angela wondered how on earth she could walk into a normal shopping centre and get her remaining Christmas presents, after all she had just seen and heard. The truth about The Family had blown her mind, and yet she didn't even know half of it. She saw where her administrative work was going. She learnt that she had initially been "apprenticed" to Barbara, once Maggie found out she was a pianist, so that she could be tested.

Both Maggie and Barbara usually made joint decisions about taking on new people. But unlike having a normal interview and being interviewed by only one or two people, or a board of managers, Angela had absolutely no idea how carefully scrutinized she had been.

She was gobsmacked when she heard how The Family made their selections. Certainly the necessary skills needed to be in place, but suitability for employment, or "membership" was determined largely upon character –something about which Maggie seemed to have largely impeccable judgement.

The grass and the trees and the modern red brick house may have been very real, but Angela felt she was in some kind of trance when Chrissie showed her around. She explained that this was one of many centres – Angela observed a mix of adults and children chopping up vegetables in a large communal kitchen, working in classrooms, tending animals and all other nature of every day normal chores necessary to keep the human cog wheels turning.

But there was a feeling Angela got as she strolled around the grounds. It was a sort of primal, organic feeling; a feeling she couldn't name. This, however, came from the very depths of her and there was something intrinsically earthy and human about it. It was like she hadn't known who she truly was until this moment.

Work as she had known it in the past was something that you endured in order to pay for the life that you really wanted. The more she had been integrated into The Family, the more her work *became* the life she wanted. Angela no longer had dominating forces like Verity demanding control as a means of coping with her own insecurities. No one put her down or belittled her. Now she was supported, encouraged – befriended.

Ironically, Angela had found she was far more productive and turning out higher quality work when she felt appreciated than when she was effectively whipped into action. If only she could tell her old bosses that.....

What struck Angela the most was that everyone in the centre seemed really happy. Even those working outside in the cold were laughing and joking, whilst the children appeared to be unusually helpful and friendly. No one seemed to be protesting in any shape or form and yet everything seemed to run like clockwork.

From this, Angela could only draw the conclusion that an establishment took on the character of its creator. As this was something Maggie had created, she had gathered people with the qualities of diligence, integrity, compassion, a dry humour and that elusive thing otherwise called The Knowing.

****

Angela staggered thorough the heavy crowds of Christmas shoppers and grasped the shiny metal handle of the entrance to the shopping centre. She stopped and looked behind her. It was the exact spot where she'd first seen Maggie narrowly avoid being hit by a vehicle. The first time they'd met. It seemed as though Angela had had a different life before that moment and it was so very different......

At once it came to her what her recurring dream about the hill and the shops was all about. Now, in real life, she was happily gliding down the hill instead of struggling up it. That all the little shops in her dream were so unique and represented her rather unusual work life and unconventional people she had met. It was therefore something of a shock to suddenly come face to face with her old life.

Sat on one of the little leather seats opposite the card shop, was Verity. At least – it looked like Verity. Only this woman was much thinner with black circles under her eyes and sunken cheekbones. The white stilettos however, unmistakably gave her away. Angela approached tentatively.

"V...Verity?" The woman who might have been Verity looked up and confirmed her identity.

"Oh, Hi. Hi Angela." She didn't sound like Verity. The voice was croaky and quiet, not booming and critical. Angela was shocked. She'd heard the phrase "being a shadow of one's former self", but this was a bit too literal.

"How are you?" she asked feeling quite foolish, given Verity's present condition. Verity didn't answer. Instead, bloodshot eyes looked up at

Angela from beneath sunken grey sockets, and Angela had her answer. She sat down beside Verity. "I'm so sorry. Have you found any more work yet?" Verity shook her head.

"I had a court letter the other day" she told Angela, "I have to move out of my flat because my landlady hasn't been paying the mortgage. It's being re-possessed." Angela gasped.

"Where will you go?"

Verity shook her head again. Without thinking, the words came involuntarily out of Angela's mouth before she had a chance to stop them. "Well then – nothing else for it. You'll have to come and stay with me." Angela looked on in horror as the shadow of Verity's former self smiled sadly, got up and followed her home.

****

Benji banged and banged on the front door. His knocking was as urgent as his voice. "Daz – open up – it's me!" His lower back still aching and painful, Daz hobbled to the door.

"Wassup Benj? What's going on?" Benji pushed the door aside and sat on the settee, breathless.

"It's The Hippy, Daz – you were right! He's not a friend. He said he was going to kill Callum!"

"Callum?"

"I saw him – he was outside Cal's new house. Remember you told me to watch what was going on there? Well, The Hippy showed up! An' he was screaming and shouting and yelling, and having a right go at Callum's neighbour." Daz turned pale.

"Christ – what does he want with Callum?"

"I dunno Daz, but he sure as hell ain't happy." Daz remembered his encounter with Mark and recalled how he couldn't find the bit of paper with Callum's address.

"The bastard . So that's how he found out. I must have dropped it. We've got to get there – fast."

"Bro – you can hardly move. I'll run back over....hopefully Callum will be home." Daz nodded and Benji grabbed his bag before shooting out of the door again. Daz wracked his brain and worried about Callum's welfare, but there was nothing else he could do. Who the hell was The Hippy? Was he something to do with the Chiefs? He knew they'd been trying to locate Callum for a while. But – kill him? Things were becoming pretty extreme. Now he needed to try and get through Christmas Presence with nasty injuries as well as try and save the life of his best friend.

****

Benji rang the doorbell of number 48 Rochester Road. He was horrified when a policewoman came to the door. Maybe he was too late. She spoke gently to him.

"Hello there – are you a friend of Callum's?" Benji nodded. "Do you know where he is?" The look of surprise, mixed with relief on Benji's face, aroused her suspicions. At least Callum was safe- for now. He must know something, if he hadn't come home. "Please – come in" the policewoman beckoned Benji inside.

He recognised Marisa Brown, but she barely acknowledged him. He didn't recognise the woman who smiled at him and who was holding Marisa's hand, but she seemed a bit overly friendly . Beverley smiled and anxiously searched Benji's face for some news.

"Isn't it a bit late for you to be out?" the policewoman asked Benji. "Does your mum know you're here? She'll be making you dinner pretty soon, I would think?" Benji realised he needed to think fast. He also needed to try and find out what was going on. He took inspiration from his older brother – what would Daz have done, faced with the same situation?

Daz was a master of quick repartee and most definitely had the gift of the gab. He could bluff his way out of almost anything. But Benji wasn't as articulate and especially when put on the spot, he'd stutter and give the game away. Instead, thinking of all the lessons he'd learned from being a Tunnel Boy, Benji stopped and engaged his brain before speaking carefully and slowly.

"We haven't seen Callum for ages. We used to play with him a lot. Someone from school saw him pop into this house, so we guessed he must be living here now. My mum just wanted to know if he fancied coming over to ours for dinner – haven't got a phone number, so decided to come round." It sort of sounded like it might wash. But it didn't sound right to Beverley.

Someone had obviously been following Callum. She knew he'd been very careful not to let anyone from Rook Hill know his whereabouts, and she was very clear about various authorities keeping quiet, once she'd taken Marisa and Callum in. She wanted to ask Benji lots of questions, but the policewoman stopped her, making it clear that was her job.

"So, Callum used to come over a lot, did he? I mean – when he lived near you?" Benji was out of his depth, and he knew it. He wanted more information, not to be questioned himself.

"Not that much" he replied. In fact, Callum had never been round at all. They'd only ever met up at the Tunnels. Marisa smiled at him. She didn't remember. Callum's mum was nice – Benji remembered that. Sometimes he wished his own mum exuded the same kind of warmth as the two women sitting opposite him....

He started to feel distinctly uncomfortable and knew he was going to have to find a way to leave – alas, without finding out anything more about The Hippy. He just said he needed to get home, satisfying the woman that he knew nothing of Callum's whereabouts. Benji had one foot out the door, when Beverley's phone rang. She looked confused as she answered and then responded in a shaking voice.

"It's a woman called Chrissie. She said Callum's with her." The policewoman made hand movements, indicating that she wanted Beverley to get more information, but that was all the information Benji needed. Quietly, he slipped out the front door and ran home as fast as he could, which was quite a distance.

****

"Eat up young man" Chrissie motioned to Callum. "Beverley's going to come and get you, but we're going to meet her at the Crosslands. It'll take her ages to find us here in the dark." Callum looked disappointed. He'd been taken in by this family, both literally and metaphorically and he really wanted to stay longer. Christian came to his rescue.

"Mum – can Callum come and visit? Whenever we want?"

"Well, that's not up to me" said Chrissie, "It's up to his mum. But he'd be very welcome." Andy took a deep gulp. Chrissie knew him well enough to know that in the time that had passed between her going out for some air, making dinner and phoning Beverley, that he had received some news that had shaken him deeply. She let the boys finish their meal and chatter as she led her partner outside.

Andy crouched on a log that served as a smoking seat and was illuminated by the outside light of the mobile home. Trembling slightly, he tried to make a roll-up, but the tobacco and paper clumped beneath his fingers and he threw them on the ground. Chrissie moved beside him and took his hand, but he wouldn't look at her. Her breath became faster as she squeezed his hand tighter, urging him to tell her what was wrong.

There was going to be no easy way, and Andy didn't need to know more. He instinctively knew who this strange boy was that had wandered into their lives from out of nowhere – he was his son. How could he live with himself, abandoning this boy and his mother, when the child was so young and his mother barely out of her teens?

It made no difference that he'd become a "reformed character" since he'd met a remarkable young woman called Chrissie – he'd still done awful things in his misguided youth. He had given up the boozing and womanising and roving, but he'd never given up his first love – the guitar. Andy was a consummate and talented musician – many of his friends had been and gone, left the country, done too many drugs – not stayed in touch.

Andy was tired of a life on the road and tired of always being on the move. But he'd never tried to contact Marisa or see his son. Maybe he was afraid he'd be unwelcome or a terrible father – always absent, often drinking, usually with other women. Yet, he was as good a father to Christian as any man could be. How then could he justify giving one son such a good life and never even seeing the other grow up?

And how would it be seeing Marisa again? He wondered just how much she hated him. This was going to affect the lives of so many, not to mention rapidly altering his own. As he turned to face his soul-mate, Andy's eyes were filled with tears. He rarely wept and Chrissie's eyes welled up too, as she knew this was serious.

There was nothing else for it. Everyone involved would have to know. No human being can erase their past – they can only make amends in the present. Andy knew that in the present he was a good man; a reliable and supportive parent and partner – someone who helped others and contributed to society.

He could only do now whatever he could to make up for lost time. Drying his eyes and telling Chrissie that his past life had just caught up with him wasn't easy. But her unconditional love and understanding gave him courage and he knew the only way to deal with the present, was to fully accept responsibility for the past.

****

Angela stared at the silent, remorseful creature sitting on her sofa. This was obviously not Verity, but some lame excuse for her. The real Verity must have been abducted by aliens and they had foolishly sent a replacement which was nothing like her. This Verity kept saying 'please' and 'thank you', which wasn't what proper Verity did. This Verity sipped quietly at mugs of tea and looked thoughtful. The proper Verity didn't think.

"This is really good of you, Angela" said improper Verity, "I promise I'll be off your back the minute I've got something sorted. I've got the local paper and I'm going to make some calls. There must be something for me somewhere...."

"I'm going to make a few calls myself" said Angela, "Some of my friends might be able to help."

"I guess it's easier for people like you in times like this" said Verity. This sounded like proper Verity. But what did she mean, people like *her*? Angela bit her top lip. When people said things like this to her, it was always meant in a judgemental, critical, sneering way. It was implied that because she didn't do things the way everyone else did them – conventionally or 'in line', then she was inviting ridicule and belittlement.

Verity continued. "I mean, you can do so many different things, can't you? You play the piano, and you've got lots of office experience and you're......" she hesitated "Very good with people." That last bit was the crunch. As Verity was finding out, skills and experience didn't count for much without the last bit. "I've spent years just being a manager at Mort and Grey. I don't know how to do anything else."

Angela couldn't believe what she was hearing. Did Verity really think that she'd had it easy, spending years being bullied by belligerent bosses? Struggling to survive as a single woman in an expensive city and hardly living up to the myth that she had a beautiful bacheloress pad, decked out in Habitat finest and an everlasting walk-in wardrobe? On the contrary, there was many a day when she had to chose between a tin of beans or a bus fare and her social life was far from swinging.

But what she lacked materially, she had in reams as a person. She was, as Verity had rightly said, "a people person". She seemed unperturbed by office politics, got along with just about everyone, was amenable, adaptable and very resourceful. This was why the Family immediately knew they had got lucky. They placed values such as these above all training. Computer skills, organisation, routine; this was something they figured could be taught – learning to be a better person, was something an individual just had to discover for themselves. Angela had come to them as a ready-made package.

What Angela really was, was a survivor. She knew how to make a casserole from nothing, source market stalls in the more run-down part of town for cheap fruit and vegetables at the end of the day, make things instead of buying them and would joyfully "muck in" whenever required. If there were ever another war, Angela would be superb in the "effort".

Unbeknown to her in the market, she would already have met Daz's father at the cut-off materials stall or bumped into Spencer's mum in the £1 shop. She was already prepared for a recession without having known it, having spent years spending time in greasy spoon cafes, charity shops and discount stores. Every penny had to stretch a long way.

These were things Verity had never had to do. During the last recession she was still at college and by the time she graduated there were plenty of jobs for bolshie, materialistic assistant managers. She'd started in retail and worked her way up to stationery, finally garnering a very good salary at the top of her tree. Now it had all gone. A few years back, she'd have walked into another job - now she couldn't even crawl into one.

Outside of work, Verity had frequented over-priced gastro pubs and paid for theatre tickets for her friends, when she wanted to make out how "cultured" she was. She only bought clothes from the higher end of the high street, or designer shops, although Angela often wondered how Verity always managed to look so cheap....

Like many people used to bonus schemes, luxuries and years of putting things on credit, Verity felt like an earthquake had erupted beneath her own personal space. She desperately tried to grasp at all her belongings, but could only watch in horror as they disappeared beneath the ever widening cracks in the ground.

Maybe for once it really was easier for Angela, but now wasn't the time to delve into their CV's. The fact was, here was a woman in Angela's home in dire need of help. Angela knew Verity had other friends and family, but it was very possible that they had also been "personal earthquake" victims, whilst she'd managed to avoid the worst hit areas. Listening to Verity, Angela almost felt as though a "hand of God" had reached down and pulled her from the brink of disaster, just before it happened. She had no idea why she'd had her bag stolen, helped Maggie Buxton and thereafter entered a chain of life with changing events and people, but someone – or something had helped her.

Months spent in close proximity to The Family made Angela look at Verity in a whole new light. Quite simply she was no longer her domineering boss, but a frightened woman without a job or home. Perhaps Verity was lucky to have been sitting in the shopping centre at that moment when Angela was walking by.

Angela boiled up the kettle again and rummaged in the kitchen cupboards for some biscuits. She'd gotten so used to eating evening meals with Chrissie and helping her make the food as well as sourcing it, that she didn't really shop just for herself anymore. For the first time ever, Verity actually looked in need of a good meal and Angela felt bad that she had nothing to offer her.

"I'll tell you what" said Angela, "Howzabout a take-away tonight? On me. Whaddaya fancy?" Angela could barely believe the words were coming out of her mouth. Verity looked down.

"Oh no – really. Don't worry. I'm fine with tea. Not really hungry." This wasn't real. Verity was *always* hungry. But shock had found her, and she couldn't physically eat. Angela uncovered a loaf hidden at the back of the freezer and popped slices into the toaster. There should at least be some butter and jam or peanut butter somewhere, as well. Verity was going to have to eat something before she was no longer recognisable as Verity.

****

Mark seemed to register no emotion as the news was delivered. This bemused his manager enough to repeat the details.

"Mark...you do understand what I'm saying, don't you? Temporary suspension. We don't want to lose you, but....the powers that be have been pressurising me to make a full report on you. This is the only way that I can maybe help you to keep your job." Eventually, Mark responded.

"If you're talking about Gardening Leave, then I don't have a bloody garden."

The manager let out a little cough of an embarrassed laugh, before turning more serious again. "If you're still finding it difficult coping with the breakdown of your relationship, then maybe...maybe you'd think about some professional counselling?"

Mark glared at the man sitting opposite. As far as he was concerned, the words "not" and "coping" did not go together. Instead, he spat back with a mouthful of venom that took the manager by surprise.

"Crap. How would you like it if your missus shacked up with some other bloke?" The manager could not immediately answer....

****

"Who the hell is Chrissie?" Daz asked Benji.

"Dunno" said Benji "But that's who Callum's with now. He's been moving around a lot, hasn't he? He must know The Hippy is after him. I wonder what he did to him?"

"Did you get an address?" asked Daz. Benji shook his head. "Some clues? Anything?" Benji affirmed again that he had no more information.

"Great, Benji. Why didn't you stick around? Find out more? How the hell are we meant to find him now?" Benji looked across angrily at Daz.

"I'm not stupid, Daz. Callum's mum and that welfare or whatever she is woman they live with are going to collect him. He's going back to the house. We need to go round there and tell them about The Hippy." Tunnel boys reveal things to adults? This just wasn't the way. And yet, Daz knew this made perfect sense. Besides, he was grappling with his own identity and exactly how he fitted into the Tunnel Boys these days.

Daz did a quick assessment of the situation, and decided his loyalties lay with his nearest and dearest. Right now that meant Benji and Callum. Benji had matured greatly and Daz trusted his gut instinct and first impressions of people. He patted his younger brother on the back. "Y'know what Benji – you're right. Let's give them a chance to get home,' cos Callum's bound to get a lot of questions about why he ran away. Chances are he knows something anyway, so I vote we head up there tomorrow after school."

Benji started to nod, but then reminded Daz they had a meeting for Christmas Presence. Daz took Benji by both shoulders. "Look, what's more important here? Callum, or that crass bunch who just did me a grave injury? They can hold off for a bit. We'll just say we had family stuff. No one can argue with that." Benji didn't look convinced, but then Daz added, "Callum's family, isn't he?"

****

Andy smiled sheepishly at his partner. "Not like you to be taking religious advice" he grinned, as Chrissie put down the phone to Anthony. Chrissie frowned.

"As if. C'mon Andy – this is a bit of a bombshell for me as well. I mean, I know you had another son, but....for him to just stumble upon us like this. It's going to take some getting used to, no matter how we're going to tell Christian."

Andy had thought about all the consequences, but not any solutions. He was kind of relying on Chrissie for those. Fortunately, she made a quick decision. "I need to call Beverley" she said, urgently pressing the numbers into her mobile, "In the meanwhile, you're going to have to find a way to tell both these boys that you are their Daddy." Andy took a deep gulp. The time to fully face up to his past had arrived.

****

Angela put the phone down to Barbara and tentatively turned to face Verity. "Well....they don't need any more help in the office, but...." Verity looked up hopefully. "There's a lady who lives near here called Mrs Mandlebaum...." Verity continued to look positive, which was somewhat disturbing. Out with it, thought Angela. "She needs some cleaning done." Angela waited for the meltdown. It didn't happen.

Instead, Verity just said very quietly "That sounds great." And so it was that Angela had found her old boss a new job. A new job for ex-manageress of Mort and Grey, Verity Macklesworth. Verity Macklesworth; high-heeled, short-tempered, man-eating, wine-swilling old boss.

Angela found herself staring at the pathetic, hunched over woman and realised that Verity looked very different without any make-up on. She seemed not to have any features, and any that there were receded into a grey spotty complexion. Without cakes of foundation, Angela could see that Verity had quite a lot of lines for her age – no doubt an accumulation of years of heavy drinking.

What was a most peculiar feeling to Angela was not only a little bit of pity for Verity's condition, but that for the first time ever in her life, she was actually the one in a better position. She could offer a place to stay, some work. She passed a slip of paper to Verity. "You need to give this woman a call – I wasn't sure when it would be a good time for you to see her."

"I can go anytime" said Verity sadly.

"Oh – sorry. Yes, of course" replied Angela, still trying to take in the surrealness of the situation.

****

"Perhaps it's best if I come over" said Chrissie to Beverley. "It's going to be a huge shock for Marisa about Andy – I can explain to her. Andy can stay with the boys and bring Callum home later. Or Callum can stay overnight with us, if you like." Beverley was aware it was getting late. She thought Marisa needed to be told. She'd be relieved he was safe and well and she wasn't sure how she'd take the news about him finding Andy.

"To be honest" continued Chrissie "It's quite a shock for us, as well. And what a small world, me having my friend Maggie in hospital and visiting at the same time you and Callum were seeing Marisa!" Beverley replaced the receiver and fumbled in her office bureau for some headache pills.

"Are you ok?" said Marisa, coming into the living room fresh out of the shower.

"I'm fine – just a bit tired."

"Look, Beverley – if you're not ok to go out then..."

"Actually Marisa, there's been a change of plan. Chrissie, the woman who's with Callum right now is going to come over here."

"With Callum?" asked Marisa.

"No, she's..." Beverley's voice trailed off. *She* was going to have to tell Marisa about Andy.

****

Verity had to walk around a bit to find Mrs Mandlebaum's road. It was in a mews that wasn't clearly marked on the A-Z and she had to stop and ask a few people en route. Verity had no other footwear other than that which contained rather high heels and by the time she found the house, her feet were aching and her toes pinched and throbbing.

A doorbell rung out a majestic chime. It seemed to take a while for anyone to get to the door, so Verity guessed Mrs Mandlebaum might be quite elderly and not find it so easy to descend the stairs. Eventually, a petite yet imposing woman with a shock of neatly coiffured white hair opened the front door. She spoke with a heavy Austrian accent.

"So. You are Verity. Come in." Verity walked across a highly polished wooden hallway furnished with ornate marble tables that were decorated with porcelain vases containing dried flowers. She looked around in horror at the size of the place. This – she was going to have to clean and she could already tell that Mrs Mandlebaum wasn't likely to take any prisoners.

She was ushered into a kitchen area and offered coffee. It was overly strong, with only a dash of milk and no sugar – the antithesis of how Verity liked it. Trying not to gag, Verity smiled sweetly as Mrs Mandlebaum gave her the once over.

"So. You know Barbara."

"Well, not exactly" said Verity "I know Angela, who works for her. I'm staying at her place at the moment." Mrs Mandlebaum raised one eyebrow so high, Verity thought it was almost going to knock a crystal off the lampshade.

"So....you are not.....married?"

Verity sighed deeply "No..."

"Hmm. Vell. Not very likely now. Still, no matter – zere are other things you can do." Mrs Mandlebaum always told it like it was. Without asking if she'd finished, Mrs Mandlebaum swiped Verity's cup away and poured the remainder down the sink. It was quite a relief. "So. Now you will come and see the house. I vill show you vat I need you to do." She glanced down at Verity's feet.

"You have some training shoes, I hope?" Verity nodded, although she'd not owned a pair of trainers since secondary school. Mrs Mandlebaum proceeded to show Verity around the three bathrooms, five bedrooms, two reception rooms, kitchen and hallway, all of which would need "cleaning most thoroughly". Mrs Mandlebaum could tell Verity was not the sort of girl used to rolling up her sleeves.

"Hmm. You are not like the girls I usually haff. Still – I shall give you a chance. You can start tomorrow?" And so it was that Verity had a new job and the perfect opportunity to sample the delights of far more suitable footwear.

****

Beverley had barely turned out of her garden gate, when her neighbour stopped her.

"Beverley....I don't want to worry you, but Mark came round here the other afternoon when you were out."

"Mark? Did he speak to you?"

"If you could call it that. He was screaming his head off and ranting about coming after Callum. He said.....he said that he was going to kill him."

"Oh my God. What does Mark want with Callum? He doesn't even know him."

"I think he's got it into his head that Callum is your new bloke. I'm not being funny, but just be careful. He doesn't seem to be in a very sound state of mind."

"I see" said Beverley. "Thank you for letting me know – I guess I'd better call him, even though I don't really want to speak to him." As if Beverley didn't have enough to worry about. She tried to put the thought of Mark's erratic behaviour out of her mind – he was no *real* threat –

oblivious to the sinister goings on in the minds of some seriously unhinged Tunnel Boys.

****

Andy nervously changed a guitar string, not knowing how long Chrissie was going to be, not knowing if she would come back with Marisa and absolutely no idea of what to say to the boys. Christian noticed his father shuffling anxiously around, but wasn't sure why he was behaving that way.

"Don't be upset, Dad – you can get new strings, right?"

"Yeah, yeah sure, son. No worries. Got a full set somewhere in here."

"Well – what's up then?"

Christian was too astute for someone so young. Andy was thrown – he just couldn't tell him without Chrissie there. But if Marisa came then....how would it be seeing her again? He was the one who'd walked out and never seen his child again until now....she must hate him with a vengeance.

Young Christian was the product of another life for Andy. A smart, bright, "other worldly" kind of kid, Christian exhibited his mother's enthusiasm and awareness as well as her large green eyes. Andy remembered when he had first laid eyes on the woman who had "saved his soul".

She was dancing barefoot at the Glastonbury festival, swaying and smiling, seeming not to have a care in the world and yet at the same time seeming to know and feel everything....

"Dad?" Christian reminded Andy that he had to deal with the present.

"Getting late little 'un – you need to get your PJ's on" Andy told his son. Christian protested. It wasn't bedtime yet and anyway, he wanted a song seeing as Andy had just put a new string on the guitar. Andy started strumming "Can't Buy Me Love", then stopped for a bit to tune the guitar better.

Callum dug down into his sports bag and pulled out Grandma's photo. He stared at her long and hard. Impatient with his father, Christian plonked himself down next to Callum. "Whozzat?" he asked.

"It's Grandma" replied Callum, nonchalantly.

"Grandma? She doesn't look like you. She's a bit scary, actually. My Grandma Maggie doesn't look like that. She's all soft n' nice. At least, she was before she got ill."

"This Grandma's not alive anymore" responded Callum dryly.

"My Grandma might not be alive any more soon" said Christian, before spontaneously bursting into tears. Seeing the commotion, Andy put the guitar down and asked Callum why he'd made Christian cry. Callum stuttered.

"S .. sorry. I didn't know about Christian's Granny." Andy placed himself down between the two boys.

"Y'know what.....I think we all need to have a talk. I think there's stuff all of us want to say. And God only knows I have something I need to tell both of you...." Christian wiped his eyes and stared up at his father, eager to listen to him. Callum held the picture of Grandma in front of him and stared for quite a while before averting his gaze to Andy. By then, he already knew. Grandma had told him.

****

Chrissie sat with Maggie, gently stroking the back of her hand. She was trying to take in the impact of recent events as well as trying to explain all to Maggie.

"So" coughed Maggie, "Andrew's son found him."

"It would seem so" said Chrissie "I've no idea how – it seems completely by accident."

"You know what I think of things happening by accident" said Maggie firmly.

"I think – I think Callum has The Knowing" said Chrissie, "In fact, I'm sure he has." Maggie smiled. A product of Andy – it should be no surprise that the boy had the gift. But Maggie was also concerned.

"Christina....you do remember what I've said about using The Knowing, don't you?"

"Always" said Chrissie "Especially when it comes to the children" Maggie nodded and then grasped Chrissie's hand as tightly as her own feeble hand could manage.

"Angela....I'm right about her too, aren't I?" said Maggie.

"Oh yes" said Chrissie. "Absolutely. Your judgement is always impeccable, Maggie."

"Jolly good....now tell me.....is she proving herself? I mean, with all this work we're putting upon her?"

"Yes, but....Maggie, it was hard when she found out about the accounts. It was an accident." Chrissie saw Maggie flinch, remembering what she'd said about "accidents".

"Perhaps we should have been upfront about that from the start. Should have told her about The Family before she even started working for us."

Maggie frowned "Christina you know how we work."

"Yes, of course, it's just that – given what we intend for Angela next...."

Maggie gave Chrissie a look that said please trust me. She needed to know that everything was being done in the way that she had asked. Chrissie reassured her that everything was in place. She tried to hide her sadness, as Maggie was keen to discuss Angela further. She harkened back to that moment – the moment when a young woman forsook her keys, credit cards, phone and material belongings to help a stranger – her.

It was important for Maggie to hear that Chrissie had no doubts about Angela, either. Chrissie felt overwhelmed with responsibility, but she would manage – with the support of Andy, Angela and The Family, they would carry out Maggie's wishes. Maggie changed the subject, asking if Chrissie had met "The Verity girl", but Chrissie shook her head. There was so much to do, and she wanted Angela to meet Callum and his mother.

"Christina....you look tired. Promise me you won't go over-working yourself" said Maggie, concerned. As if that were possible. But Chrissie lightly kissed the back of Maggie's hand and said that she should stop worrying. Maggie was so frail, so exhausted. The legacy of The Family needed to be continued and of course there would be deadlines, difficulties and dramas.

But that was a small price to pay for such a beautiful life. And for continuing the life's work of this wonderful woman.

****

Andy trembled slightly when he first saw Marisa. Apart from the fact he hadn't seen her in a very long time, he was shocked at her appearance. She had always been petite, but now she was emaciated with deep dark hollows beneath her pretty brown eyes. The sense of guilt overwhelmed Andy immediately. He vowed then and there that he would make up for every single lost moment that he could and be an impeccable father to Callum.

Marisa was less overwhelmed. Maybe it was years of life as a single mother, the harsh reality of her daily life or the kindness of strangers, but she had no feelings towards Andy at all. Their liaison had been passionate, but short lived – flesh and blood, a child was the result of many such an encounter.

Beverley was immensely relived that Marisa was so calm and left the various parents to discuss the future. As she moved to another part of the caravan, she saw the corner of a photo frame poking out of the top of Callum's bag. She recognised it immediately. Beverley reached into the bag and fished out Grandma.

"Callum – why did you take this?" The boy's face reddened and he lowered his head. Beverley continued. "Why on earth would you want it?" Callum felt really embarrassed that she'd brought this up in front of everyone else.

"I...I liked it" he stuttered.

"Oh come on" Beverley scorned "You can do better than that. You're not the sort of boy to take something just because you fancy the look of it – I know that." Callum conceded that he was just going to have to tell the truth.

"I took it because....she tells me things." Beverley gasped and then took a deep gulp. This was a secret that belonged to her and Grandma. When she was younger, Grandma had "told" her many things. Beverley had heard how her ancestors had the gift of foresight and that they could predict floods, famine and other natural occurrences.

Grandma herself was a "sensitive" and had terrible trouble coming to terms with the great culture shock that was England. She told Beverley that she was "the protector of the little children" and that she would protect Beverley and any children with "The Knowing" who found her or summoned her.

Beverley tried to push this primitive way of life to the back of her mind and deal with the now. After all, it wasn't just Grandma who'd gotten into trouble with all her so called "Hocus Pocus". It had spelled the end of Beverley's relationship. But immediately she felt that something Grandma had told her would manifest, had now happened.

Before she passed over, Grandma told Beverley that she would watch her – guide her. Lead her to the people who would be right for her. Looking across the room at Chrissie and Andy, she immediately sensed that she was with other people who had The Knowing. And now little Callum was also one of those people. Had Grandma led him to his father?

Beverley gently put the photo down. "It's OK Callum. I understand. We'll talk about it." Callum seemed to heave a sigh of relief. But no one was quite prepared for how Christian would take it. He grinned broadly and simply said, "Yeah. I know about that. My Grandma Maggie's got The Knowing, too."

****

The days leading up to Christmas Eve when Angela planned to see her mother, were spent getting to know Callum, Beverley and Marisa by helping out at the allotment and playing with the boys and looking after Verity by attending to her feet. Whilst feeling slightly sorry for Verity, Angela couldn't help laughing at the fact that Verity was so used to having spent most of her life in stilettos, the trainers were giving her blisters. Two days a week, after having spent hours polishing, scrubbing and vacuuming, Verity would crawl back exhausted to Angela's flat and collapse on the settee.

The usual routine was that when Angela got in, she'd be armed with plasters, foot ointment, callous pads and....biscuits. Verity made the tea, but this afternoon she could barely hobble into the kitchen.

"Maybe you need to get larger size trainers?" suggested Angela.

"No...its not that...." said Verity. Then Angela saw Verity do something she had never seen her do. Not even when a one night stand had failed to phone her. Verity broke down in tears. "I admire you so much, Angela. You've held it altogether, despite everything. You've got a job and a home. You've got wonderful friends. I do envy you."

Angela could hardly believe what she was hearing. It was true that life had changed rapidly in a very short time. But the new life now felt so natural and easy, like it was the life that she was always meant to have. If only she could explain to Verity how it all just came together when you had The Knowing....

Angela had no idea why that phrase had popped into her head, yet it immediately and instinctively felt right. It was like it was something she was born with – something that had spent years being repressed and now been re-activated. But it was no use trying to explain that to Verity. Verity didn't have The Knowing. That much was obvious.

Still, Angela knew that all the members of The Family were very compassionate and tried to help people – whoever they were. For now, she could give Verity somewhere to stay and help her get some work. Only, the old Verity Macklesworth no longer existed. She was being forced to change and perhaps she needed to be in some kind of transition. At least The Family could help with that. More important than who Verity Macklesworth was becoming, was who Angela Morgan had *become*.

****

Beverley was just about to collect Callum from Christian's home when there was a knock at the door. Peering through the peep hole, she couldn't see anyone and so concluded that it was either someone very short or a child. She opened the door to Benji.

"Hiya Miss. Callum in?"

"No" said Beverley "He's with a friend."

"Oh good, can I come in?" Benji just pushed past Beverley into the hallway and before she could say anything, an older boy followed Benji in.

"Sorry about my brother" said Daz, "He's just keen. Doesn't mean to be rude." Beverley folded her arms, angered at this sudden intrusion.

"Callum's *not* in" she said firmly.

"Yeah..." said Daz. He lowered his head. "To tell you the truth Miss, that's a good thing." Puzzled, Beverley gestured towards the sofa. She noticed Daz lower himself very carefully to sit, as though he had some kind of back injury. The three of them sat silent for a moment as Beverley took in these unexpected visitors.

She was immediately struck by Daz, as most people were. He was a beautiful looking teenager and usually had a deep sparkle in his eyes. Beverley couldn't help wondering if a boy like that had The Knowing. Maybe that's why he was friends with Callum. As a little brother, Benji was very different.

It wasn't just to do with his age, but somehow Benji was far less "deep" – he was like a little puppy dog, eager to please and join in. He spent the whole time looking at Daz, as if he needed to learn what Daz was going to say, for future reference. Daz went straight in. "We're worried about Callum. Apparently, there's this bloke after him that wants to hurt him."

"Bloke?" said Beverley.

"We don't really know him – not that well. He used to hang around the local park and chat to us sometimes, but if you ask me he's not...not all that right in the head."

"He's a hippy" added Benji.

"Hmm...." Beverley leaned forward. "Now....my neighbour said something about a bloke hanging around here....she said he was making some kind of threats regarding Callum. D'ya think we could be talking about the same bloke?"

"Yeah! I do!" said Benji, proud of his own spying skills.

"Ah..." replied Beverley, now relaxing a little more. "So – how well do you boys know this – bloke?"

"Sometimes he'd kick my football around a bit with me. Sit on the bench. Chat a bit. And sometimes he'd give us...." Benji suddenly cut off, remembering he shouldn't mention this bit.

"He gives us cigarettes" said Daz, aware that they weren't going to get out of that one.

"But he doesn't smoke" said Beverley. Daz described Mark in as full detail as possible, leaving absolutely no doubt that the bloke and Mark were one and the same. After hearing this, Beverley relaxed a lot more.

"Well, thank you boys for bringing this to my attention, but really – I don't think you need to worry."

"Not worry?" Daz looked angry. "Callum is our friend, of course we're worried."

"I didn't mean that" said Beverley, "I can tell you really care about him. What I mean is, I know exactly who this bloke is. He's harmless. Let's just say that he's not taking the break up with his girlfriend too well....."

****

"Where the hell are Daz and Benji?" growled one of the Chiefs down Spencer's ear.

"Dunno. I ain't seen them, but s'pect they'll be here soon" replied Spencer. He felt the hot heavy breath of the Chief on the back of his neck, as the teenager came way too close for comfort.

"Well, you'd better not be lying" said the boy, "Cos you know what happens to liars, don't you?" Spencer nodded. But he was furious with Daz. He reckoned he'd just about had it with Daz's Callum obsession. Didn't Daz realise that if he was late, or worse still a no-show, that it was going to look really bad on Spencer as well?

He spat on the ground as another boy laughed and pulled his hood up over his head. "We're ready to roll, Spence. If Daz and Benji ain't here in five minutes, we're going without them. They're gonna get what they deserve." But Daz and Benji arrived as he spoke.

"Sorry" said Daz, puffing as he ran up the hill "Mum's out and Gran got taken bad....had to sort her out." Spencer glared at him. He knew Daz's grandmother was in a home.

"Alright alright" said the Chief "No time for that now. Get your gear and get in line." Spencer, Daz and Benji joined the other boys in collecting bricks wrapped in cloth, a selection of knives and knuckle dusters and bags full of broken bottles. It all seemed so primitive compared to the earlier raids. But they didn't argue. Nobody dared.

The boys marched into town whilst simultaneously chanting their version of "The Twelve Days of Christmas". They looked like they were in some gritty, nasty film as pensioners shouted at them, mothers screamed and grabbed their children and others dived into shop doorways, out of the way of the marching parade. Graffiti on a wall on the high street depicted a bloodthirsty scene and the words "Got ya!"

Once the gang hit the high street, it was every man for himself. Each boy needed to steal at least one worthwhile item and then leg it back to headquarters without being caught. Only it was a ridiculous plan. Of course someone would get caught. It was only a few days before Christmas eve and the town was teaming with security.

Some of the boys even secretly hoped they'd be caught, because then there wouldn't be any more Tunnel Boys and they could live their lives free of bullying. Best to just switch onto autopilot. Become a robot. Go along with it. The rampage began in the smaller shops before running riot in the larger department stores. Before loads of police were alerted.

Daz got off lightly by having a younger boy, Benji, with him. All he needed to do was carefully watch his nimble-fingered brother, as his child's hands reached up into a Christmas shopper's pocket or handbag and pulled out a purse. He'd go barely unnoticed. Benji managed to lift a particularly expensive looking wallet and Daz just hoped its owner had taken out a wad of cash.

The two brothers counted as "one unit" and therefore Daz didn't have to steal anything himself. On account of being so small and slight, Benji was valuable to the gang in tasks such as these. Mission accomplished, they could have quite happily just strolled back to H.Q then and there, but Daz clocked Spencer stuffing a Nintendo Wii up his jumper and looking for somewhere to duck into.

He also saw a security guard looking over at Spencer and Spencer freezing to the spot. Risking being seen himself, Daz reached out and yanked at Spencer's sleeve, dragging him behind a pile of haphazardly piled toys and through the double doors onto the stairwell where Benji was waiting. "Quick Spence, over here" whispered Daz, pushing him to a place of safety.

Then the three boys tore as fast as they could through all the quieter, shopper-free streets, taking a less direct way back to H.Q, where they awaited the fates of the others. They were safe.

****

"Terrible, so terrible" muttered Mrs Mandlebaum, flicking through the local paper the morning after. "After all we went through in zee wars. Ze children now.....I don't know. Zey just take. Zey do not want to earn anything for themselves. I don't know vy zey sink zey should haff, without working."

Verity nodded in agreement as she sipped at a luke warm tea. She was exhausted and didn't take a lot of notice of what Mrs Mandlebaum was saying. But then as Mrs Mandlebaum leaned over to empty her own teacup, she saw, clear as day, the dark numbers tattooed on her forearm. Verity gasped and her cup dropped to the floor.

"Oh, oh Mrs Mandlebaum, I'm so very sorry – I'll clear that up right away."

"My! Verity –vatever made you jump so?" And then Mrs Mandlebaum saw the way her bracelet had fallen down her wrist as she'd pushed her sleeve up and how she had exposed the signs of her history that would be etched onto her for life.

"Ah.....yes, vell. So you know, now. I am a Holocaust survivor." Verity didn't know what to say. It seemed that her own life flashed before her eyes in sudden, startling shots of spending it either sitting at her desk or sitting at a bar. She was raised in a place that she hadn't moved far away from, had friends only from college or work and just a few months ago was full of her own self-importance. Her managerial status. Her wardrobe.

How far the mighty fall. If living with her former P.A hadn't humbled her, this certainly had. Mrs Mandlebaum didn't seem to notice that Verity was having a life-changing moment, as she recalled her past. "I lost all my family, you know. My parents. My brother and sister. But I married the British officer who liberated us at the camp."

In her wildest nightmares, Verity could never imagine a life like Mrs Mandlebaum's. Mrs Madlebaum had only been spared, as she had trained as a nurse and had medical knowledge. She changed the subject. "Now – tell me Verity, vat did you do before you came to me?" Verity explained that she had spent many years being an office manager.

"I thought so " said Mrs Mandlebaum. Verity sat up, thinking that maybe someone was recognising her place in society again. She was realizing that people knew other people who needed someone – it wasn't like the old days where you emailed a C.V.

"So – why do you think that?" said Verity, smiling.

"Because you're a terrible cleaner" replied Mrs Mandlebaum, running a finger over the draining board. As Verity's shoulders sunk back down, the phone rang. Mrs Mandlebaum excused herself. Verity only heard snippets of the conversation, but she picked up on the urgency of the call. Mrs Mandlebaum was talking to someone called Barbara.

"I see, I see. Yes. I vill be zere as soon as I can." She came back into the kitchen and Verity noticed all the colour had drained from her face. "I'm sorry Verity, I must get a taxi right away and I vill haff to leave you here. You can carry on and finish, yes?"

"Mrs Mandlebaum....if there's anything else I can do....."

"No...just stay here, please. I'm sorry Verity, but ..... I really don't know how long I vill be...."

****

Daz, Spencer and Benji waited. And waited. But few boys had made it back to H.Q. It was a given, really. There would be so many arrests and questioning and it was going to be such a miserable Christmas that the remaining stalwarts would find it hard to rejoice in their escape. The Tunnel Boys, if they were to continue existing after this recent escapade, were never going to be the same again and Spencer needed to find someone to point the finger of blame at.

He scowled long and hard at Daz, but Daz had just saved his bacon. So, Daz might have been very loyal, but sometimes he was just a bit too loyal. There was only one person to blame for the collapse of the Tunnel Boys and the lifeline out of his miserable existence. That person was Callum.

****

It was January 4th and Angela was just returning to the flat after spending Christmas with her mother. After a mild Christmas and Boxing Day, the weather had suddenly turned on New Year's Eve, when Angela was catching up with old friends. She told Verity to put on as much heating as she needed whilst she was away and despite the bills, Angela secretly hoped Verity had it on full blast, as she was frozen to the bone.

A stranger started chatting as she sat on the bus. "Looks like snow" said the elderly gentleman next to her, scanning the whiteness of the sky out the window.

"You reckon?" replied Angela, "I thought it was too cold to snow."

"Nothing to do with that" replied the man. "We've just had a bereavement in the family and it always snows the day after. It's just them letting us know that they're still around." Angela shivered and it wasn't because of the cold. She really couldn't wait to get home now. Not only was the flat nice and toasty, but Verity had got in some of Angela's favourite biscuits.

She told Angela about Mrs Mandlebaum taking a call from Barbara and rushing off. As she listened to how Mrs Mandlebaum had turned very pale and gone suddenly, Angela suddenly felt sick. She ran into the bedroom and repeatedly dialled Chrissie's number, but it just kept going to answer phone. Verity was abandoned without explanation for the second time.

When Angela arrived at the hospital, instead of getting the lift to the ward as usual, she bolted up the three flights of stairs, then pushed open the double doors, omitting to squirt anti-bacterial liquid on her hands. As she took long strides down the endless corridor, she tried not to panic, although an acid taste of vomit rose to her throat and her heart seemed to beat faster than ever.

When she saw Maggie's bed empty, she took a deep breath and reminded herself that Maggie had been moved to other wards before. But when she saw a nurse that she knew quietly sniffing in a corner and trying to wipe her tears before Angela saw her, she knew Maggie wasn't in another ward.

Angela was ushered into a little side room where Chrissie and Barbara sat sobbing and Anthony and Mrs Mandlebaum sat holding hands silently. Anthony got up and gently led Angela away. He took her hands in his and spoke directly and softly. "Maggie passed away about half an hour ago." Angela gave a gasp and he squeezed her. "Chrissie and Barbara were with her all night. It was very peaceful – very gentle. She just went in her sleep." Angela started to cry. Anthony put his arm around her shoulders and they walked towards a window.

He chuckled softly with the memory of Maggie. "Y'know, she said she couldn't possibly pop her mortal coil until she was quite satisfied we all knew what we were doing. So, she stuck around until she was certain she could let go."

"B....but – she didn't know if I could live up to her wishes, if I knew what I was doing" sobbed Angela.

"Oh my dear, when Maggie knew something, she knew with absolutely one hundred percent certainty. You can be sure of that." Anthony pulled a freshly ironed hankie from his top pocket – the likes of which Angela hadn't seen since she'd been a little girl. She took it and dabbed her eyes and looked past Anthony through the large glass window. Outside, it had started snowing.

****

Mark's redundancy had forced him back into reality. It was like he'd been in some kind of bizarre, drug-induced state and hadn't been himself for several months. He started to question why he'd even left Beverley in the first place and how on earth he could possibly have let his career slip through his fingers.

All his current behaviour was fuelled by his obsession with Beverley. So what if she had a new man? She was a warm, intelligent, attractive young woman and it would hardly be natural if other men weren't attracted. Pouring himself a large cup of freshly ground coffee, Mark realised that before he could even get his head around being unemployed or looking for another job, he needed to resolve his issues with Beverley.

Their relationship was over – he knew that, but he hoped they could be friends – he couldn't bear the thought of losing her completely. Mark had behaved so completely out of character for such a long time, that he wondered if Grandma had put a curse on him. If anyone had led him to that God-awful cafe, then it had to be Grandma.....

Mark resolved to put his life right again. Heal his relationships, re-think his job and then, as soon as he was more secure, get out from under his parents' feet. To start with, he needed to do the thing he would find the hardest and that was to call Beverley. He reached for the receiver, but the ring tone beat him to it. Who was calling? His heart leapt to his mouth, as he saw Beverley's number on caller display.

"Bev?"

"Mark. Glad I got hold of you. I need to speak to you urgently, so I hope you've got a minute."

"I've got all the time in the world, now" Mark said sadly. Beverley was harsh.

"Well – no doubt you do if you've got the time to come round and threaten my lodger."

"Yeah – about that Bev, I......"

"What the hell did you think you were doing? Like Callum hasn't been through enough."

"I'm really, really sorry Bev. I wasn't thinking straight. The old green-eyed monster just took over and.....the thought of you being with someone else is really hard to deal with." Beverley went quiet. Mark couldn't see her putting her head in her hands. Then she muttered something to herself, before revealing all.

"Oh Christ, Mark......Callum Brown is eleven years old!"

"He's.....what?"

"A little boy and his mother are living with me. Callum is an old student of mine." It was Mark's turn to go quiet. He told Beverley he wanted to make it up to her. Somehow....There was a pause before she told him he could stop coming round and threatening murder, for a start. Once he'd placed the receiver back down, Mark let his head fall into his hands.

The sudden realisation of sabotaging his own life suddenly hit him. If Grandma had put a curse on him, then maybe she was now giving him the chance to have it lifted and if he possibly ever could, he would find a way back into Beverley's heart, if not completely back into her life.

****

Spencer's anger towards Daz had now diluted. All rage was now directed towards Callum and he knew he had to find him. He also desperately needed to find a way to save what was left of the Tunnel Boys and his uncertain future. He needed to find Callum and he knew Daz knew where Callum was.

He also knew Daz wasn't that enamoured by the remains of the gang, and would have done anything to get out, if he could. Spencer cornered Daz as he crossed the forecourt of the Drayton Estate on his way to school. "Glad I caught you, Daz. 'Fraid I've got some really bad news." Daz asked what it was. "It's about Callum. Some of the boys have found out where he is."

"Whhhattt?! How come? How did they find out?" Daz's eyes widened as his heart skipped a beat. Spencer said he had no more information – just heard about it through the grapevine. Then he told Daz the boys said they knew where to find Callum – and that they'd make him pay. Daz shook his head. He'd never let on to anyone and he knew Benji wouldn't either. Someone must've seen him – followed him. Spencer continued.

"We need to warn him, Daz. Can you get him to come here?"

"Here?" said Daz "Isn't that a bit dangerous?"

"On the contrary" said Spencer "No one will ever think he comes round this way anymore, for that very reason. We need to bunk off early and get him to do the same. We can warn him and he can get home before his mum or that woman even know it." Spencer could see the complicated cog wheels of Daz's brain turning. He was trying to weigh things up.

"Wednesday, 2pm would be good. My mum goes to bingo. We can meet with him alone." Spencer sounded convincing. "You know how important it is, Daz – we *have* to protect him." Spencer could see he was getting just to the part of Daz that he wanted to reach. He knew Daz trusted him, despite their recent differences and he knew Daz would want to protect Callum against all costs. Once you were a blud, you were bonded for life.

He couldn't understand just why Daz cared so much for Callum, but then he didn't know that Daz had already sussed a long time ago that Callum had The Knowing.....Incredibly, Daz fell for Spencer's plan. He said he'd sort it with Callum. Now all Spencer had to do was go and tell the Chiefs where they could find Callum that Wednesday afternoon....

****

Callum listened patiently whilst a red-eyed Christian told him all about Granny Maggie. Callum was too young to remember the death of his own grandmother, and this would be the first funeral he'd been to. He didn't know much about it, except that his new family and friends would all be there – Chrissie, Andy, Christian and the new lady Angela. He liked her because she was funny and didn't speak to him like he was a child. He sussed that she also had The Knowing – most members of The Family did.

Beverley was going to come – she was keen to start doing some volunteering for The Family. And Marisa seemed to be able to talk to Andy just fine and that made Callum feel strong and good. His mother was also much healthier and marvelling at this way of life that she had never seen, but maybe dreamed about. She thought that if she was well enough to work again, maybe she could do something here – she had never wanted to work anywhere else more. And if she had work then they could get out from under Beverley's feet and perhaps finally have somewhere of their own to live again...

Beverley had really lost her rag with the council when they told her they weren't obligated to re-house Marisa and Callum as they had left the flat "voluntarily". As far as she was concerned, they could stay as long as they liked, but she knew Marisa longed to get her life back, and she vowed to keep fighting for them.

Instructions from Chrissie about the funeral were that no one should wear black. On the morning, gatherers arrived in bright colours and with bunches of loosely tied flowers, rather than traditional funeral wreaths. Anthony conducted the service, and anyone who hadn't known Maggie that well would have been surprised at how the vicar spoke.

It was more like political oratory, than a tribute to an old woman. He had people cheering and raising their fists in the air – promising to continue the work of Maggie and The Family. Far from weeping and grieving, there seemed to be a joyous atmosphere and a strong sense of purpose. There was even a "Three cheers for Maggie!" as Anthony finished speaking.

But then tears were shed as Andy played the guitar and sang. He sang a beautiful, haunting Irish tune – a barely known folk song, but one that was a favourite of Maggie's. When she'd first met Andy and realised he knew that tune, Maggie had asked him to play it over and over and they both joined in the chorus.

The lyrics spoke of the Irish struggle, but they could just have easily applied to The Family. The majority of them had spent their lives in extreme hardship and suffered whilst fighting for their own values, as well. There were people like Marisa who had lived amongst violence and deprivation, impoverished children and also many gentle and brave souls who Maggie had found along her life's journey.

There were others with less deprived upbringings, but who had no desire to live within the conformities of the society they had been raised in. There were people like Chrissie and Andy who worked hard to put something back into the society that Angela knew, but who were labelled lazy or scroungers, purely because they couldn't be pigeon-holed. Andy considered his old rock and roll lifestyle no less immoral than the City Boys he saw squandering huge bonuses and abusing people in bars.

All members of The Family were very carefully "vetted". They may have been guaranteed a roof over their heads for themselves and their families, but not without their necessary input. There was a sort of communal ethos involved, and yet individuals were free to continue jobs anywhere they wanted, provided they also undertook whatever was required in order to sustain The Family.

Maggie knew specifically what kind of people she wanted and surrounded herself with helpers like Barbara, Anthony and Mrs Mandlebaum. But they couldn't run things forever – Chrissie was the hope for the next generation and Callum and Christian after her. The lineage would continue.

After Andy had finished singing, all child members of The Family were invited to place flowers on the grave to say their final farewells, until Maggie was eventually buried beneath a deep sea of winter blooms. Angela and Chrissie wept and held each other, after which Chrissie pulled away and nodded towards Andy. Then, something extraordinary happened.

At least twenty children ran out of the church and came back out with a multitude of musical instruments. Then, upon Andy's instruction, they all began to play, walking forwards across the graveyard and leading a procession down the high road, crossing around the back of the main shopping centre and in the direction of the Drayton Estate.

This wasn't some school orchestra – the music was haunting, beautiful and melodious. It sounded like the youngsters were professional musicians. Angela was moved to tears by the purity of the sound and followed behind, joining at least one hundred other people. Not all were members of The Family – it seemed Maggie was a very well loved and well known figure of the local community and had many friends.

As they approached the Drayton Estate, where many members had their origin, Angela guessed this must be a tribute to Maggie's own roots and a sort of returning her "home". As he heard the sound echoing around the back window of his house, Daz leapt up and ran to the window.

As he peered out, he saw Callum and Marisa in the sea of people. He wondered what on earth it was they were partaking in. All he knew was that the music suddenly touched him deep inside – and confused him. He never listened to music like that – he was an R & B boy who liked modern bands and rap. But this moved him to such an extent that he couldn't explain.

Then he realised the sound was flickering around his very soul, suddenly illuminating all that was important to him. He knew in that moment that his friendships held the utmost level of importance. Now that he had a contact number from Beverley, Daz sent Callum a text marked "H. P.D.C.". He knew Callum could interpret the Tunnel Boy lingo. "High Priority Daz to Callum."

****

Beverley may have erased her past with Mark, but no one can totally predict the future. As she'd put the phone down on him that afternoon, he'd vowed to regain control of himself and his life from that moment on. He decided to take a stroll around his favourite thinking place – the blustery park. It was a bitterly cold day, but at least it was just starting to get a little lighter in the evenings and the shortest day of the year and winter solstice had passed. Mark could definitely feel a new beginning in the air.

He tried to think back and analyse what had kick-started his behaviour. He remembered the charismatic teenager, Daz – the day he'd first seen him, the few times he'd spoken to him. The impact Daz had made on him. Try as he could, Mark could not find the words to describe his feelings. He only knew this chance meeting had ignited something within; his "shadow side".

This was his anger and his darkest thoughts, but suddenly he realised it was all about the opposite. It seemed he had to go through these trials to reach the clarity he had now. Buried deep inside him was The Knowing. It took a relationship break up, redundancy and a boy like Daz for Mark to understand this.

As he sat on "his" bench, he reached into his pocket and pulled out a pack of cigarettes. They belonged to a time he didn't need any more. He crumpled them up and slung them in a bin. Now approaching the upper end of the park and getting closer to the tunnels was the funeral procession. The group of children played on and Mark turned towards the heavenly sound.

Amongst the throng he clocked Beverley and she saw him too. Only, she didn't look away. Instead, she smiled softly and in that smile, he knew she'd forgiven him. Their eyes held each other for some time. There was a shift, a healing. And although he didn't know it then, the initiation of Mark's introduction to The Family had just begun.

****

Spencer congratulated himself on the practically flawless precision of his organisational skills. Callum trusted Daz implicitly – he would be there on time. Daz would trust Spencer – believe that he would have more information about the future plans of the Chiefs.

Daz had somewhat fallen out of rank, but his rescuing of Spencer at Christmas Presence had afforded him some grace. If Daz could do anything to help Callum, then now was the best time, to cash in on his being back in favour. Callum arrived at the Drayton Estate exactly on time and made his way over to Spencer's flat.

Only, Spencer was already strolling briskly through the courtyard. "Hey – Cal, glad you're here."

"Yeah – I'm here" replied Callum. "Daz's text stressed how urgent it was, but I can't say I'm too happy about coming back *here* again."

"Trust me" Spencer smiled. "You've got nothing to worry about. Just come down this way." A few steps more and Callum would be just where Spencer wanted. At that precise moment, Daz felt a pain in his kidneys so sharp, he thought he would pass out. Instinctively, he knew something was wrong. Some bizarre gut instinct was telling him not to trust Spencer.

He could swear he'd heard the voice of an elderly African woman telling him he needed to find Callum immediately. He didn't even question it.

 A few feet beyond the courtyard, Callum suddenly realised everything. At least five Chiefs and several Seconders circled round him. His eyes darted towards Spencer, but all he saw was a twisted, sickly smile on his face and Callum didn't need to know anymore. A veritable Judas. He had been betrayed.

The Chiefs began taunting and one of them took his hand and shook it, cruelly laughing. "Callum, mate! Good to see ya again!"

"Yeah, it's good alright" snarled another Chief. The circle tightened. On the concrete balcony outside Spencer's flat, Daz thought he was going to throw up. The lift was smashed and broken, but he wouldn't have waited for it anyway – he tore down two flights of stairs and then, despite his pain, willed his body to run faster than it had ever run before.

Callum saw the gang had knives and his eyes shot towards Spencer, then back at the knives. As he saw a blade rise up into the air and glisten in the cold winter daylight, he waited to meet his maker – waited for the cold steel to pierce his heart.

Instead, he felt the heavy thud of the concrete beneath his back as Daz hurled himself on top of Callum, pushing him to the ground and taking the full thrust of the knife in his own back. As Callum lifted his neck, he saw the handle sticking out and felt Daz gasping heavily for breath, hot on his face.

To the outside world, it was yet another brutal stabbing of an Inner City teenager. Another gangland murder in a rough area. To the younger boy who howled whilst angry tears streamed down his face, it was the killing of his older brother. To the woman who arrived at the scene to cradle the boy in her arms moments before he took his final breath, it was the loss of her eldest son. To Callum, it was the ultimate sacrifice of his best friend.

****

For the person who had given his life in order to save his, Callum wanted Daz's funeral to be extra special. He asked Daz's family for permission to have the musicians from The Family and Maggie's funeral – he felt that Daz deserved no less of a procession. Only, he asked Andy if they could learn the sort of music that Daz really liked and play something appropriate.

Daz's death marked the end of the Tunnel Boys. Unable to cope with the guilt and grief, Spencer turned himself in and became another jail-bird, like his brother. The other boys were either sentenced or fled and there was an eerie calm that descended on the concrete canvas of the Drayton Estate.

Callum now had a new purpose, family and identity, having found his father and half-brother. He wished he could have introduced Daz to this way of life, but Daz had gone now and would never be forgotten. He would have approved of the brave, new hopeful life that Callum had ahead of him.

****

Angela returned from the church office one day to find a letter on her doorstep. It was an eviction order from her landlady saying that she had to sell the flat. She and Verity would have to find a new home. It was nothing new to Angela – she'd always had to move around, but she was so weary now and still grieving for Maggie.

This place had been home for nearly five years and she didn't know where the next one would be. Suddenly she remembered the sound of Maggie's voice telling her to be strong and not give up and she felt more hopeful – perhaps Chrissie could help her look, or maybe some of The Family might know someone. Deep inside, Angela had a strange feeling that life was about to change even more dramatically – she just didn't know how.

Angela decided to have a few biscuits and cup of tea before breaking the news to Verity. She was just about to brew up again, when the phone went. Angela answered to a man called Mr Bradbury. He said he was Maggie's solicitor.

****

It took Angela a little while to find "Bradbury and Bourne" as it was off the main road and tucked at the bottom of a cul de sac. She had expected Mr Bradbury to be a character out of "Great Expectations", sat in a leather armchair, smoking a pipe and surrounded by papers and dust. Therefore, when a handsome man in his mid-thirties opened the door to a plush, modern office, it came as something of a surprise.

"Thank you for coming so soon Miss Morgan" he said, beckoning towards the empty seat. "Can I offer you some tea? Coffee?" Mr Bradbury was utterly charming, not to mention extremely good-looking. Of course, he wouldn't be single, but Angela could have her little fantasy....

He pulled open his office drawer and pulled out a large wodge of documents. "Now...as I'm sure you know, Mrs Buxton had no next of kin."

"Yes, but she had a huge family." said Angela in quick response.

Mr Bradbury smiled. "Indeed. And it seems there are certain members of this family to which she wished to bequeath some gifts. You're named in her will as one of these people."

"Me?" gasped Angela "But I hardly knew her – not for very long, anyway."

"Well....clearly you were very important to her, Miss Morgan."

"I am? I mean, I was?"

"She has listed you here as....a very special lady." Angela looked gobsmacked. Surely whatever paltry material things Maggie had would have gone to Chrissie and Andy. And she couldn't imagine that would be much. She knew about the lump sum that had gone into the setting up of The Family, but all of that needed to be invested. Maggie was just a pensioner and even if the council flat on the Drayton Estate was at the cheaper end of the rental market, she still wouldn't have had much to live on.

There must have been something of sentimental value left to her. Some china, jewellery. Something like that. She smiled. If she knew Maggie, it would have been something small and delicate and very poignant. Mr Bradbury fished in his jacket pocket for his car keys. "Now, in order for you to collect this item, we need to go to Mrs Buxton's home. I can drive us there now, if you're free."

Angela shrugged and then nodded – she didn't know why it hadn't been brought over to the solicitor's office. As he opened the door of his rather shiny B.M.W, Mr Bradbury asked Angela if she had the afternoon off, or if she was a "lady of leisure."

"I suppose I am – sort of. In that, I love what I do. So I guess that's leisurely, isn't it?" Mr Bradbury smiled again, which made Angela feel a little bit dizzy. She sunk back into the soft leather car seat and clicked on the seat belt with relish. Even if it was just a short spin, the ride to the Drayton Estate would certainly be a most pleasant one.

She thought about the area they were going to and felt glad to have a big, strong man with her. Mr Bradbury took a different turning off the roundabout to the one she thought led to the estate. "Isn't it that way?" asked Angela.

"Just going the quickest route I know" replied Mr Bradbury.

"Oh right" said Angela. "I trust you." She tried to stop blushing. The car turned off the high street and Angela clocked a little piece of graffiti on a viaduct wall.

It said; "Last Graffiti Before Motorway". She smiled at the wit of the artist. When Mr Bradbury did actually turn onto the motorway, she felt sure they were going the wrong way, but then he came off it at the first exit. Maybe he didn't know his way. They went quite a way down an "A" road and into countryside.

"Mr Bradbury....I'm pretty sure this *isn't* the way to the Drayton Estate. You wouldn't be leading me astray now, would you?"

Mr Bradbury laughed. "Don't worry – I'm quite sure I know where we're going. I used to visit Mrs Buxton a lot. Anyway, got Sat Nav, just in case we *do* get lost." He put the radio on and told Angela to relax. They were definitely a few miles out of town now. If Mr Bradbury was going to pull into a lay by and make unseemly suggestions towards her, then Angela really wouldn't mind at all.

But at the end of the journey there was important business to conduct. Business that involved Maggie. Suddenly Mr Bradbury took a sharp left turn and stared driving through a little village. As they started descending a steep hill, Angela gasped. It was the street in her dream. The little cake shop. The children's toy shop, the brightly coloured awnings – they were all there. As they reached the bottom of the road, she saw the street sign –

"Angela Street". She tried to memorise the route they had taken to get there, so that she could verify if it was real and visit again.

"That street we just went down....I think I know it....."

"Do you? Quaint little place, isn't it? Not very well known. It's run by a group of people known as The Family. They wanted to have a street full of all their ideal shops and so they run them, and make the things that go in them, and sell them amongst themselves. Quite unique. Not many people know it's a back route to the Drayton Estate."

If it was a back route, it was a very long one. But Angela had felt a shiver run down her spine when they'd descended that hill – obviously she was meant to see it – it was time to go there for real. She wasn't dreaming, but something extraordinary was most definitely happening.

Eventually, after several more miles down winding country lines, Mr Bradbury drove up a long gravel path to what appeared to be the entrance of a stately home. He stopped at two huge gilded gates and then made a call on his mobile. A moment later, the gates opened and Mr Bradbury pulled up outside the house. He got out and walked around the car to open the passenger door for Angela.

"OK, Mr Bradbury, the joke's gone far enough. Who are you really? And why have you brought me here? You said we were going to collect something. You said you were taking me to the Drayton Estate – Maggie Buxton's home?"

Mr Bradbury paused before offering an explanation. "I think you mean *Lady* Margaret Buxton-Drayton. Dropped the Drayton part after her husband died. This *is* her home. *The* Drayton Estate."

Angela got out her seat, but immediately fell back down again. Mr Bradbury gently lifted her to her feet. Angela felt she had lost her voice. Luckily, Mr Bradbury spoke, "I'm afraid I did mislead you slightly – part of what she left you is in my jacket pocket, but we did have to come here to collect the main item." He gestured to Angela to open her hand, before dropping a large bunch of keys into her open palm.

"Now....I think you'll find the keys are marked South West Wing. That part of the mansion is now in your name. Other members of The Family live in other parts – I believe you know some of them." Angela would have collapsed again, had she not seen little Christian running towards her with his arms outstretched.

"Come Auntie Angela, quick!" he grabbed her hand and led her into a huge hallway. The place looked like more of a nursery than a Manor House. The walls were covered in children's paintings and there seemed to be a huge and busy canteen to the left of the main entrance. Offices and school rooms appeared out of every corridor, until Christian eventually led Angela up two flights of stairs and pointed to a locked door.

She unlocked it with the key Mr Bradbury had given her and walked into a bedroom three times the size of her whole flat. An en-suite bathroom was so large there was a sofa in it. Through what at first appeared to be a cupboard, was a fully stocked galley kitchen that led to a dining area with another sofa and office bureau.

Chrissie came up the stairs and put her hands on Christian's shoulders. "This is yours now, Angela. Your home – if you want it. For as long as you like." Tears welled up in Angela's eyes. Before she could say anything, Christian dragged her back into the bedroom where she saw a large gift-wrapped box on the four poster bed.

"Open it! Open it!" said Christian, barely able to contain his excitement. Angela pulled off the ribbon, lifted the lid and gasped as she saw the sparkly blue Celine Dion dress in all its glory. She held it against her body and turned towards Chrissie.

"Maggie wanted you to have it" said Chrissie simply. "Why don't you try it on?" This time Angela did let the tears come as she grabbed Chrissie and her son, pulling them close towards her for a bear hug. Christian quietly slipped from their grasp and ran into a room across the way, where Callum was sticking some photos in frames.

On the huge, ornate mantelpiece, Callum placed the newly framed picture of Grandma next to Maggie. "Yeah, s'good there" said Christian. He pulled Callum away, eager to show him the excitement going on in the rest of the house.

And Maggie Buxton and Grandma smiled from their frames, watching over the next generation of The Knowing Family.

****

9 781908 147141